About the Author

Lisa Nicholas lives in Lancashire with her husband, two big dogs, and two cats. Following a career in advertising, *Don't Forget Me* is her debut novel. When not writing or devouring novels, she enjoys hilly hikes rewarded with long lunches and wine.

Don't Forget Me

Lisa Nicholas

Don't Forget Me

Olympia Publishers
London

www.olympiapublishers.com
OLYMPIA PAPERBACK EDITION

ISBN: 978-1-80074-074-7

First Published in 2021

Olympia Publishers
Tallis House
2 Tallis Street
London
EC4Y 0AB
Printed in Great Britain

To Steve, who made everything possible.

Part One

2019
The present day

Olivia

Megan's dead, and Adam has run away.

Yesterday, I saw him for the first time in months. He has lost weight, but it suits him, I suppose. He's also started wearing trendy clothes, which don't. He blended in as he strutted through the streets of London; you'd never have known what he'd done. The lines on his face were cut no deeper than the last time I saw him. You'd guess he didn't have a care in the world, if you didn't know him. But I do know him, and even from across the street I could make out the scars on his hands, creeping up underneath the cuffs of his bright white shirt, as if trying to crawl away in shame.

I've been sitting for hours on a wooden bench decorated with pigeon shit, staring at the towering building across the freshly cut lawn that nobody walks on. His lights are on, but I didn't need them to tell me he was home. I'd have seen him if he left the flat, exiting from the large glass doors, which swing open and closed beneath a stack of glistening windows. They stand tall, peppered with balconies home to steel-grey deckchairs that stay empty, their owners safely within their fortress, shutting out the noise of the cars beeping and growling. They give me a headache.

Today is Saturday and it's not yet nine a.m. I don't know what he does on Saturdays anymore. He used to spend them with me. Megan was always busy on a Saturday with her horses at the livery yard, so Adam and I would do something we both knew she'd hate. He used to joke she loved the four-legged beasts more than him. We'd travel by train to London, and spend hours slowly meandering through our favourite galleries. I loved our secret escapes from my dull village life in Yorkshire, and I loved our lunches in exquisite little restaurants with too many tables draped in white and packed close together, strangers' elbows almost touching. The bustle of the city overwhelmed my senses and I had no idea how to find my way around, but he would hold my hand and wink at me, like he knew it all.

He doesn't need to escape for the day to London anymore. He's made it his home. Finally, he would probably say. He had always wanted to. He'd argued with Megan about it, and I pretended to be on his side, but I was glad she refused to leave Yorkshire because I couldn't stand to be left behind. Until I started to wonder if perhaps it would be Adam and I who would go to London, leaving Megan behind instead. Life is full of surprises, and in the end, he left us both behind. I hadn't factored that possible ending into my deliberations and calculations. I've missed him. Every day I have thought about him, and not once have I blamed him for what happened but I expect he blames himself. I blame Megan. She wanted to drive me away, but in the end, it was Adam who absconded. And now, I'm left alone.

I felt lost not knowing where he had gone. I went back to the old house every day for 221 days, and I'd watched autumn turn to winter turn to spring. The large front garden was overgrown now, but the sandstone walls of the house still drew the eye in, winking through the tiny windows that remained intact, covered in diamond-shaped lead, not a straight line to be found across the whole house. It was big, old, and wonky; we had loved it. I was sure that one day I'd find him there, looking for me as I looked for him. If nothing else, I thought he'd have to come back to commission and oversee the repairs, to salvage anything that might have escaped the lick of the flames, but he didn't come back. Not once.

The seasons changed, but the house remained black and white, dilapidated, and sorry for itself. It was still standing, remarkably, though I hadn't been back inside. I wondered if the expensive blue and white wallpaper in the hallway that Megan had spent months choosing and thousands paying for not so long ago had completely perished, or would a trained eye still make out the textured lines? I thought about the wide staircase that would greet us as we walked over black and white floor tiles and tried to imagine the walnut-wood bannisters adorned with hand-carved spindles no longer erect.

The fire had started in the living room, and travelled over at least two antique rugs to make it into the corridors that connected the many rooms. The snug, the utility room, the dining room. I wonder if it destroyed the kitchen — the heart of the home — or if the shiny marble-topped space withstood the attack of the flames. From outside you can see that the bedrooms didn't fare well, at least the three at the front. Ragged material, once heavy, lined curtains, made to measure, blew gently through the broken windows whenever there was a breeze. Still, it was beautiful, and I didn't believe it was lost forever.

I walked through winding lanes encased by fields full of sheep and cows to pass the house each day. I'd squint and blur my eyes to make its colours reappear. The blue door, the coral pink roses climbing the walls, and the sing-song voice that would great me as I walked up the once pretty pathway, scattered with wild flowers at the right time of year, or covered with snow.

'Come on in darling, I've just put the kettle on!'

Megan had been my closest ally once. Like everyone else, I'd orbited her; she was my sun. Until I realised how little I meant, like Pluto, not even a proper planet. I wanted to be the fucking moon. Adam, over time, had embraced my quirks. We became very close, especially when Megan started to fall apart. He'd needed me then, just as I need him now.

I used to write funny notes for him. I'd hide them in his suit jacket pocket so that he'd smile as he reached for a pen to sign one of his tediously dull and incomprehensible work documents, or find it when he reached for loose change to give to a homeless person. I slid notes into his jean pockets too, reminding him that I was always thinking about him, even when times were tough. His warm winter coat had huge zip-up pockets stuffed with waterproof gloves. I'd roll up a note and insert it deep into the thumb. His gloves reminded me of how large his hands were, warm and comforting. I adored him; still do.

'You're incredible,' he'd say, marvelling at our new-found connection, in the midst of their struggles. I was incredible for him. Everything I was, by then, it was all for him. But who wants to be incredible anyway? Beyond belief, lacking in credibility, seemingly impossible. Megan was the real deal for him from the very beginning, and I was a delusion he wanted to believe in. I think deep down he still wants to believe.

Once, feeling brave, I left a note in the jewellery box containing her anniversary gift before he popped it in his dinner suit jacket. She didn't notice it, or me. She barely noticed him at all in the end, which was painfully unfair when I spent my days and nights noticing everything about him. I heard her tell a woman at book club that he was a tad nondescript. By then I knew how much I loved him, and felt fiercely protective towards him. I could have slam-dunked her pretty, heart-shaped face through the wine-laden glass coffee table. She wasn't as nice as she used to be, her true bold colours starting to bleed through the pastel façade.

When Adam encouraged me to move away, I thought he meant well. He wanted me to take the opportunity, make a success of my artistic vocation. He believed in me, they both did. I believed them. Why wouldn't I? They said I would fit in there, and that I looked beautiful. I've never felt beautiful but it's nice to pretend for a moment, to forget my intimidating stature, and to believe in the vision of adoration and adulations that they painted with encouraging words. Still, their friends sneered at me. Bea, Elizabeth, and Antonia, Megan's hateful book club friends, called me clingy, and said three might be becoming a crowd. Our relationship wasn't normal, they'd say, when they thought I wasn't listening. It wasn't *normal*, whatever *normal* means, it was better.

That's why I came back when things didn't work out. I'd been away for months, unhappily pursuing my dreams on the advice of those I thought loved me the most. Turns out I was just in their way. I'd missed them both, the only two people who understood me. When I returned, success for me was still elusive, but to bask in theirs had always been enough. I'd been back less than a year when Megan died, and since then

15

life has stalled. He doesn't want my notes anymore, he's made that perfectly clear. Yet I never stopped trusting that he'd come back for me, eventually, so I waited. And I waited, and I waited, and I waited. I would wait forever, for him.

Last Tuesday, something finally happened. As I sat and watched the old house, in my usual spot on the drystone wall across the lane, waiting for Adam to finally come home, the colours I had conjured faded and the voices I used to love to remember were silenced. The skinny man in the shiny ill-fitting suit stood back to admire his work. The sign he had knocked into the soil blocked my view and the rage stymied my imagination. Adam wasn't coming back. He was a coward after all. A wimp, a deserter, a total bastard. It said offers welcome, quick sale preferred. I went to the estate agents, determined to find a forwarding address. I didn't need to lie, or cheat, rummage or steal. Right there on the out tray for post, a clearly addressed letter to a Mr Adam Sykes. So much for all the grave promises of privacy policies and data protection. I took a note of his new address and headed straight to London. I arrived on Thursday.

His flat is in Canary Wharf and the rentals advertisement billboard just out of residents' view on the corner tells passers-by that they probably couldn't dream of affording one of these *luxury penthouse apartments*. The weekly rent was eye watering. I guess he sold Megan's livery yard after all, though now I can see why he might need to sell the old wreck too, whatever it's worth now. He has a river view punctuated with the 02 Arena, its yellow arms reaching to the sky from its bloated white belly. I could see his silhouette in the window. As I took it all in, I dared to believe he might be over the worst of his grief and his guilt. He was selling up, starting afresh. He was ready to move forward.

My heart had danced with joy but then I saw her. They didn't emerge until ten o'clock on Saturday morning. It had been a long night. She was small, like a child. Even as a child I don't recall having shoulders so narrow. Her ponytail was long and thick, and should have frizzed and fought its way out of order as mine always had, but of course her caramel highlights were shimmering in the morning sun as if she belonged in a shampoo advert. She was much younger than Megan, but he clearly has a type. Do these tiny birdlike women make him feel tall?

Until now, I've been unable to move on, I didn't even know where he was. I couldn't get *closure,* as some say, particularly idiots and Americans. Meanwhile, he, the supposedly tortured widower, is practically skipping from his fancy new apartment to his cool new office. Judging by Slutty-McSlut-Face hanging off his arm, it seems I was right about him being ready to forget the past.

I spent last Christmas alone, following the crescendo of the unravelling, discordant melody of my imperfect world. Imperfect, but the only world I had, and the only one I knew I'd ever have. I've been left alone too long, but I will not be forgotten. I want my life back. I spent last Christmas alone but it was the one before that I hate to think of the most. That's when it all began. Megan ruined everything, but soon, Adam and I will be together again.

Adam

'Jesus, you are so fucking sexy.' He shifted his weight to his knees and extracted himself. Stretching his long body, he knocked over the lamp on the bedside table, which knocked over the half-full glass, spilling water onto the beige carpet.

'Fuckity-fuck'. Clambering, uncouth, unkempt, his short grey-speckled dark hair stood on end. He looked at Lucy, she was rolling her big eyes, smudged with mascara, and half smiling. Her lips were flushed dark pink, she had a stubble rash on her neck. 'You are simply beautiful, especially when you roll your eyes disdainfully at your loser boyfriend.'

With a charitable sigh, she rolled to her side and casually brushed his arm. Her hair fell over her tanned shoulders, hiding her pretty freckles. Adam paused, always easily distracted, before stepping into the soggy pile and half hopping into the large en suite to locate a towel, grabbing the empty glass. Although the rooms in the flat were spacious and cluttered with few obstacles, he filled them. His broad shoulders and thick sturdy legs created a frame that despite its promise often abandoned grace.

'Fancy dinner tonight?' Lucy was already clipping her bra, deliciously naked from the waist down. Her mismatched bottoms lay at the bottom of the bed. Her other clothes were piled on a chair in the corner of the room.

'Not tonight, Luce, I'm meeting Peter.'

It pained him to turn her down. He'd forgotten the

addictive nature of falling in love; it had been so long. But the favour he needed to ask of Peter, like Lucy, was part of the get your shit together programme he'd set himself three months ago, as the first daffodils bloomed in sad little concrete flower beds, splashing busy London roads with not enough colour. He had known Lucy for just ten weeks. They'd met online. She was only his second match on the dating app he'd felt silly using, yet he had turned his profile off the same evening he met her. She'd bowled him over with her enthusiasm for life. She was so full of life in fact, there simply wasn't room for endless curiosity, which was useful. She knew he'd been married, she knew Megan was dead, and she didn't notice that his knees cracked when he sat down. He'd insisted on paying.

'I'm looking forward, but let's take things slowly,' he'd told her over the Chateaubriand they shared on their second date at Gaucho's Steakhouse. He'd told her just enough about how he'd ended up in London, the city you're supposed to start a new life in when you're young, not in your depressingly late forties, and trying to start again. He hadn't known what to expect. An interrogation? None came, not then, not now. It was almost too good to be true. He hadn't mentioned Olivia.

By the third date, after checking almost daily, Adam saw that Lucy's profile was finally absent from the dating app search. He never mentioned it but from then on started to experiment with how the word girlfriend rolled off his tongue. It didn't. He practiced in his head, but avoided it until she introduced him as her new chap when he met her work friends, sipping cider outside a cheap and cheerful bar on Broadwick Street in Soho.

He squeezed Lucy's big toe as he stood at the bottom of the bed to pull up his boxer shorts. He dressed in a loose, grey, long-sleeved jersey top, creased from its position on the floor, self-consciously stretching the cuffs over the disfigured tissue that didn't have the decency to finish at his wrists, instead creeping onto the tops of his hands. Large, sturdy feet met wood as he sauntered into the open plan living room. He headed to the kitchen end, glancing through the mass of glass that made up the entire length of wall, from floor to ceiling, through which he had spent many hours this year observing the human ants below, as he sat alone in his identikit ready-furnished, rented bachelor pad.

'Tea, babe?' he called to Lucy.

In the not so far away past, he didn't use words like babe, and he feared he shouldn't start now, at his age, but it had fallen into his vernacular, imitating the easy way Lucy spoke, without a trace of self-consciousness. He envied that about her. Adam was working hard at being less self-absorbed. His strongest desire was to forget about himself and all of the pieces of his messed-up life that had connected together to make him who he now was, and who he forever wished he could escape.

'Can't stop, actually, sorry. Meeting Tom for coffee.' Lucy was glancing at her watch as she walked towards Adam. She was fully clothed now, last night's denim pencil skirt dressed down with one of his shirts. She'd tied it in the middle, revealing glimpses of taut stomach as the material moved. She had no idea how much that shirt had cost. She hadn't asked to borrow it.

Too preoccupied with this beautiful creature's next moves to care a great deal, Adam brushed away the petty jealousy and tried not to form comparisons between himself and the lithe young man forming part of Lucy's house share, who was unencumbered by the crinkles, wrinkles, and speckles of age, and able to pull off a trendy beard. Jealousy was something he hadn't experienced in a while. In the past couple of years nothing so trivial could have held his attention. It could be a good sign. He was ready to once again focus on the mundane ups and downs of everyday life.

He'd met Tom at a thirtieth birthday party Lucy had taken him to, someone from their wider circle of friends. He'd forgotten the birthday boy's name five minutes after meeting him briefly in the hustle of the dark, painfully fashionable underground bar. He'd been the oldest there and felt conspicuous. Tom didn't like him, and he could well suspect why, seeing the lovelorn look in his doleful eyes. He'd also met the other two housemates: another man, Josh, who wore his hair too long, in Adam's opinion — which had only lowered when the youth left the party on a Segway — and Celia, who he could see was fiercely intelligent, and annoyingly forthcoming with it. Adam had been aware his judgements were unfair. He'd probably been just as unbearable to people his age, at theirs. And besides, they were worth putting up with if it meant he passed the test with Lucy. She made him laugh.

Until recently, he hadn't laughed much. He hadn't anything much. Adam had been shocked to notice the tightening of his belt notches, assuming a man who sat still for so many hours a day over so many months would not lose weight. The days had gone very slowly since Megan died. He still couldn't look his mother in the eye. He hadn't seen his brother in months. He always wore long sleeves. When Lucy had asked about his scar, he'd quickly changed the subject. He couldn't stand to be the pitied failed hero in her eyes, the way he was viewed by his family, and with Peter. Not their fault, the fiction was of his own creation.

Adam had never considered himself a pep-talk kind of guy but the money he'd left with wasn't going to last forever. The savings he and Megan had were depleted before she died, and the sale of the livery yard and the horses were substantial but not infinite. He doubted he'd get much for the old house. Do or die, he had told himself some months ago. Adam didn't promise to try and forgive himself. Some people deserve to live with their guilt but that didn't mean he couldn't live at all. He decided he needed to connect with people again, get a job, put something other than condiments and leftover takeaways in his oversized fridge. So here he was, a girlfriend adding colour to his stark rooms, and maybe a job, depending on Peter.

He looked at Lucy as she tied the shoelace of her clean white pumps, and she glanced up. Not a line on her carefree face. He was too old for her really, he knew that. He was mildly embarrassed by the gap, him clinging on to his forties, she not yet thirty. He had been around Lucy's age when Megan first brought Olivia into their lives. He had no idea how much she would change things, in the end. He didn't used to look that far forward. Like Lucy, he'd blissfully lived in the moment.

Lucy smiled. 'Good luck with Peter.' She kissed him on the cheek and touched his arm. 'I'm sure he'll be happy to help you out, sweetie.'

She hadn't showered, and smelt faintly of sex, adding to his anxiety about Tom; they were all so insouciant, and he feared through her eyes he may look uptight. He hoped she might instead interpret his reticence for nonchalance as a man in control. Masterful, at a push. He looked down to her upturned face and held her soft cheeks in his hands. A fatherly gesture, he suddenly thought, removing them and sliding them to her waist. She mimicked him, cupped his stubbly cheeks, and looked into those worried eyes.

'I just really want this job. It's the perfect fit for me. MD level, great package. I really fancy working for one of the bigger banks now. Been a big fish in a small pond for far too long. I need a new challenge, you know?'

It was true, he'd wanted this for a long time, and for a long time he'd resented Yorkshire and everyone in it for making his goals so difficult to reach. He kept his tone light, burying the feeling of unease he felt at being questioned later by Peter about how he was feeling, and if he was ready. The mask of togetherness would be secured in place, but even if he didn't feel like a fraud, he would hate to ask his oldest friend for a favour. He didn't like to feel needy.

Lucy threw her bag over her shoulder, and pulled her long hair into a neat ponytail that swung low down her back, tendrils falling in a way that his wife would have found impossible to tolerate. Lucy was light on her feet, easy going. She rarely worried, and if she felt low, she'd put her trainers on and run around the block. She was the antipode to Megan, and to Olivia. She was exactly what he needed.

'Call me tomorrow, let me know how it goes! Good luck!'

The door slammed, and the single chime of the lift being called was just about audible. Adam sat for a moment. Time to get ready. The flat was quiet now. Until Lucy had started visiting, it had always been this way. He hated the flat. Not the silence, which had been welcome after previous torturous months — months that had ultimately led to his dash to London — but the stark white and grey angles everywhere. Large mirrors provided unwanted reflections, and the impractically small statement rugs exposed the shine of the pale panels underfoot. It was cold.

'Fancy!' Lucy had commented the first time she'd seen it, noting the space, the light. All Adam saw was a blank canvas he had no inclination to paint. He'd paid for the convenience of a fully-furnished flat, and had barely looked at the photos that appeared in his inbox from keen estate agents who knew an easy sell when they saw one. Even now, after living here for months, if you asked Adam to list the furniture they'd chosen for him, he'd have to think hard, and even then, he'd discover he hadn't really noticed it all. He'd tell you he had an uncomfortable sofa in pale grey, and opposite a large, curved plasma screen in the centre of the end wall.

Finishing the tea he'd made for himself, he placed the mug in the dishwasher carefully, and had a quick shower. A towel wrapped around his waist, he stood at the wardrobe, flicking through shirt after shirt, save the one Lucy was currently modelling, all beautifully presented, rarely worn, as Adam hadn't worked since arriving in London, after leaving his predictable, senior-management banking role because of events he couldn't have predicted at all. Lucy seemed content with his explanation that he was exploring his options. Something about a well-dressed middle-aged man with a black credit card and a well-honed air of self-confidence to turn unemployed into self-sufficient would-be entrepreneur.

She wasn't naive, he'd thought, she just didn't care much, and that was a nice change too.

He fastened a cufflink, a gift from Megan for his fortieth birthday. They'd been married for over fifteen years by then, and she'd had his initials engraved on the platinum ovals, a small topaz stone in each; his birthstone. They'd been young when they met, younger than Lucy was now. They'd married young too, shocking friends and family, all chasing far more interesting dreams than kitchen renovations.

She'd been dancing with a group of girls he didn't know the first time he saw her. Adam's hair was too long at the front and too short at the sides. He'd thought himself quite cool, but not cool enough to dance. Especially not with her. Her friends made him think of sharks circling. He wanted no part of it. He'd watched her though, and later she told him she'd felt his eyes on her. In the early days she told the story romantically, eyes meeting across a smoky bar, before smoking was banned and everyone would go home smelling like overflowing ashtrays. Years later she evolved the story to him being a bit creepy to make those same sharks laugh.

Adam and Megan had spent three years living in the same student block in Fallowfield, the corner of Manchester reserved for students, vagrants, and rats. They had attended seminars in the same lecture theatres, but always at different times, Adam's Mathematics timetable never colliding with Megan's English Literature. A few short weeks after final exams, enjoying endless days and nights of summer student deals, they met. She didn't just light up a room, she redirected all the electricity so that everyone else dimmed. Like a red-carpet darling, she compelled the glare of people's lenses. So Adam was shocked when she arrived by his side at the bar and said something as simple and life changing as hello.

The bar was noisy and dark, and everything was sticky: the floor, the bar, even the glasses. Adam persuaded Megan to go outside to the beer garden where there was some artificial light, and only the faint beat of the drums and the distant wail of the guitars. Her hair was softly layered, a celebrity copycat style chosen by every second woman that year. It was dark blonde, which she later highlighted. Megan's face was small, and the bones beneath sharp. Pale skinned, she was striking, and he couldn't stop looking at her. He wanted to touch her. Megan's soft, rounded drawl betrayed her public-school background. He teased her, and told her that he was far too lower-middle class for such aristocratic standing. She had slapped his hand, playfully.

'Silly, don't you know? I'm from *Up North*,' she'd rebuked him, adopting a wonderful Yorkshire accent, exaggerating every vowel with precision.

Misled by her playful humility, she wickedly giggled with laughter at his shock when he arrived at her family's large house in Yorkshire to meet the formidable father. He took Adam on a tour of his livery yard, introducing him to horses worth more than his dream car. Her father didn't conceal his high hopes for his only daughter to follow in his footsteps, buying and selling horses, training, competing, and renting spare stables to other fine beasts owned by other fine people. Megan's parents welcomed Adam, they tried to make him feel at home. He told himself he belonged. The antique furniture in her ramshackle bedroom, chipped and painted with little care for its provenance, contrasted with his mind's image of his own home bedroom: pine modern matching drawers and desk, fitted wardrobes and a single bed, always neatly made.

'Would you ever leave Yorkshire?' he asked her as they lay in her large, mahogany bed, his stomach curled around her back, her hair tickling his nose, baffled by the enormity of what he might well be about to take on. His parents had sacrificed everything to supplement his scholarship to Cheltenham College, where he had been a day boy and Peter had boarded. He'd been the first in his family to go to university. His parents had taught him to work hard, and be house proud. He, in fact, was immensely proud of them. Megan's family broke all the rules, original paintings covered in dust, not revered. His mother would have had a fit. She would probably start cleaning when they weren't looking, were she to be invited one day, he'd mused.

'Would you ever leave me?' she had simply retorted.

'Never,' he promised.

At the time he'd meant it. Megan had changed everything: dreams to move to the city forgotten in place of simply being anywhere she was and doing anything to make her smile. But that was a quarter of a century ago, before the grey at the temples had started to spread, and before he knew what tragedy meant. He remembered how naive he'd been, and how happy in such a simple way.

Chastising himself for wallowing in self-pity, he unclipped the cufflinks, and instead opted for a pair he'd been given by his mother. They'd belonged to his father, a death he wasn't responsible for.

Adam knew he looked good as he arrived at One Lombard Street, shaven, a mist of Issey Miyake clinging to his skin.

He'd been told, once or twice, that he was handsome in an unconventional way, and that was a good enough compliment for him. He'd got better with age, his jaw gaining strength and determination, years of expensive holidays leaving him with skin a shade or two darker giving the impression of health, vitality. A couple of heads turned at the bar to catch his eye, but he avoided them, instead searching for Peter's familiar face. Peter was sat at the bar grandly occupying centre stage of the large dining room, beneath the high glass dome skylight. The restaurant was full, and city workers stood at the bar laughing loudly, waiting for their turn to be seated.

'Adam! Adam, Adam, I can't believe it, you look like a new man!'

Peter looked exactly the same. Somewhere unidentifiable between forty-five and fifty-five for most people. The dark jeans a tad too tight, but well-coordinated with the tan shoes and clearly new, an expensive shirt, and a heavy, deep blue silk-lined jacket with a coral handkerchief prettily clashing. These days his nose was slightly red, but he was still attractive; an alluring cheeky smile, kind eyes.

'Come, come, sit down.' He patted the seat next to him, which he'd impressively managed to keep hold of despite the shortage. 'What'll it be?' He smiled, he chatted, and Adam almost felt at ease. Peter recommended the Smoky Sour, and Adam allowed him to order it for both of them.

Sipping his drink, and agreeing that it was the best he'd ever had, Adam began his speech. He was feeling much better now, he enthused, convincing both of them that it was all in the past. Moved on, name's Lucy. Young, yoga, the very definition of breezy, easy going. 'Yes,' he'd acquiesced ignoring Peter's crude sniggers, 'I am a lucky man.'

He told Peter in confident tones that he was ready to go back to work. It was an amazing offer, but they'd heard about the hasty exit from his last role, and saw he had done nothing since. That's why he needed Peter. Adam had taken leave when Megan died. He had planned to go back, but that had all had to change. He hadn't resigned, he just never turned up again. He chucked his work phone in the bin and got a new one. Adam had needed to cut all ties. Peter was the only one he couldn't bring himself to sever.

'So you've been *taking stock*?' The interviewer had not been impressed. 'I understand you had a tumultuous year, but this is an intimidating environment and, for this role, you need balls of steel, quite frankly. On paper, you look perfect, but we need to know you're ready.'

They needed a reference, reassurance. Adam needed Peter. Stalwart friend, a mentor of sorts despite being the same age, the picture of success in finance, contacts everywhere, and the only one who knew him then, had known him long before, and still knew him now.

'But Adam, you're really ready? Tell me, mate, be honest, because ours is a small world, and I don't want to end up looking like a fucking imbecile because you have a meltdown, or all that shit comes back to haunt you.' He paused to sip from his glass, and as he placed it back down, he caught the look in Adam's eye. 'Don't look shocked, mate, this is exactly what I mean. This, this is how we talk, don't you remember? If you go back, the gloves are off. They might not know everything about you but they know enough to be watching, testing you. So tell me now, are you ready? Because, shit Adam, it was all so bloody awful, so sad,' he tailed off, and patted his eyes with a napkin. It didn't need to be said, not again. 'Adam, you're not desperate for cash, are you? You're doing ok, no one would blame you for just keeping a low profile, taking it easy for a little longer.'

'Don't get me wrong,' Adam was treading carefully. Too easily fixed, over it, and it would look strange. He dabbed at his own eyes, and swallowed the lump in his throat slowly as he continued, 'I'll never get over what happened, and I'll never forgive myself. But I need to move forward. I need something to focus on, something other than the memories.'

Peter drained the last of his cocktail in response. Adam suspected Peter hadn't quite forgiven him either for Megan's unravelling. He'd adored Adam's wife almost as much as Adam had, or as much as Adam had before things started to go wrong in their home. Nevertheless, he repeated the empty mantra of friends and family everywhere, 'You mustn't blame yourself.'

'I'm ready. You'll have to come see the flat, meet the lovely Lucy. She's great.' Had he winked as he'd said lovely Lucy? Had he forgotten how much he hated this shit? Probably. It used to come naturally, now it felt like he was reading a script. His mood was fragile, moments lifting him high on the crest of a wave before drowning him in fear and self-pity.

'Okay, okay.' Peter looked into Adam's eyes a second too long, and then asked him how his mother was.

Peter always had been charming. Adam's mother adored him, 'Call me Helen,' she had repeatedly admonished, as Peter continued to address her as Mrs Sykes, and kiss both her cheeks upon greeting, telling her she looked wonderful. Now she was a widow, his father dead of lung cancer for over a decade. He was not doing his duty as a son and he knew it. Her grief swallowed his own, drained him. Her questions, her need to make sense of it exhausted him, when Adam knew it was a pointless task. He hated to lie to her. Easier to keep a distance. He sent flowers for her birthday just last week, but let the phone ring out when she called to thank him.

'She's well, thanks mate.'

'Not been up there lately then?'

'I've been busy,' Adam's voice was quiet, and it merged into a long sigh. Adam had not been busy but he was grateful that Peter knew what a dead horse looked like, and stopped flogging. They drew an invisible line under the conversation, as a short waiter with slick black hair approached to indicate that their table was ready.

'It's not too far, gentlemen,' he said with a slight accent, Adam assumed to be French, as he led them to a table close to the bar.

'Let's eat, the John Dory is fucking amazing,' Peter advised as the menus were opened onto their laps.

Peter was given the wine list, and chose an expensive Sancerre to Adam's nod. He tasted it, and it was poured just before they ordered. Rules going back decades demonstrated to Adam that Peter intended to pay for their meal. They always had agreed that he who chooses the wine pays for dinner, based upon their increasing one-upmanship when it came to the price of grapes. Adam made a mental note to at least offer his half when the bill came. He didn't want any more charity tonight.

The John Dory was delicious, baked in salt and moist. They shared a whole one and picked at the greens, demolishing the wine too quickly and summoning the

31

sommelier to order a second, barely breaking their conversation to do so. It was good to talk about nothing much, peppered with Peter's hatred of London.

'I'm here until the end of the week, and then straight home to air you can breathe. This wine, and seeing you, that's the only saving grace to this week. Be bloody pleased when this project is over — I'm in this dreadful city five days a week at the minute! Even had to rent a place at an absolutely eye-watering cost. Charging that straight back to the client, I can tell you. Making him a damn fortune.'

Like his dead wife, Peter was Yorkshire born and bred, and nowhere else lived up to its high standards and impossibly pure air. Apparently. Brought up in the Cotswolds Adam was teased by the pair of them for being a southern softie. He hadn't minded at all. Through their years together at school they'd become like brothers, excelling in the same subjects, following similar career paths, playing on the same rugby teams, and being each other's wing men.

Adam wasn't anywhere near so close with his actual younger brother, Michael, who had been quiet and studious, and now taught languages to sixth-formers and, between travelling Europe to take short term, low-paid contracts, was based in a village not far from where they'd grown up.

However, Peter had been willing to travel more and stay later than Adam, in part thanks, he joked, to his lack of a good woman, and teased he didn't need one so long as he could continue to share Megan.

They didn't resist a peek at the dessert menu, and opted for cheese plates, ordering ruby ports to wash it down with from their efficient, little waiter. Adam felt a warmth, which had been lacking for a while in that cool flat in his anonymous city. They talked of politics, argued about the economic fallout of the continued Brexit debacle, with Peter declaring himself the winner of a debate about Yorkshire's inward investment scheme given Adam's total failure to bloody visit the bloody place in months — so what would he know anyway — guffawing, spitting a little wine, and thumping the table in victory, eating irons chiming in agreement.

Adam amused Peter with his tales of woe as he attempted to immerse himself in millennial culture to impress Lucy. 'She's wonderful, my Luce, she's just a good person who wants to have fun. Please God let it stay that way! But can someone tell me what the fuck plant-based diets are all about?' He threw his wine down his neck, wiped his mouth.

'Does she know?' Peter asked, as a quiet, serious tone stilled their table, their minds.

'Some. Enough.'

'I suppose it's hard to explain. It's impossible for anyone to really understand.' Peter looked like he wanted to go on, but he was stopped by Adam's booming voice, louder than Adam had intended.

'Yes, quite. No one really understands. It's futile to try. I'd be grateful if you didn't mention it when you meet her.' The full stop to the conversation was audible.

Was that a raised eyebrow? Disapproval? Adam wasn't sure, perhaps Peter thought him uncaring or conversely too bottled up to let his thoughts breathe. He tried not to overthink it. Adam and Peter had always been good at avoiding difficult conversations. Returning home from a night out with Peter, Megan used to ask Adam what they'd talked about. He'd never been able to remember a single proper conversation. She hadn't been able to understand it. It was wonderfully straightforward for Adam. They attempted to get back onto the lighter subjects, and miraculously succeeded.

Peter signalled for two more ports, the bottle was delivered in mere minutes. While the waiter poured quietly, Adam checked his watch, and he noticed the date. He couldn't help but remember it was Olivia's birthday. He pushed the thought from his mind, and all those other thoughts threatening to spill forth from this time last year, when he knew nothing but thought he knew everything.

Peter raised his glass. 'A toast then, to Adam, and his swanky new life in London. Long may it last!'

Their mouths smiled simultaneously and their eyes locked as they clinked their glasses, revealing an unspoken and intuitively understood addendum to Megan. Adam knew what Peter was thinking. She should still be here. And Adam knew that because of him — because of him and Olivia — she was dead. If Megan had been here, there would be no need to welcome Lucy or see a new flat. Because everything would have stayed as it was: better.

Adam didn't disagree with Peter's silent reproach. When Olivia had returned to their lives that Christmas, the one before last, he and Megan had been arguing a lot. They'd wanted different things, the synergies they shared through their history and in age somehow propelling them in opposite directions. How desperately he'd craved a new start, fought for change, excitement, something for *him*. It had seemed that Megan was going to prevent him from having any of it. Olivia, on the other hand, had said she would follow him anywhere.

Olivia

One Lombard Street is very nice. He never took me anywhere that nice. I watch them greet each other, old friends, loyal forever. Of course, Peter wasn't loyal to me. Neither of them were, but Adam had his reasons. Peter was just a stuck-up, festering, old cantankerous git. I am close enough to listen to some of their conversation but they don't see me. I used to be the only thing Adam would see in a room, but now I'm invisible to him.

As I sit alone in the restaurant, unseen within the hubbub of the busy curved bar beneath the vertigo-inducing glass ceiling, I see how well Adam and Peter fit into this world. Megan would have too. I wonder if Peter and Adam are thinking the same thing. I don't fit in at all, but there's nothing new in that. The smells are rich as they waft past held high by nimble waiters doing their best to blend into the background, so food appears on diners' tables as if by magic.

I'm sure I hear Peter mention mental health at one point. He's got a nerve. Peter thinks all women are mad. Megan, me, the poor flings who haven't lived up to his exacting standards or, should we say, Megan's benchmark. We could all see he fancied her, it was pathetic. Every time he'd come for dinner, ignore me completely, and hang off her every word, whilst her poor oblivious husband poured him more wine, and laughed at his terrible jokes. Not that Megan would have ever strayed; she liked her life just as it was, everything in its rightful place. Including me. My problem was I grew out of my little box.

The veal Milanese here looks delicious. I had that once, when Adam took me to a little Italian in Leeds, but that feels like a long time ago. Tonight, I'm not ordering anything to eat and I don't give a damn what anyone thinks in this room, not that they seem to notice. Even the waiters are oblivious to me. Although it is a nice place to have a birthday, even if there's no one to toast you.

Frankly I shouldn't expect anything more; last year wasn't much better. Megan had been pretty self-obsessed by that stage, my last birthday, and we'd had a difficult, few months since I'd come back and she'd started to slip into the wine soaked, pilled-up cliché she finished up as. Adam was rarely around, but I was hurt that night, sat in her kitchen, that he hadn't made the effort for my birthday. I remember catching myself becoming momentarily almost as bitter as Megan, irked by his absence, the pull of the city.

Megan constantly moaned that he was always in London, that he might as well live there. I tried to avoid pointing out that her refusal to move was the main reason they were making each other so miserable. There was no point, she wouldn't have accepted any blame. It wasn't in her nature to compromise yet she genuinely didn't see anything wrong with expecting him to. After all, eventually something always has to give.

A year ago today, as we sat together in the kitchen, I'd perched on the tall stool, elbows on the cold, hard mottled surface of the large island, having helped myself to a cushion from the large, cosy armchair in the corner by the French doors. The island stools were hard and uncomfortable, but the chair was too low to sit on and be part of the action. Megan's kitchen was always alive with action. Spotlights twinkled in different formations depending on the time of day, or her mood. The ceiling was high yet integrated wooden wine racks reached it from their base at the floor, breaking up the homely creamy doors of what often felt like hundreds of cupboards.

I'd let myself in earlier that evening, and thrown my large imitation Mulberry bag onto the floor. Megan had the real version, a brown leather satchel with a suede interior and delicate gold lettering that wouldn't dare to fade. Most people wouldn't be able to tell the difference, but she could and so could I; mine wasn't even real leather, and it certainly didn't have a suede interior. As I greeted her, Megan didn't wish me a happy birthday, instead she told me that her doctor not only thought she was mad but now a liar too. She didn't want to worry me, she said, but she'd told the doctor about her symptoms and he had accused her of drinking too much, and asked her if she was supplementing her prescription.

'He doesn't believe me. He thinks I need to focus on my relationships more. Perhaps take some time off work. He thinks I'm just stressed. He said I mustn't drink so much. I told him, my relationships are all fine, and I don't drink very much at all! It must be side effects. He's given me an alternative, but I could see he wasn't convinced. How dare he question my integrity? As if I'd take drugs other than my prescriptions! For heaven's sakes!'

I remember her reaction to this particular appointment with the renowned Dr Lewis, partly because it overshadowed my birthday, and partly because I had always been quite taken with the good doctor's old-fashioned attitude. Lock her up; the female is hysterical! Heaven forbid we might explore the option that something really might be happening to her. Something that poor Mrs Sykes can't fix with positive thinking and some time off. I wonder why they bother training in medicine at all if some happy pills and a supportive home life can cure all ills. But Megan was weak by now, and question the great Dr Lewis she did not. Instead, she took her new lightweight prescription without argument, went home, put on her best smile, and started *sharing*. Lucky. Fucking. Us.

A brilliant man, really, who can turn patient-reported worsening symptoms of a middle-aged woman in therapy, who was losing weight as well as her marbles — it seemed to me — into the direct result of her lack of positive social interaction with her husband and too much stress at work for the little lady. He thought she was a liar, drugged up to hide from an unhappy marriage. He wasn't far wrong, but he wasn't right either. By now, though, I knew the marriage could be in trouble.

Yet, compared with tales of marital woe told at her regular book club after the last drops of the third bottle of Chenin Blanc were shaken out into lipgloss-rimmed glasses, their marriage could have been worse.

'Of course, the dynamics change after years of marriage, and everything changes after children,' one of her coiffured clones would drone.

On they all plodded, not looking for change, not minding the imperfections, whilst I waited in the wings, the outsider, for my turn. I always believed one day it would come.

'Darling,' she'd whined that night — my birthday — as I poured her another large glass of sauvignon, 'You know I love you, and wonderful Dr Lewis said I mustn't block out my family, my friends, I mustn't struggle alone. I've been trying so hard to be strong, for all of you really. I don't want to be a burden.'

I knew that I was supposed to say something reassuring here, coax the words from her quivering lips. I knocked over the bottle of wine instead and busied myself with kitchen towels.

Undistracted, entitled, and used to constant attention, she continued, 'I get these terrible nightmares you see, and daily I'm plagued by all sorts of silly things. I know I must be going perfectly mad.' She laughed, a self-conscious tinkle.

Another queue to reassure, I thought absent-mindedly, and placed the sodden kitchen towels in the bin.

'I feel side-lined, sometimes. In the way. I used to sparkle, my darling; I used to *enthral.*' The final word elongated.

All my effort allowed me to succeed in suppressing a roll of the eyes. I was her confidante — the shoulder to de-burden to. I needed to try harder.

'I've become forgetful, like an old lady. I lose things; I swear they move! I make appointments and forget. I change appointments and forget. Just yesterday I saw my brand-new basil plant was withered, I looked closely, and I'd watered it with warm disinfectant, sweetheart! Can you believe it? I worry it's the pills, but Dr Lewis isn't convinced. I'm just so tired all the time, so muddled.' She looked sad.

I felt deeply sorry for her, mixed with an overpowering sense of revulsion, like one might have for a mangled, dying kitten. I wanted to put her out of her misery. Just over six months ago I'd come back to Yorkshire expecting our happy dynamic to fall back into place, but I found something very different. She seemed to have greyed, or perhaps she just wasn't attending her salon as often. Even her face was grey. But most importantly the colour had gone from their conversations.

We all used to laugh. By this point we never did. The atmosphere was dreadful, and they were rarely in the same room as each other. I'd tried to ensure I was always there for both of them. I saw each of them far more often than they saw each other. I was the only one who could see how quickly they were coming undone. I only ever wanted us all to be happy. For some reason, Megan pulled against that, and made everyone as miserable as she was.

How could he live with her, still, as she transformed to this poor, unfortunate soul? Well, I suppose he didn't that much, what with all the time he spent away. It was too hard to watch but I had no choice. I'd learned one thing in the last few months, that whatever else was happening, I couldn't let Megan take Adam down with her or chase him away for good. Like I said, Adam and I had become close, and even more so following the incident in book club, a few weeks earlier.

The more she pushed him away, the more he ran to me. The more she turned her back on me, the more I found myself seeking his comfort and reassurances. I couldn't understand what she wanted. I'd hear her whispered conversations about needing more time alone with him, just the two of them, feeling crushed to be in the way, then the next thing she'd scream and shout at him, and he'd be in London, or with me. The good listener, to all sides. I probably understood more about their marriage than anyone in it.

'Maybe you should stop taking them, then, and see if you feel better,' I told her. 'You don't want to be thrown in the lunatic asylum now, do you?' I'd smiled. I knew Adam would agree with me.

'Oh Olivia! You have always said the funniest things,' she said.

I wasn't joking, but she didn't make it that far anyway.

'I remember when you first came into our lives, sweetie. Gosh, things were different then. What fun we had, all of us! I basically insisted on muscling you in everywhere we went, but I was right to, they all loved you!'

Even in her moments of self-pity, as she questions her own sanity, she still managed to try and make me feel grateful for her acceptance, for being part of her coveted life.

'Antonia has always hated me though.' I looked at her straight, daring her to deny it. Antonia was a bitch, and I did not fit into her idea of perfect; she suspected me, though to begin with, I really didn't know what of. She'd never liked me, ever since I'd known her, she'd been positively icy cold. Perhaps like a dog, she could just sense something in our group was off. She certainly had no proof of any wrong doing.

'Antonia doesn't hate you, Olivia,' she lied. 'Some might say she's rather sharp, not unlike you. Perhaps you're just too similar? Though she needn't have been so rude about your outfit last week. That I will give you.'

I tried not to glare, and she tried not to smile. She'd only just contained her mirth at the time, Antonia and Bea had outright laughed, before awkwardly clearing their throats and apologising, seeing the fury in my face, the wetness threatening to spill over my bottom lashes. I'd said nothing though, as after the previous incident at book club we were all on tenterhooks. They'd waved goodbye, as the crossing beeped, and we'd made our way across the road, leaving them to gossip.

Megan and her friends had a uniform, and it wasn't one I cared for. They were prim but just sexy enough — neutral colours, age appropriate, modest heels, neat, tailored trousers and skirts hugging their narrow, slender hips. Prominent collar bones cast enticing shadows accented by some delicate chain hinting at pert not-too-large breasts enhanced with well-fitting bras, and the odd surgeon's lift.

They seemed to forget I was younger, able to carry off a more youthful, cutting-edge ensemble. I had my own style, which I'd artistically woven together through influences I admired. They mistakenly called it grungy, most likely due to their age and sheltered, echo-chamber based existences. I was also taller than I wished to be, hips wider, my shape somehow uncontained compared to their tight, ordered flesh and bones.

Megan helped me realise I needed to grow up. Under her gaze, and that of her friends, I started to doubt my more bohemian style. I'd tell myself I looked the part I was born to play, but I'd never sold a painting, only given them away. I had started to envy them. Their perfect hair must have been professionally blow-dried. I knew Megan's was. I went with her to the salon once but they couldn't tame my mane. I didn't go back. Places like that, all white and shiny, and full of tiny people, make me feel like a monster.

I admit, I copied her a little. But she encouraged me to. She loved to be adored and what greater flattery is there than subtle imitation? In the end I gave the style my own twist. In fact, I improved it. Usually, I found the group's evangelising on fashion irritated me. It was only stuff, and mainly stuff that I couldn't afford and, unlike most of their kind, I had no adoring husband to buy it for me. But the moment I had seen her oversized 'simply-divine-darling' Mulberry bag I'd fallen for it. It truly was a thing of beauty. Pragmatic, useful beauty: the best kind. Wasted on her, as she only carried lipstick and car keys. My replica version was stuffed full of my work, my writings, my diaries; it allowed me to keep my most precious belongings with me at all times.

I would record moments as they happened, reality shaped by ink and lead. Unlike the others, who were a motley crew of housewives, livery stable directors, GPs, and public-school teachers, I was an artist, or trying to be. In common they had tradition, wealth, and a need to conform to their social position and age. In contrast I had nothing except that which I created. As well as producing vast canvases of darks and lights, expressing my troubled inner thoughts and how they clashed with the soft, unsatisfactory textures of the world around me, I wrote poetry and short stories, mixing my inner workings with the outside world. I created truth.

So far unsuccessful, at least in the conventional sense, in my endeavours, I at least looked the part. I favoured loose-fitting, long, swinging dresses and tops, paired with thick tights or leggings, and statement ankle boots. The rest of the group had shiny hair, falling in perfect, well-cut shapes around their shoulders. Un-highlighted, a muddy brown, mine was unkempt, half up, half down. My breasts were large, my legs long. On paper, I had the goods, but context is everything, and next to Megan, Antonia, Bea, and Elizabeth,

I was self-consciously ginormous. And eminence evaded me.

Kicking my boots off to lighten the load on my legs as they swung from the stool, I pretended to absorb the notion that Antonia and I could be similar as if I was really considering it. I didn't need to overdo my consideration of her ridiculous proposition that I was in any way like that paper-faced, fake-tanned, hateful woman, who did nothing all day but admire herself, spend her husband's money, and fawn over her babies. It took about forty-five seconds to return to Megan's favourite topic these days: Megan.

She moved slowly yet gracefully across the stone floor, choosing spices from the rack, pouring olive oil into the heavy orange pan on the hob. She had many recipe books on high shelves across the room, but rarely used them. She liked to experiment in the kitchen. Even by June last year, when Megan really wasn't operating at full capacity, she cooked tremendously. As she chopped and grated and stirred, her questioning went on, answers unnecessary. Was it the pills, and had her doctor given any consideration to the possibility of a genetic disposition towards mental illnesses in her family? Was she simply tired, anxious, stressed? Was her mind playing tricks on her? Was she paranoid? Was she imagining things? Why would the doctor accuse her of lying?

But even Megan, who had historically occupied the moral high ground knew why. Everyone knows it is far too easy to get hold of Mother's Little Helpers without a real prescription. You can't always blame the hapless doctors when our sparkling ladies are dulled on the inside, procuring their spoils from book clubs, mothers at the school gate, or artistic cocktail makers just wanting to help. You can even get them online if you know where to look.

I had started to think it was going to be a very long night, then Adam arrived. I heard the door, and Megan rushed out to greet him, leaving me sat alone. I thought my birthday would be rescued after all. I heard whispers, then raised whispers, staccato and fast.

'Oh Megan!' She was being reprimanded.

More whispers and footsteps running up the stairs, and back down again, then silence. They entered the kitchen together, clutching a gift, singing happy birthday. When they'd finished, they embraced me in a group hug and, for a moment, it felt like the old days. I tore off the paper, the bow fell to the floor. I didn't bother to pick it up. It was a jewellery box. I didn't have any real jewellery. I slowly opened the lid of the long thin box to reveal a diamond hanging from a pale, thin chain.

'It's the one of mine you love so much, we want it to be yours,' Megan said, and started to take it from the box and fasten it around my neck. Her breath was sweet and alcoholic. Adam made a show of appraising me.

I knew what this was. She'd accused me of coveting it before, and not so long ago she'd accused me of far worse. This gift may be worth a lot of money but its real value is a slap in the face. Hand-me-downs and sympathy: Megan's favourite gifts. Had she just run upstairs to wrap it now, hastily, reminded by Adam that it was my birthday dinner? She hadn't even offered to cook a favourite of mine. We were having chilli prawn and courgette pasta, hardly pushing the boat out, and I always found it a little too spicy. She'd completely forgotten that my birthday was the whole point of this dinner. That, and to put the book club row well behind us; a chance for Meghan and I to bond once more. But Adam was back, and he'd remembered. Necklace be damned, things could have been worse.

And of course, now they are. Much worse.

Beneath the ambient lighting of One Lombard Street, I watch Adam and Peter dab tears for Megan away. I watch them toast Adam's new life. I watch them scramble in their pockets for phones, and try to find dates to meet *lovely Lucy.* They don't talk about me. They don't toast my birthday. They don't reminisce about happier times. They don't think of me, and they don't see me. No one ever does.

When Adam gets up, he has to steady himself by holding onto the chair. After almost tumbling down the limestone steps, he zig-zags up the pavement, waving goodbye to an equally precarious Peter. He stops once, suddenly, and I don't notice and so I'm next to him staring into the same shop window and I see him see me in the glass, our forms morphed into hall of mirrors monstrosities by light pollution. He squints at our reflection. I can smell him.

He steps back without grace, still gazing at the reflection, but then throws himself forward, muttering something about weird, and I know he's fooled himself, too drunk to see anything, never mind the truth, but instead only shades and shapes reflecting against the confusing bodies of mannequins and frippery. He makes it to the roadside and flags a taxi, shouting his home address more loudly than he needs to. I follow him, wherever he goes. I wonder if he's drunk too much to dream, or if he will dream of me tonight? Last year, after my birthday, Adam replaced the diamond necklace Megan gave to me with a larger, more beautiful one presented to her on a holiday they took without me. Platinum chain, no white gold that easily dulls. I wore it to her funeral. I haven't taken it off since.

Adam

The spring in his step was such a surprise to him he almost tripped over it as he walked down the immaculately maintained pavements that connected one skyscraper after another. Was he whistling? Frankly, he thought to himself, he didn't give a damn, and swung the door to the local newsagent's wide open, allowing it to swing back too quickly. As he jumped back to save the day and prevent the bang of the door, he chuckled aloud. The girl at the checkout narrowed her eyes, dubious of yet another deranged customer in the local shop. A man about to go over the edge, or typical end-of-week bottle of Merlot? Her guess was as good as anyone's in this corner of London; burnout a daily regime alongside spin classes, deadlines, promotions, and demotions. Checkout girl took her turn to smirk as he grabbed a bottle of Merlot and placed it on the counter.

'Anything else?' She had quickly rearranged her face back to her preferred stony expression. Adam didn't notice.

'Oh no, this bottle at home, then off out to celebrate with my girlfriend!' He proudly announced before feeling marginally self-conscious about how much of a middle-aged twat he sounded. Why couldn't he have just said 'no thanks'? Briefly he considered marrying Lucy just to never have to say the word girlfriend out loud in public again. The thought passed quickly. As he skipped out of the shop, his foot met with something hard, unbalancing him, and made a sound a bit like a cough, but not quite.

'Shit, what the —'

A flash of the dangerous mood of the last months suddenly darkening his face, revealing itself to be alive and well beneath the current happy veneer, fooling everyone, including himself. He stopped and saw with shame it was a man sat on the otherwise pristine pavement in soiled and torn trousers, dirty paper cup held out. Adam automatically fished in his pocket for change. He threw a couple of coins into the cup carefully avoiding the man's eyes but noticing his black fingernails, and scrawny neck. As the man politely thanked and blessed him in a voice of tar, he thought of the odd little notes he used to find in his pockets, planted by Olivia.

Adam was sure at first there had been a reason for her to write him a note, but he'd forgotten what it was, and for a while they were funny, cute even, but later it got a bit weird. He'd never said anything, didn't want to hurt her feelings. Perhaps he should have. He never told Megan either. Lying by omission. Something he'd had to do a lot of since then. But it had worked and Adam was once again gainfully employed. The call had come at three fifty-three this afternoon, almost exactly three hours ago. They were pleased, wait — no — they were thrilled, to have him on board.

Wine in one hand, he keyed in the codes to get into his tower, and then through his door. He popped the cork to let the wine breathe and slumped onto the sofa, throwing an unwanted cushion to the floor, and taking in the views ahead as the sky started to darken, cloaking the river. Forty-five minutes before Lucy arrived, enough time to shower, dress and catch up on the latest financial news. And what a lot of catching up he had to do. Once a slave to every stock market app, a beep that became white noise as everything but his guilt faded into irrelevance for months and months on end. His laptop lay sleeping on the glass side table next to the sofa. He woke it up.

Oil rose yet again, settling at $52.59 a barrel, for its ninth-straight gain. That hasn't happened since January 2010, he thought. *GE rose 5.2%, is the worst over?* The journalist speculated. Did he care as much as before, he pondered? Probably not. But it was good to have something to think about other than how Megan should still be alive.

Megan had been radiant. Not just beautiful, but quick witted, never still, like electricity. But when it had all changed, that was difficult to pinpoint. Years pass, excitement dulls, and suddenly dimples become wrinkles, and those funny little quirks become habits you might murder for. It hadn't happened overnight. They'd both worked hard, he at a Leeds Stockbrokers, learning his trade, and she heading up the day-to-day running of her father's livery stables. A cottage not far from Ilkley, in the village of Askwith, a world away from their peers' lives of city lights, making them feel grown-up, secure, whilst the novelty of playing house provided interest. Breakfast tables were laid, rather than coffee grabbed on the go, and nights in front of the wood burner were hot, then naked and sweaty.

The nineties were a good time for Adam and Megan. They didn't have much money, but they were full of energy, and loved each other more than anyone else. Towards the end of the decade, everyone fretted over the possibility of the millennial bug, and they met Olivia for the first time. The millennial bug turned out to be nothing to worry about. Adam wished he could say the same for Olivia. In the year 2000, the world partied and so did the happy couple, full of hope for the future. Now almost twenty years have passed since the night they danced under Y2K banners and popped balloons, and Adam can't fathom a world that Olivia hadn't destroyed, at least for him.

Megan had tired of him long before she said her final goodbyes: his constant demands to move to London, to start afresh. She'd tired of everything, he'd thought at the time. He couldn't blame Olivia for everything. He could have done more. Or less. Depends how you look at it, he'd often thought to himself.

How long before Lucy tired of him? Tutted at him for breathing too loudly and favoured a late-night girls' text conference to his touch? And when would her most perfect disposition, endless confidence turn, like sour milk, into insecurity and neediness, driving him to emerge through the surface, towards the light, as if he were escaping from drowning in the dark sea having jumped into a glorious, safe swimming pool. A favourite metaphor of Adam's, offered by way of explanation on why a man should never marry by Peter.

'They're a shallow swimming pool when you first look at them, mate,' Peter had originally explained, perhaps as long ago as sixth form days. 'You can see your reflection in their eyes, and it looks good. You just want to jump on in, knowing you can easily climb out to safety. But once you're in, they transform, like Ursula, and you're in the Atlantic Ocean. It's deep, unfathomable, and all the rescue ships have long gone. You're going to drown, mate, in the end, the question is: can you keep afloat a while longer?'

Never a cynic, Adam had laughed then and repeatedly as the metaphor was replayed, unable to imagine a world in which Megan's light no longer brightened his existence. He had turned a blind eye at first, but as the evidence mounted, Adam had seen his wife's increased neuroticism, fragility and unpredictability as inevitable; part of the female progression. And so he had lived with it, and then Olivia, who'd started as an extra in the story of their lives, started to offer hope. Hope of a connection, one not marred by seething under-currents of marital irritation. He had clung to it, at the expense of all else. A lifeline, though it turned out to be something else.

Adam clicked the laptop shut, news digested though his mind still too easily led astray by his meandering memories. So what if Lucy tired of him? Or he her. No longer were life-defining forever-declarations and being the chosen one at the centre of another's universe components of the good life. Adam had a second chance, and his main plan was to live a normal, quiet life, with a normal job, a normal girlfriend, in a normal flat. No more magical swimming pools to swallow him alive, just basic, safe, dry-land connections, like puddles splashing and occasionally overlapping.

He replaced the laptop on the table and hopped into his room to shower and dress. The intercom went just as he buttoned and then unbuttoned the collarbone button of his starchy pink shirt and tucked it into his jeans. A little chest hair springily winked at him in the mirror. Too much, he thought? And then, dashing to the door to see that glorious smile, he thought, fuck it.

She screamed with delight as he picked her up and twirled her around and around.

'I did it, Luce, and we are celebrating!'

'You are so brilliant!' She kissed him hard on the mouth, tilted her head back and grinned at him, 'I knew you would.' Matter of fact, Lucy stepped back and appraised him. 'Looking good, mister, now pour me some wine, and tell me everything.'

They glugged back wine, kissed hungrily, and shared secret smiles as they readied themselves for a night of gluttony at a new Japanese restaurant in the heart of Canary Wharf, just fifteen minutes' walk away from the flat. Adam had happily noted Lucy's small wedged sandals beneath her long, elegant summery wrap dress, and knew that she wouldn't demand a taxi. It was a beautiful evening to walk. Lucy twiddled with the chunky gold bracelet she always wore on her right wrist as she attentively listened to his excited tales of everything he knew so far about his new job and team. Her bare arms looked so delicate poking out from the wide wings of the sleeves of her dress. She was pleased, he could tell. Genuinely pleased *for* him, no agenda. As he locked the door, and took hold of her hand, he stepped forward, and for the first time in a long time he didn't look back.

Olivia

Was he actually sprightly? That's not how I remember him. Adam was always a serious man. I used to love his sober, furrowed brow. He brooded, evaded questions. He was mysterious, just out of reach. His stature demanded respect, not ridicule, and tonight he's behaving ridiculously. Even the spotty, greasy-haired shop assistant had nothing but disdain for him. I hope he's not on the verge of a breakdown. And could *Luce* be any more of a cliché? They walked hand in hand like schoolgirls. She was giggling. She laughs at everything he says. She agrees with him, nodding like those dreadful toy puppies that sit mournfully looking out of the back window of a car. She's so amenable. I hate her.

Megan wasn't amenable, she was a woman in charge.

'Adam, really?' I once overheard her snap in a whisper shortly after I'd come back from my trip. 'You can't just work late every night, without a sniff of a promotion, and then refuse to engage at home as well.'

He'd paused. From my position in the hallway, I couldn't see him, but I imagined he was turning on his heel and planning to walk out of the room. He obviously changed his mind.

'I need to move to London to earn more, Megan, as I keep telling you! We said we'd think about it this year. And now! Now you've dug your heels in, and it's all about you!'

They were no longer whispering now, as Megan retorted,

'You damn well know we can't move to London with everything else we have to deal with right now!'

It was no wonder to me that Adam was getting utterly fed up as I couldn't see what she could mean about having so much to deal with other than her own neuroses and escalating dependence on booze and pills. Everything else other than the struggles she was creating herself was pretty straightforward as far as I could see. And I saw most things that happened. As I said, I'm very observant. They'd looked up when I walked into the kitchen, where this little altercation was taking place, just offstage, as the dinner party in the adjacent dining room roared on.

'Can I help with anything?' I'd asked, and he'd grabbed a bottle of red from the rack and muttered something about getting back to his hosting. She'd looked at me quizzically, trying to read what I'd heard, what I thought, though I doubt she really cared. She was pretty forthcoming in her critique of her husband to anyone who'd listen when he was out of earshot.

I'd started keeping a diary at a young age, and still did at this point. I recorded things that happened, to me, and to others. I extrapolated from the insights that I had things that easily could be happening behind closed doors. As an artist, as an intellectual, I understood reality was a human construct, understanding and perceptions the building blocks of truth. Megan thought that they had built a life in Yorkshire and that Adam was being selfish. Adam thought that he needed something else, something different, and that Megan was holding him back. I thought I could help. I had always been determined to be there for both of them and to help them keep everything the way it was. Until Megan changed.

Adam had made the celebratory reservation for tonight by telephone on his way back from the shop. Apparently, he knew he was lucky to get a table at such short notice. I get to the restaurant before them. If you will stop to snog in the street, then you will not catch the worm. Honestly, it's embarrassing, at his age. She's got no excuse either. High school hair, the popular girl's shiny, thick curls, defying logic as they bounced yet stayed in place perfectly, but that perfectly applied natural look make up wasn't fooling me, whatever her yoga regime and juice diet books had promised her, her skin wasn't great. She probably thought she had it all, but I was always one step ahead these days. Always.

Apparently, Lucy is easy going, especially compared to Megan, who was the definition of high maintenance. Supposedly, Lucy is not needy. I heard Peter call me needy once, and Adam didn't correct him. I'd been unfairly labelled. My love, adoration, dedication misinterpreted as smothering; too much. Perhaps, as he keeps telling any old loser who'll listen, 'Lucy is just what he needs', but I know it's a lie. The breezy appearance a mask, easily removed with the right little nudges. No woman in Adam's thrall is breezy, she's just camouflaged, ready to pounce.

I use my spare minutes to appraise the venue, or at least I try my best to in the gloomy atmospheric lighting. It is a chain restaurant claiming exclusivity. Familiar enough to not require guests to leave their comfort zones, but a price point and critique write-up only an independent can usually command. Risk-averse show-offs are the main target audience, I quickly conclude. They finally emerge from the lift onto the second floor and approach the maître d', a stout woman dressed in formal black and white with a stern face, onto which she paints a fake smile as they step close enough to make out the line of her lips in the dark corridor leading to the main restaurant. My little test begins. Unseen, not atypical these days, my viewing is slightly impaired as I sit around the corner in the bar, but I can hear the exchange.

'Welcome sir!'

'Reservation for Sykes, eight p.m.' Matter of fact, commanding, still sprightly.

Face down, our stout penguin runs her index finger down the page seeking out Sykes. 'Ah yes, there you are sir, Mr Adam Sykes and Mrs Olivia Sykes, you are very, very welcome, please come.'

A beautifully abrupt stop, without a word uttered, but that human instinct particularly fine-tuned in those who spend their days and nights interacting with strangers, putting them at ease. Her fake smile dissolved, her face ashen, mouth agape. The maître d' turns to *Luce*, who is starting to look like she's having a minor stroke, as she struggles to keep her composure and waits for the explanation that will tell her it's all okay, and that there isn't a Mrs Olivia Sykes concealed just off stage, or worse still, hiding back at his other home, the one she hasn't been invited to. Perhaps another Mr Sykes is in tonight? Perhaps, perhaps, but no.

'There's been a mistake. I reserved a table for two under my name. There is no Mrs Sykes.' Adam is being masterful. A swan seen only above the water. I wonder what is happening beneath that calm surface to propel him through this little storm.

Penguin shuffles through her book, busies herself with some meaningless scribbles, and hurriedly apologises. I imagine she is confused, as she would have found the note next to the booking, which clearly explained that the eminent couple liked the personal touch, so the use of the familiar should be encouraged. Not wishing to delve further, she probably sees all sorts of relationships, deceit and characters, she adopts her more usual formal tone, and tells them she'll show them to the best table in the house.

Curiosity gets the better of me, so I get up and move as if to go to the lifts, turning to see them walk away. I watch Lucy flinch as Adam's hand touches the small of her back, allowing her to slightly step ahead. It was imperceptible. Had her mask slipped just a little, a hint that she too might have the urge to possess him? A simple mistake, her composure soon regained, quickly forgotten if it remains a one-off. But in this moment, he's not quite as sprightly. As they are escorted through to their table I take in the layout of the restaurant, and decide to stay a while, exploring the dark nooks and crannies, close enough to hear how they handle their first adverse event.

I wonder if he is transported back to that last year with Megan, the texts she denied sending, claimed to have no memory of. The emails he found in her archive, badly buried. The disasters at her business, always someone else's fault, apart from the witness who tells you otherwise. The proof is there: you did this, you must have. Accusation hanging between them, denials weak. Explanations sought in illness, in drink, in malice, but none agreeable to both parties. Just for a moment, does he feel what she felt? Alone, confused, discombobulated. If he does, not for long. He orders champagne, they clink glasses. He touches her hand too many times. He tells her that Olivia is no one. He's beginning to get on my nerves.

57

I left the second-floor cave-like destination and waited outside as they ate. I've become very good at waiting, and time no longer seems to go so slowly, not now that I am close by again, now that I have a plan. Still, I wish it was me sat inside with him, sipping champagne and improving my fairly shabby chopstick skills.

He hasn't taken me for a meal since late last August. He'd left Megan at that point. I'd made a special effort, dressing up, trying to be patient and sympathetic about the complicated circumstances circling all of us. It had been hard not to let my resentment show as he evaded my questions and refused to make plans with me. I don't like change as a rule, and I like it even less when I don't know what's coming. It was around that time that I started to suspect he might like change. He was drifting away from me as well as putting distance between himself and Megan. I had to stop him, yet I failed. I would have come to London with him if he'd asked. We could have started again together. I tried to make him see, but within a month of that last, difficult dinner she was dead and he was gone.

Adam

Adam's spring in his step had diminished as soon as he'd heard Olivia's name. He didn't understand how he could have possibly made such a momentous error. Olivia's name was banished from his daily dialect, and there had been no Mrs Sykes for a while. Not once had he forgotten this painful fact. It's really not the sort of thing a man forgets easily. He had tried to forget Olivia.

Foolish man, he berated himself. He was unstable, then, was he? As Peter had asked, and confidently he'd said no. He was still plagued, he had talked of a Mrs Sykes, he had mentioned Olivia's name, and of this he had no memory. He cannot have said Mrs Olivia Sykes; that was impossible. But could he have said Mr and Mrs? Possible, it used to roll off the tongue, and that day he had felt almost like his old self. Lucy had handled it well, having no real reason to assume it was anything other than the mistake of an overstretched receptionist at the restaurant.

'Unless there's something you're not telling me' she'd joked.

Until then, the omission of Olivia had seemed natural, and now it felt dishonest. Correction: it was dishonest, and he didn't know how he would ever put it right. They'd talked of his new role, Lucy had told him about her day at the office involving an unruly minor C-list celebrity playing havoc with the media plan she'd been working on for months, in her 'not glamorous at all really, babe' PR office. They'd drank just a little too much, but Lucy's constitution wasn't quite of Adam's long-standing capacity. It had taken three attempts to type in the code to get into her flat.

'I could do with waking up at home, I've got spin class down the road really early, God help me,' she'd slurred in the taxi, 'And you may as well see what a dreadful slob I am before you get too attached.'

If Adam was relieved to still be officially with Lucy after the reservation debacle, he had been over the moon to be welcomed into her home, despite, as a rule, preferring to play host himself, and wake up in his own bed. As Lucy had gingerly felt along the hallway wall for a light switch, Adam avoided the piles of shoes threatening to cause an accident, and in doing so the bottom of his shoe came into contact with something soft and angry. An inhumane noise, and the light switched on.

'Argh, shit, I stood on your cat!'

'Shhhhh.' Lucy stroked the cat, who stalked off, indignant tail in air. 'That's William, he's your main competition.'

Giggling, they'd tumbled through the second door on the left, Lucy's room, and onto her unmade bed but she'd quickly jumped up, muttering something indecipherable about the bathroom. He'd lay alone for a few minutes, taking in the scene. She was right, the room was a bit cluttered, but it was endearing to Adam. Photo frames bursting with smiles and laughter covered every surface, and between them he could see that dusting wasn't a priority. Her work clothes, presumably from earlier, had been flung on top of her miniature washing basket for one in the corner of the room rather than placed inside, and he wondered if it was full or if she just felt that opening the lid was too great an effort in the grand scheme of things. Make-up lids lay next to their pots, tubes and pallets on the dressing table next to it. The mirror had been cleaned in a rush, the smears in the corner giving the corner-cutter away.

When she'd reappeared, there was a little toothpaste on her bottom lip, and Adam had an overwhelming urge to kiss it away. She was perfect in that moment, bedraggled and wobbly, but still so self-assured. She had lay next to him, close, and sleepily stroked his chest, undoing the buttons on his shirt. He had automatically pulled her even closer, fumbling with the tie on the back of her dress. She undid it for him and the dress, fell open, and as their breath quickened, Adam wasted no time peeling off his own jeans and socks, and pushing them to the bottom of the bed with his feet. Things had started to look up, until they didn't. He'd hastily pulled the covers over the two of them, hiding his lack of erection and his shame. Olivia had hijacked this simple moment.

Lucy, too drunk to be concerned and eyes already closing, sleepily reassured him, 'Don't worry, it's just the booze.'

He'd slept little that Friday night at Lucy's house. Saturday morning, he'd managed to show some enthusiasm to make up for his failed attempt at sex, and whilst not his best performance, or their most connected, he'd at least moved utter failure to the time before last, rather than the most recent memory. Lucy had pulled on his shirt straight after and padded out to make tea.

Early, just seven fifteen, the house share was up,

everyone planning on hitting the gym or juicing, or whatever their holy schedules demanded, Adam had thought uncharitably. His head had been sore, and although desperate to pull the covers back over his head, he somehow resisted, mentally getting ready to swing home, get out of Lucy's hair, and do some more background reading before Monday morning. As he'd grappled in sheets for lost items of clothing, he'd heard Lucy laugh at something a housemate said.

'Seriously, Lucy, you're sure he's not married?'

They had all laughed. Great, early scepticism from the friends. Brilliant bloody start.

He spent the rest of the weekend moping about his flat, trying to forget the last twenty-four hours and remember what he did for a living, and that he used to be good at it.

A bright Monday morning finally arrived, and sat at his new desk, surrounded by new faces, he wasn't so sure even he was convinced by his protestations of competence. The open plan design meant he'd got a sense of the pace quickly. Fast. The lights were too bright, and the walls too white. His desk was large though, and well positioned near a wide window with views down onto a patch of green often used for concerts and outdoor cinema nights in the warmer months. People walked past his desk in a blur, and the background noise was high. It was an attack on the senses, and Adam wasn't used to it these days, but he had missed it. He could see that now.

'Ah Adam!' James, Head of Equities, slapped Adam hard on the back, bringing him back to the room from his thoughts.

Despite the humid air that surrounded them outside, James was in a full three-piece suit, waistcoat buttoned snugly, tie knot unfeasibly fat. His facial hair was only partially grown, or perhaps it was only partially trimmed. Most likely, either way, it was supposed to look like that. Adam was still catching up with fashion, having happily avoided it for a number of years, but he knew that whatever he discovered, he had no intention of ditching his tried and tested clean shaven look.

'I'd like to meet later, once you're settled. This role is jam-packed with great opportunities.' James emphasised his last two words as if requiring ironic speech bubbles to be mimed with a raised eyebrow. 'Just needs the right person...' he went on.

Adam almost hallucinated the sardonic mime on *right person* this time. If he wasn't careful, he'd end up performing it and getting in a confrontation on his first day.

James was still talking, '...to really go balls deep.'

Jesus, Adam thought, struggling to keep his face straight, what an utter wanker.

'So swing by my office, say three? Let's hear your strategy. Heard you used to head up equities back in the sticks before your sabbatical.' Sabbatical was emphasised, without empathy. 'Based out of Leeds though? It's tougher here, some right nuts if I'm honest mate, but Pete said you're the bollocks.'

More testicles in this conversation than in his trousers, Adam thought. As Head of European Equities beneath James' Head of Equities, but a fellow MD all the same, James' assumption of seniority over Adam was technically correct, but his involvement in Adam's strategy was neither expected nor typical. Yet, a year out of the loop, with targets more than five times over his prior comfort zone, though it irked him to swallow pride, Adam's testicles felt very small. James swaggered off, more back-slapping offering a percussion bass behind the constant, loud, and indiscernible chatter of the floor. Suits, sweat, swearing. The youth astounded him. When did he get so much older than everyone else in this godforsaken industry?

Refusing to work out of London hadn't helped. Megan's life was in Yorkshire, and her heart too, she'd often told him. His heart was wherever she was, back then in the beginning. Her livery business, inherited from her wealthy, now dead, father, was her heart and soul. He wished he had been that to her.

Of course, the irony grew as Adam's ability to progress and compete with the London-based husbands of their friends was increasingly hampered by Megan's romantic view that they should both work, and they should live side by side, all week, not just home visits when the banks shut for forty-eight hours. He hadn't complained at first, but there came a point where he really believed it was his turn to choose. Not that he blamed her, at least not entirely, but Adam had become dissatisfied, and he hadn't hidden it very well.

The bracing winds on the moors, the daily riding, business challenges overcome, new clients recruited and eventing wins had kept Megan young, slender and most of all, happy for a time, a long time. He hadn't noticed when she stopped eventing herself, preferring to watch from the side lines, bringing on young riders instead. There was a lot he hadn't noticed back then, as he'd stopped going along to cheer, stopped being by her side.

'I'm lonely, Adam,' she had complained, more than once. He'd felt her to be selfish and unreasonable. Not only would she not go with him to London, but she demanded he stayed trapped by her side. They'd been married over two decades when he ramped up his campaign to relocate; they were no longer on a honeymoon. He lived where it suited her, worked where it didn't suit him, and entertained her friends. They had work, other priorities. Now he lived with guilt for not putting Megan first. She was the kind of woman who expected to be put first, and now he saw that she had always deserved to be put first. He should have listened.

His rebellion had heightened her sense of isolation, exacerbated her behaviour. He could have listened, but she had sounded quite awful at times, accusations flying, struggling to keep paranoia kept at bay. And the lies, all he'd heard that year was lies. He shouldn't have come to rely on Olivia during those dark months, he knew that now.

When Olivia first arrived, she'd been his wife's project. She was taken under the wing of the whole of Megan's gang, like an injured bird. He didn't get involved, really, to begin with. He'd left the girls to it. But eventually he'd been persuaded by Megan that her oddities were charming. They'd become close. It was nice to have someone other than Peter to talk to, to hang out with. It made a change to be not entirely reliant on Megan, Megan's oldest school friends, Megan's bloody Yorkshire. His outrage, when Megan threw accusations, was contained. After all, Megan wasn't well.

'You're the one who brought her back here,' he'd chided her, but gently. Inside, though, he'd been seething. Megan was paranoid, he'd thought. How unfair that Megan should go to such efforts to avoid being alone with him, whilst refusing him the opportunity to be alone with anyone else.

Their house had continuously bustled with life, squeezing Adam out of the main fold. Until it didn't contain any life at all.

Plagued by memories of Megan, and paralysed with fear that his mind could be so diseased that it would add Olivia's name to his dinner reservations after months of purposeful oblivion from her image, her memory, his thinking was impaired. Adam turned his attention to a spreadsheet on one monitor, Reuters' financial live updates on another, and the FTSE screen on the wall, Adam, started to sketch out some thoughts for James. By the time three o'clock arrived, he had some thoughts, but they were ill-conceived. Even the new boy from Yorkshire could see that.

Unable to polish the turd on his desk, his head swimming, Adam had few palatable options: brazen it out and blag it, or bravely run away. If only there was a choice. James was waiting, and before he knew it, he was striding into the meeting room the other man had reserved, hoping for enough vague yet promising-sounding nuggets to keep James from asking too much, should he seem lacking in initiative. If all else fails, confuse the shit out of them, wink, and walk out purposefully. Peter had taught him well.

Olivia

I waited outside all day for him to emerge. Even I can see his new office is pretty cool. Who would have thought he would be on the forty-fifth floor right in the centre of his beloved Canary Wharf? He had come a long way from his complaints of little league back home, though I suppose this is his home now. The sun was shining, but his vitality had been dulled when I followed him this morning.

I hadn't known he would go back to Lucy's *digs* on Friday night. I hadn't actually heard her call them that, but I imagined it was the sort of posh, London slang she and her wholesome friends would use. I had, however, known just how to get into his flat having paid very close attention over the last few days, and seeing as there wasn't anything further to view of the happy couple, at least not for the fainthearted, now seemed as good a time as any to finally see this new world close up.

I slipped in easily, unseen. I entered into an enormous open-plan kitchen and living room, the space under used, and a gulf between the kitchen and the sitting area. Windows replaced walls and the view, in my opinion, was grim, but undoubtedly the right side of London; you could tell by the percentage of skyscrapers made of glass versus concrete forming the foreground to the river's backdrop. But still so grey, so square, out there, and so bright, so angular in here. The complete opposite to the rolling hills of home, and the soft furnishings lovingly chosen by Megan, and handmade by someone else.

Cartoon pink lips in the shape of Lucy's mouth marked the rim of a wine glass, almost empty, next to a bottle and another glass drained, this one unmarked. I wandered, leisurely, through the room, taking in the expensive furniture, noticing the lack of clutter, or personal things. The few pieces of furniture were utilitarian, masculine. I could appreciate that, I like practical things. The sofas were large and not too squishy. Firm and with only two cushions, unlike the piles of mismatched squares and rectangles that bedecked Megan's huge, body-enveloping sofas.

From this gigantic hollow space, there was a corridor: wide, wooden-floored, leading to a series of doors. A large bathroom, towels neatly folded on a shelf next to the shower. There was an empty soap dish, and a toothbrush holder integrated into the wall, but no toothbrush or paste. The toilet roll had not been opened, there wasn't even a splash of water in the sink. I assumed he had an en suite.

I was right, and in it there was the faint remaining scent of him, his deodorant, his aftershave. Even now, after everything, it comforted me, made me feel at home, safe. In his bedroom, a low, modern bed — bigger than any I've seen before — still left ample space to walk around the room. I take in the lines that make up his life, devoid of colour: the fitted wardrobes, the full-length mirror and a large television on the wall. In his wardrobe I scan the shirts and come to the coats, the jackets. Notes no longer hidden (I checked), the magic of before gone, erased. One jacket though, linen, bloodstains never washed out. The one he must have worn that fateful day, returning from his mother's home, to find

Megan. That's a bit Lewinsky-esque, if you ask me. He really could have chucked it out if he couldn't face the dry-cleaners. I can imagine it now.

'Oh, dear, sir, this is a bit of a mess.'

'Yes, I was wearing it when I discovered my dead wife. Such a shame; this jacket was very expensive.'

I looked closely, checked the pockets. No note, but her gift was still there, never opened, never returned. She died just two days before her birthday. He hadn't wrapped it yet, and I imagine he'd bought it that very day. He'd probably forgotten it was here in all the commotion. I look closer. Huge diamond earrings to match the chain around my neck but twice the price. Even now, she is worth more than I.

He'd made a fake haven for himself in his new pad. The other bedroom was similarly furnished, to give the impression of a home lived in, but this jacket, her blood, and the unworn earrings are the only reminders — the only proof — of that time, of us, of a real life in a real home, and of love. I look through drawers and inside cupboards. There's no trace of me.

I still have some of the notes, the ones he accidentally threw away. I knew he usually kept them, hidden, as keepsakes. I'd seen one when I was looking in his bedside drawer mixed in between receipts. One of the receipts was for a perfect night we spent in London. I took that as a souvenir, but left the note. The receipt I stuck in my diary, annotating and drawing around it adding colour from my memories and imagination. I found one of my notes crumpled in the kitchen bin amongst a stack of old train tickets. I knew he had thrown it away by accident yet I couldn't give it back to him, with splashes of egg yolk on the corner. That might have seemed odd. I worked hard to be less odd, on Megan's advice. I often helped tidy up after dinner or drinks parties whilst everyone else drank more and sat around doing nothing. So, as it happened, I found a few more old notes, over time. I kept them all.

Looking at this bare home, this empty life, save for a temporary distraction-piece girlfriend and almost certainly soon to be soul-destroying job, I know he needs a reminder of what he's left behind, and what he's thrown away. Literally and metaphorically. Given the circumstances, I decide maybe now it's okay to be odd. Perhaps Megan would have advised differently, but she's no longer here to control me, and make me more like everyone else. I select one of the notes from my one surviving book, its leather exterior somehow preserving at least some of its guts. I keep it with me still. The remaining delicate charred pages tear at the spine as I gently open it, and remove a hidden note to place in the pocket of a silk-lined royal blue suit jacket, before quietly leaving.

The weekend passed slowly. He rarely left his apartment, so I passed some time getting to know the remarkable Lucy instead. She has a cat called William, and three housemates almost as irritating as she. Not much else to report really. She could possibly do with some PR herself, add a bit of interest to her predictable and overused mould.

When Monday morning arrived I was positioned in my new favourite spot, underneath a chestnut tree, just left of the concierge reception doors. Almost with him, I walked his new route to his new office. As I said, very cool. And populated with the cream of London, I guess. All day long, well dressed, slim young bankers, girls and boys, popped in and out, making calls, grabbing coffee to go, hungrily smoking a cigarette sat on a bench or a wall, steeling themselves for the next challenge of the day. Some of them looked purposeful, all of them neat. They reminded me of a younger version of Megan, and of the others. Of a world I never could belong to. I don't care much anymore, so long as I can belong to Adam again.

I thought about him, up there, surrounded by new faces. I wondered if he still saw mine. Finally, at about two minutes past five he came into sight. Not exactly going the extra mile on his first day, he must be exhausted. Poor thing. I felt an overwhelming desire to look after him. Still lacking in vigour, but with a determined face, he was scrambling in his pocket, and out popped his lifeline. He swiped, and held it to his ear. At least he wasn't using the wireless earbuds that the other suited and booted favoured. They looked like utter morons.

Closer, unseen by him, I listened to his side of the conversation.

'Peter, yeah, okay, okay.' A pause. 'Well first day and all that, mate, I was getting the lay of the land — did what was needed, but I reckon I'll have it sussed in a week or so.' His brow furrows as he listens, thinking. 'James? Yeah, bit of a cunt.' He laughed. I scowled, it's not a word I approve of. Then he drew breath and his hand went to his face. 'Oh, mate, I'm sorry. I did see your message, I forgot to be honest, just had stuff on my mind this weekend.' A sigh captured but not quite in time. 'I know, I know, it would have been so good to get your last-minute thoughts but—' Peter must have interrupted him. He always had been rude. 'Honestly I'm fine. It's all fine.'

71

He went quiet for a while. Peter was probably droning on about how awful it all is, and how poor Adam must look after himself. How little the old mouth-breather really knows. Adam and Megan looking after their respective number ones is what got us into this mess.

'No, I know, and it's nothing to do with her. Just a thing with Lucy. I promise.' Liar. He's so good at it now. It's everything to do with me. 'Lying by omission, maybe, but to be honest, you're the only person I'm still in touch with from back then. She doesn't need to know. I just need someone in my life who doesn't know.' Nobody knows, though, not even Peter. This is Oscar-worthy. I think he may believe his own propaganda. 'Yeah, I know, but right now, I just need to focus on the job. And Luce. You must come for dinner next time you're down, meet the lady herself. You'll love her.' Another pause to listen to more platitudes and promises. 'Honestly, I'm fine…'

He took an unexpected corner, and I lost him for a moment. When he came back into sight, he was slipping his phone back into his jacket pocket, and heading into a small off-licence. Drinking too much, in my view. Just like Megan, before she succumbed. Not a good path to take. And still sucking up to Peter — some things never change. Never liked him myself. He always went to great lengths to make me feel like I shouldn't be there, visibly perplexed at why I should be seated between Megan and Adam when he was invited for dinner, as if he alone had the rights to their company.

Peter is unashamedly self-assured, untroubled by the opinions of others. Antonia was the same, my least favourite of dear Megan's friends. It was always these types, less concerned with heeding the common view, more likely to raise an objection, it was *these types* that had always singled me out, got me into trouble, and turned my real friends against me. I'd become cautious around people like that, but my vigilance invariably would worsen their suspicions, as if it were a crime, an unfavourable trait, to have layers they couldn't see and name within five minutes of meeting me. The kind of people who said of art, 'I don't know a lot, but I know what I like.' Well, they didn't like me. If they'd bothered to look, I very much doubt they'd have liked my art either.

I first encountered one of these content, oblivious types at school. I was ten years old, and Jennifer was my new best friend. Jennifer was one of the most popular girls. She played Mary in the nativity play, and goal attack in the netball team. I was in the chorus, and on the bench. When Jennifer's parents divorced in our penultimate year of primary school, Jennifer didn't take it well. They don't, the spoilt ones; can't fathom something not going their way. I knew that, even then.

Jennifer started crying in class, dropping grades, but when she wet herself allegedly during a panic attack (more practical parents and teachers may have called it a tantrum) her life was over. Until then if she'd noticed me, she hadn't bothered to say so. She presumably thought me odd, too quiet, if she thought anything at all, someone to give a wide berth to, in case social inadequacy was catching. Nonetheless, I helped her. I needed a friend, and so did she. I taught her how to draw her feelings, how to write down her thoughts, keep diaries. What I lacked in showmanship and athleticism I made up for in creativity, and in my ability to think fast. For some reason, my academic achievements and my creative endeavours never impressed anyone, unlike the achievements of those nimble-footed, singing, dancing exhibitionists. Until then, aged ten, when they finally had a use.

Jennifer became the perfect friend. She let me read her diaries, review her drawings, as if at ten years old, I was qualified to make it all better. As it happened though, I was, and it worked. Jennifer stopped crying, and starting scoring goals again. The other girls started hanging around art corner, where Jennifer and I had taken to spending our break times.

'Come on, we're playing kiss-chase!' a girl called Sally said, pulling at Jennifer's ugly school jumper. 'Let's go out, it's boring in here.'

Jennifer looked at me for approval, she wasn't devoid of loyalty, not yet anyway. I resisted, she stayed, that day, and for a few more, but she was slipping away, soon to be swallowed by the mediocre masses of the playground. I had thought that she was better than that, just like I was.

That year at school we'd been taught about the Great Fire of London. Samuel Pepys' diary is considered one of the most valuable primary sources for those studying the Great Fire of London, and the years shortly before and after. However, what people don't always consider about diaries, particularly since we all started devouring other peoples in the name of research, is that they aren't true. A diary is an opinion, or worse still, an idea of an opinion you want someone to think you had.

Jennifer's Divorce Chronicles, as we called them, were a girl laid bare. But that girl wasn't Jennifer, who was a simple creature, pissed off that life wasn't quite how she liked it. Her diaries actually made for terrible reading — shockingly dull.

The girl in the diaries was a poet, a tad melodramatic, and dedicated to vigorous masturbation, nightly. They were edited of course, by me, and photocopied in the school office the day I had a headache and was excused from class. My handwriting, my style, perfectly matched to hers.

I didn't plan to hurt Jennifer, I just wanted to be friends. I learnt a lot at school that year. Always keep a diary, always a written record. Always have evidence. Obviously, soon after her betrayal Jennifer's life was over once more. No one believed her, not even her parents (who blamed themselves I overheard the teachers whisper) for her obsessive self-abuse.

Her parents telephoned mine, but I was keenly defended. Rumours of my psychological testing had gone around when my mother told another who couldn't be trusted, but as my parents reiterated, the tests had turned out to be nothing. I was perfectly normal. They sent Jennifer to counselling. Eventually, I heard, they moved away. Don't they all?

I've given up writing in my diaries now. I thought once that my truth mattered, but in the end, Adam destroyed it and replaced it with his own version of the truth, the very same one that drives Peter to pity him, and excuses his lies and forgetfulness. The truth that ensures my name is never mentioned. Both truths may be as flawed as one another, though mine at least was born out of love.

As we near his flat around twenty past five, I desperately want to follow him in. I count the seconds that he'll wait for the lift, and the short whoosh of time as he travels upwards at speed until I know he's home. I sit on the bench looking up at his window, I imagine walking to the front doors and calling his intercom, hearing his reaction through the crackle of the device. I see his face in my head and I conjure his smile like I always did before, when I had left him notes and pictured him finding them, and remembering to think about me. I hope he remembers me tonight. I want to hold my breath until the moment his eyes show me that he found my note. He has a lot of suits though, so it could be days, or even weeks. I hope not. I can't wait that long to be with him again, but then I worry that he might not be ready yet, and it scares me.

I think I've only got one more chance. The note will remind him of the future he promised was ours. I know I said he was a liar, but you can't make promises like that and not keep them. It's not fair and I'm not going to let it happen.

Adam

Adam sat with his face in his hands on the edge of the bed, a crumpled note by his right big toe. He thought the notes were all destroyed. Tossed away, or burned. Now, sat here in his suit trousers, socks, and a pale blue shirt, stunned midway through dressing for work on a regular Friday morning, he marvelled at how he'd missed one, how this note was here, today, in his favourite jacket pocket. Once a source of pleasure, he'd read them, smiling, basking in the fact that to someone he was always top of mind. Over time, he'd grown concerned over Olivia's neediness. Not wishing to cause an argument with Megan, he'd kept them out of sight, mainly crumpled with other rubbish in the bottom of a bin. It was one of the last few ones she'd written to him.

> *Don't forget I love you, whatever happens. I always will.*

The morning that he found that note had followed the night on which Adam had inadvertently chosen his side, the wrong side, and Megan had never fully trusted him again. Accusations had been bursting with unrequited malice, a pack waiting to pounce on their prey. Adam had been appalled at their treatment of Olivia that fateful book club night. He had arrived back to the scene of the argument, his own home, around ten, in a taxi, only a tad worse for wear after a few pints and a shared bottle of red with Peter at a local pub, famous for homemade pies. The commotion was in the garden in front of the house, thankfully detached and at least a hundred yards from the nearest neighbours. In the shadows of the late May evening, Adam could see that Elizabeth had a towel wrapped around her arm, and was stepping into the passenger seat of Bea's car. Even at the time, in his initial confusion, Adam wondered if any of the women at his wife's book club should drive home, given the inevitable clinking of the recycling bin each morning after.

He had told the taxi driver to keep the change, pushed the car door shut and walked up the garden path. An angry exchange was taking place between Megan and Antonia, both visibly tense, even from a distance, standing too close to each other, arms in turn folded then wildly gesticulating. Olivia stood back from the two women, staring, arms hanging dispassionately by her side. She looked small from where Adam was, despite being tall. He'd walked quickly, catching tails of ugly whispered recriminations.

'On purpose——' Antonia.

'No, she wouldn't——' Megan.

'Sociopathic tendencies——' Antonia again.

'Fuck you.' A new, yet entirely familiar, voice. Olivia had joined the twosome now, squaring up to them in a most uncharacteristic manner.

She was cut off with a sharp slap. Adam saw his previously impeccably behaved, beautifully dressed, kind and clever wife's hand had struck Olivia's cheek. The first real violence in her he'd ever witnessed, his was not a household accustomed to physical recriminations. As it turned out, the months that followed would see that change. Adam, choosing with his feet, rushed to Olivia. He couldn't stop himself. Her cheek was ablaze, and tears ran over the mottled redness. She shrugged off his protective arm quickly, stepping back, looking unsure whether she should go or stay. Antonia called to Bea to wait just in time, and jumped into the back seat, as they started the engine and, without indicating, drove off, far too quickly.

Adam had tried to make sense of what had just occurred. Megan had started to ramble, accusations at odds with her earlier defence flew across the garden path, as Olivia stood dumb. They all drank too much, apart from Olivia, who was probably the only reliable witness to this evening, Adam had thought. The words tumbling towards him made little sense. Had these women now bored of their project to make another of their own kind from this dishevelled and unusual beast? And in their failure to meet their own challenge had their determination turned to disappointment, even to anger?

Within this chain of thought, Adam discovered his victim. Poor Olivia had been left out, teased, and now accused. Adam asked himself, why should he believe these intoxicated women who he'd heard bully and bitch a thousand times, over sober, violated Olivia, who just didn't seem to fit in? He made his choice. As he'd automatically run to Olivia, she knew. As he berated Megan, she knew. And things would never be the same again.

Olivia had left the note under his car windscreen wiper, and he'd discovered it the next morning. He'd thought her insecure, troubled by what had happened the night before, afraid he wouldn't believe her and instead that he would side with her accusers. He worried that she was frightened that she might lose him because of it. Adam had gone to her that evening, held her tight, and promised her that it would all be ok. She blamed herself, Olivia said, she'd cried.

'I know she's not herself. I don't blame her for hitting me, I'm making everything worse. I never should have come back.'

Adam had felt in awe of Olivia in that moment, still so loyal. 'With or without you coming back, Megan wouldn't be herself right now. It's complicated,' he'd told her. 'Don't blame yourself. Imagine what I'd have done these last few months without you? You've been wonderful. You've been my rock.' He'd brushed away her hair from her face and wiped away her tears.

That small piece of paper had cried out for reassurance, but now it weighed heavily with menace. And here she was, her shape forming in his mind, larger than life, powered by the returned note. The words jumped out at him: *whatever happens*. Could she have known then what would? Dizziness overcame him. He got to the bathroom just in time to project his vomit into the clean white bowl of the toilet.

The royal blue suit jacket was discarded, misshapen on the bed. Adam angrily swiped it from the bed to the floor, as if it had purposely concealed the surviving note. He selected a different suit, dressed and looked in the mirror. He hated what he saw so he turned away. He manoeuvred a stubborn Olivia from the centre of his mind to its hidden bowels with great mental effort and started his journey into his office, that lion's den reduced to a basket of kittens in light of the torture of being here alone, thoughts whirling.

Day five, the end of a long week, and arriving at his desk, Adam knew he needed to put the discovery of the note behind him. He'd blagged the strategy, managed not to punch James in the face, got to know a couple of the other MDs, Leanne and Hugo, and found a young, ambitious vice president in Jean-Paul, newly settled in London from Paris, willing to provide some crunch support in return for some daily mentoring.

Adam was a bright man, he had charm, and he had experience. His confidence was building, or it had been until this morning. He wasn't looking for deep friendships now, but someone to have a drink with who wouldn't ask him if he was alright, or spend the evening cocking their head in sympathy. He didn't want nor deserve sympathy, but he couldn't tell anyone why, and so they took his protestations as a sign of admirable strength.

His old roles considered provincial, the political battles perhaps not as bloody, but ultimately, he knew enough to pull this off. Peter already seemed more relaxed on their calls, and through their frequent texts.

James not giving you a hard time?
Coping with the pace, mate?

His old friend was staying in town for the weekend, in fact, and joining Adam, James, and, according to James, 'some right bellends from the team' for Friday night drinks at a godawful chain bar in the centre of Canary Wharf, full of traders and banking tourists looking to bag a rich boy. As he queued in the canteen for a coffee, around eleven, a hand on his shoulder made him jump. He turned to see Leanne.

'Alright?' she asked. She was striking, and a little frightening. She wore a sleeveless grey dress that followed the line of her legs to just beneath the knee, pinched in the middle with a thick black belt. Sharp calf muscles in nude tights met the mandatory black high heels of the female contingent of banks everywhere in London. Although not formally required after a campaign to save women's feet, few took advantage of the relaxation of rules, preferring to add not diminish stature: killer instincts, killer heels, and looks that could kill. The kind of woman Adam had never been able to resist: fierce and unscrupulous. Now he preferred softer edges and fewer hidden layers.

'Leanne, sorry, you made me jump.'

She laughed, baring large, straight white teeth. 'You look like you've seen a ghost! I hope you're not that easily scared. Want to join me for a fag?'

He did. Adam didn't smoke, but he liked the way the smoke curled out from her lips. Her mouth moved quickly and contained a hundred expressions. His Fitbit told him she made his heart beat just a little faster. She touched his arm as she asked him what had brought him here. 'I heard you'd had some time off,' she'd added, not exactly fishing.

He batted her question away. No more pity was required, especially from someone like Leanne, who he doubted harboured much compassion anyway. They conspired about their colleagues, Leanne filling the gaps in the paint-by-numbers' characters Adam had started to construct in the last few days.

'James doesn't like anyone, don't waste a second worrying about him, because we all hate him too. Though somehow, he's got the ear of Giles, which is astounding given the sexual harassment charges he somehow managed to bury last year.'

Giles was the CFO, an enigma. To have his ear would be amazing, but to go unnoticed almost as good, especially for those, like Adam, who had started to realise that huge leaps up the ladder at this late stage were unlikely to be achieved.

'Let's do this again,' Leanne said. 'Nice to have a non-smoking smoking buddy. My cigs will last far longer than with the other tight scavengers in there. Never buy their own. Social smokers apparently. The kind who drink a smoothie for breakfast then ten pints of lager for dinner.' She sighed extravagantly, then winked.

Adam thought she might be flirting. He forgot to think about Lucy, but he also forgot to think about Olivia. A mental state he managed to retain for the rest of the day.

Hours passed quickly as the week drew to a close, final stock market figures powering high fives as excited weekend chatter increased in volume and speed. Adam felt soothed by the inane worries, arguments, and stresses. In-fighting for promotions, minor undermining, and whether some bloke called Dave had a hope in hell with the pretty, new receptionist. The general feeling seemed to be no, particularly from the women, who said Dave was a creep. They walked out of the office together, guided by instinct to the nearest bar, a soulless place that had become their local through mere proximity to their front door.

Standing shoulder to shoulder yet still straining to hear the words bouncing across his small, jostling group, Adam was relieved to feel that familiar heavy hand on his shoulder. Familiar cries of long-lost business associates, separated only by weeks and a few miles welcomed Peter with exaggerated fondness. Adam wondered how much of this was for his benefit; the prodigal father returns, twice the man with three times as many friends. Not in their carefully conceived nature to be overly kind in public, drinks bought, the conversation soon turned.

'Trousers tight enough, Peter?' Leanne quipped, her eyes sly and teasing.

'I remember the days when I used to be able to say sexist shit like that, Leanne, but those days are gone, shame on you.'

And so, it continued. Adam observed, he laughed, he even made the odd joke but was the butt of far more.

'How does a Yorkshireman find a sheep in long grass?' James bellowed.

Adam interrupted, 'I'm not actually from York—'. It didn't matter.

'Very satisfying!' They all roared, heads back, drinks sloshing over rims. Adam's clipped southern accent doing nothing to dissuade them.

'Are you getting t'drinks in?' they challenged.

'Eh-by-gum, he's got short arms and long pockets!' they jeered.

A persona carved and appointed. Job done. Everyone had one. Peter the old Lothario: unmarried, tight jeans. Leanne the ice queen, almost inevitable, sadly, Adam thought, for an intelligent and ambitious woman who had plans to conquer this industry. James the lad: self-proclaimed, but said with irony by others. Hugo, the posh boy, despite his accent being clearly affected. And Jean-Paul, Johnny-Foreigner, Frog, grateful to Adam for a night off from being impersonated.

It was about ten past nine as the sun began to set. They had moved to a table outside to accommodate the social smokers, their temporary addiction kicking in after the fourth drink. Adam hadn't eaten. Breakfast was forgotten in light of the vomiting, which now, hours later, back in the world, made Adam feel faintly pathetic. He'd been too busy for lunch, and dinner had consisted of five hours of fast-paced drinking. After three pints, he'd moved onto vodka tonics, and was nursing his second large one, squinting into the low sun.

Not really paying attention to the conversation around him, he allowed his vision to gently swim, enjoying being with people that didn't matter to him, and to whom he didn't matter either. Then he found he was suddenly alert, fight or flight, as he sensed eyes bore into him. The unmistakable, unnerving sense of being watched threw him back into reality, albeit a blurred version of it. He turned around and fleetingly, for the briefest of moments he locked eyes with his viewer. Olivia. Then she was gone.

He knocked over his drink as he shakily stood. Cheers abound as he steadied himself on someone's jacket arm, and allowed the jeers about not handling his drink to rapidly fade behind him as James led the group in a specially personalised version of *On Ilkla Moor Baht'at* changing the words to 'Adam is a fucking twat'. Adam would have despaired, had he not been dizzy with shock, as he scrambled through the groups of drunken professionals clogging up the pathway leading out of the front beer garden. He was desperate to get out into the space beyond where there was room to breathe, away from the nauseating tobacco smoke.

Adam's short walk to his flat flashed by as he walked haphazardly getting in the way of late-night joggers. He didn't see them, eyes to the ground, ensuring he couldn't see her again. The streets became quieter as he headed inland to the residential blocks far away enough from the banks and the bars to offer peace, close enough and high enough to provide the best views. The walk didn't give him nearly enough time to sober up, but enough to still his beating heart. Adam allowed the door to slowly and heavily swing closed behind him, barely recalling the lift he must have just taken. He closed the blinds, afraid of what form the twinkling lights and city shapes would take in the glass reflection.

Olivia had been dressed exactly as she was, the very last time he'd seen her. Inappropriately dark clothes for a warm, summer evening. Boots, rather than pumps or sandals, and legs covered with thick tights. He'd loved her quirky style, and her refusal to defer to something as uncontrollable as the weather. Then he'd looked again, and she hadn't been there anymore. There were people milling. There were pop-up bars, and city trees.

Against his better judgement, he poured a large whisky into a crystal tumbler, no ice, no water. The worries came fast then, but his self-prescribed mental anaesthetic helped him to bear them. First Peter, who will think he's nuts. Secondly, everyone else, who will think he's weak, not up to the standard. If you can't hold your drink, can you stand the rest of the pace? Third, and most importantly, Olivia. Even now she managed to take up more space than anyone else in his cluttered mind. Her capacity to swell and spread and infiltrate was greater than he had realised. He'd thought he had been in control but he'd simply been the host to her parasite.

Wondering what he'd say to her now, Adam remembered what he'd said to her the last time he'd talked to her, and the promises he'd made to never tell a soul the truth about what had happened. He'd kept that promise, wasn't that enough?

The hatred he'd felt for her the last time he'd seen her felt insurmountable at the time but Adam was no longer sure he had that intensity of emotion in him. He'd hated her only briefly, he'd loved her for much longer, when all added up. He sipped his whisky, the smell made him gag. He'd had far too much tonight. He placed it on the glass coffee table with a clanking sound, and pushed it away. The smell followed the glass, and he breathed deeply. Replacing the medicinal smell of strong spirits, there was an unfamiliar scent, feminine. He recognised it. Lucy, he instinctively thought, but he knew that it wasn't Lucy's scent he was recalling as it drifted away again. Hers was heady and modern, a purple bottle that looked expensive on her dressing table top. This smell was fruity and cheap.

He lay back, closed his eyes, allowed himself to see Olivia in his mind's eye. Not the villain he'd banished to darkness, but as she was to him before, as he wished she had really been. He heard her soft voice whisper I love you, so long ago now. He listened for her laugh: unrestrained, an involuntary snort, her hand moving quickly to cover her amused embarrassment. Saw those eyes, reflecting his besotted adoration. For the first time since he'd left, he allowed himself to remember her, unmarred by the guilt to come, as she was before everything changed and his world turned upside down. The tears fell and he didn't bother to wipe them away. Heavily, he breathed that fruity, cheap perfume in, too drunk to recognise it, and felt those ancient butterfly kisses on his stubbly cheek.

Olivia

I still love him, you know. That's why I've come back. This long, shared history, everything we endured together, it is the tapestry of our lives, and I simply won't allow him to unravel it and start again. What a waste. But he's fragile, despite his protestations, and so I must be gentle, slow. Remind him who we once were, and could be again. I'd been watching for a while when he saw me, concerned about his drinking, appalled by the raucous banter. The others looked like vultures on damaged prey to me, and my protective instincts drew me out into the open, close enough to hear their bullying chants, which weren't particularly clever, and certainly weren't funny.

He was quiet in response to their chorus. I know he's read my note, in fact I'd known since the morning as I followed him to work. At the bar, he had an almost poetic look, though I know from my days with Megan and her clan that the misty-eyed look of the drunk can take on a romance if you're not careful. He misses me, I can tell. It's as if he's looking through the others around him, passing hours rather than living them. It was never like that before, when we were together. His eyes were intense, his gaze strong and direct, and his attention complete. I was good for him. I don't like hiding in the shadows. Tonight, the artificial glare of closed offices helps the moon to light the streets, illuminated twenty-four hours a day despite the signage throughout their foyers claiming to plant a tree every time they send someone to Japan on a business class flight, or something. Hypocrites.

Retaking my place outside of the glow of lights, blending into the background, I decide to accompany Adam home. He's drunk and he's had a shock. As he stumbles, I wish I could steady him. I've always been dependable and, unlike some, I like to be needed. I'd let him lean on me. When he is safely at his door, he pushes the code in, once, twice, three times. His fingers were always clumsy, and tonight he is less dexterous than ever. I didn't mean for him to see me back at the bar, but I can't say I'm sorry he did now. I slip inside behind him before the door clicks shut with a pleasant, muted thud. Even the sounds of the flat are designed with meticulous attention to detail.

He doesn't switch on the lights in his flat, and he doesn't look at me. He sits on his neat sofa, I stand behind him, my back to the wall, sure that he wouldn't notice me, there. I'm right. Adam drinks, and I slowly move around, he doesn't see me watching from the dark corner in the bottom right of the room as he looks straight ahead at nothing. I know I don't belong here, uninvited, but still, it feels wrong to be so close yet not walk towards him and reach out to comfort him as his tears fall. I hate to see him cry. I only saw him cry once before, and those tears were shed for me too. I'm torn between feeling pleased that I'm in control of my situation again, impressed by my own ability to be patient, and raw anger that he is blind to me. I remain unwatched, watching instead. I used to feel Adam's eyes watch me wherever I went. I pretended not to notice at the time. He says nothing, but his breathing is hoarse. When his eyes close I know he finally sees me again. This time he doesn't startle or jump, he doesn't run away. His face doesn't contort into anguish, it unfolds. His mouth is slightly open and his fists uncurl. He sees me, I know he does, and he still loves me.

The first time I dared to believe that he saw me for who I really was and, more to the point, that he liked what he saw, was many years ago. Until then — despite the years I'd been Megan's bosom buddy — we hadn't bonded. I'd been sitting in their kitchen, while Megan finished blow-drying her hair upstairs. I was idly flicking through a magazine, doodling on the flawless faces of ethereal celebrities, posing unnaturally on red carpets. I gave them all glasses and moustaches. He walked in, not seeing me at first. He was humming something out of tune that I only recognised because he'd hummed it before. Adam rarely seemed to be around back then, always dashing off to catch a train, to meet Peter, or to his study upstairs to finish up some work, calling to us over his shoulder, jokingly, that he was 'hiding from the girls'. He paid me little attention until that night. The humming stopped and he turned and took a sharp breath.

'Olivia! I didn't see you there. Sorry! What are you doing?'

'Art,' I quipped. Back then, years ago, I hadn't honed my craft, but I had aspirations. I tended to hide behind self-deprecation and sarcasm. I was afraid I'd never be good enough. He looked over my shoulder.

'I have something to show you,' he said, and left the room.

When he returned, he was carrying a book. It was a large hardback book, in perfect condition, every page full of breath-taking Renaissance paintings. As he flicked through a few pages, I couldn't catch all the words but I've never felt

90

so desperate to read something. He treasured the book he told me. He and Megan had bought it as a souvenir back in 2001 when they'd visited the Dante's *Divine Comedy* exhibition in London, many moons ago. He allowed the pages to fall through his fingers, seeking out one in particular.

'*Mystic Nativity* by Botticelli, my absolute favourite. Of course, he was a bit of a religious nut by this point, and shortly after went a bit mad, I think, died in poverty. Not the cheeriest of stories I'm afraid. But still beautiful, poignant.'

I was spellbound. He looked a little embarrassed, so I stopped staring at him.

'You can borrow it if you like? For inspiration. You're very talented, Olivia, you must believe in yourself more.'

He was sat next to me, close. He held my gaze, and brushed a hair that had fallen in front of my eyes away. He looked at me with such intensity, and delivered his message clearly yet gently. I didn't know until then that he cared. I was shocked that he'd noticed me at all, let alone my talent, raw as it was.

It was in that moment that I first fell foul to what would become my life's addiction: Adam's undivided attention. It was better than anything I'd felt before, and it came out of nowhere. I didn't seek it out, it found me. He believed in me, he gave me the book. He made it possible for me to believe in myself. I needed him from then on, and for a time, I was convinced he felt the same. He still needs me now, but he's forgotten why.

Megan had eventually sauntered into the kitchen. He moved to her quickly, kissing her cheek without much care.

'Ah Botticelli! How wonderful to see this book again!' She slid it away from me and started to look through it, sighing.

'I'll take good care of it,' I told her solemnly, a little afraid she might be about to reclaim my revered prize. She passed it back to me, and looked over my head at Adam. I couldn't quite read her expression. I closed the book and wrapped my arms around it. Her eyes narrowed, and I imagined Adam mouthing something back, placating her. It might have been the first time I experienced Adam's full attention, but it was also the first time I experienced Megan's resentment. I hadn't put the two together at the time, so fixated on holding onto my feeling of pleasure at being in the receipt of such a magnificent gift. Megan's meanness didn't fully register. I felt loved, not begrudged.

'Bye girls!' Adam called, as the stand-off silently ended. I hadn't realised he wouldn't stay, it saddened me more than it had before. Megan's face had transformed as the door closed behind him.

'Lovely to see that you have a shared interest.' She smiled, broad and genuine. Small, whitened, straight teeth on show, her pink tongue licked her tastefully plumped lips, which were perfectly outlined and painted with a deep burgundy and sat beneath her small nose, punctuated with a ski slope upturn. My nose was larger, and had a small bump in it, but my freckles, I'd been told, were pretty.

'You could go with him to a gallery maybe. We used to go, but it's not really my thing these days, and I'm far too busy. I'm sure he'd like that, if you don't mind him boring on about every historical detail of every artist.' She laughed.

I tried not to scowl, suddenly protective of the new object of my affection. How could he bore anyone? He was amazing. She could be so careless with her words.

'I thought it would be nice, just the two of us for dinner. His team are going to a local awards bash actually, with Peter too. He hasn't stopped talking about it. Apparently, they're convinced they're both going to win a gold.'

I was sorely disappointed, but I hoped he'd win an award. I think he did.

She continued to speak: 'It's been so long since we talked, and I know how much the girls bore you —'

I tried to interrupt, but a manicured hand gestured that there was no need.

'I really want to hear about your art, see what you're working on. Let's have a whole evening where we talk about interesting stuff, not all of that dull middle-aged woman stuff. I've got into rather bad habits over the years. You can be my saviour Olivia, stop me from getting old and bitter before my time.'

It was a wonderful evening, the earlier frostiness was quickly forgotten. Megan and I had an unparalleled relationship at this time. When she showered you with affection, you'd have to be dead inside not to feel elevated. She shared hilarious stories from her youth, talked conspiratorially about the others, and listened to me, heard me. Later, after dinner, as Megan finished the last of the bottle of Pinot, I researched art exhibitions, and found one at the National Gallery in London. I was desperate to tell him, to be of use to him, as he had been to me without even realising it, but it was getting late and he didn't come home.

I wished her goodnight, kissing her soft cheek, smelling her musky perfume. I didn't want to leave the gallery information in Megan's hands, as it seemed insensitive given her earlier jokey comments about the amount of time her 'dreadfully neglectful husband spent away in London', and I suspected she'd probably meant a more local exhibition when she suggested that we go together. So, I wrote the details on a scrap of paper, and popped it into the pocket of the coat hanging by the front door, the one I'd seen him wear at the weekends, often. My first note, ready for him to find.

I think he liked it. He appreciated my thoughtfulness. He wanted me to go with him, and so I did. An early morning Saturday train, home in time for bed. Megan didn't mind, he'd said, she was at an eventing competition that day anyway. We'd walked down the Strand after exhausting the gallery, arrived at Gordon's Wine Bar, where we sat in the garden, eating — he said — the best cheese plate in central London, in the oldest wine bar.

'Isn't that marvellous?' he'd asked. For me, that little plate of cheese was one of the finest things I had ever eaten. When he told me he'd taken Megan there after the exhibition they'd visited in 2001, the one where they'd bought the book, I felt closer to them than ever. I still had the book. I wanted to keep it forever. I listened as he told me what they'd eaten, and how they'd drank so much wine that they didn't realise the time, missed the train and had to wander the streets until the morning. Although it was cold, he explained, they didn't notice, wrapped up in their coats and scarves and each other. The happy memories imprinted on his eyes, his lips, and the dimples in his cheeks. For the first time I wanted something of their life for myself.

It wasn't a secret, our first trip, or any of those that followed, but it felt like one. The part of a secret that matters is the shared experience, and even when retold, it is never quite reimagined correctly. The day was perfect, so I wrote its story onto the pages of my diary, creating sketches to go with it. We talked of Dante's Hell at length on the train on the way home for it had captivated me. I never imagined eventually I'd become one of the damned myself. But then, and for many years, Megan encouraged our relationship.

'You're saving me a job,' she told me once or twice.

He loved the city, she despised it. I loved him. Everyone was happy. Our days out were infrequent but important, to both of us, and eventually, inevitably, they weren't quite enough, and the days turned into nights and weekends away. Megan didn't seem to mind at all. Most of the time, Megan and I, along with the ghastly ghoulish old gang carried on as usual but my relationship with Adam meant that she was free to spend more and more time at the yard, and it was easier for her to gossip with the others when I was absent. They were strangely guarded in my presence. They needn't have been so protective of their skeletons. I really didn't care. I was listening but I had no use for their information. I'd come to realise they were just a necessary evil in my life. All I cared about was being with Megan and Adam, occupying their world.

I created long and beautiful prose about all of them, illustrated with fantastical interpretations of our days, in my diaries. The edges bled. His stories of Megan, his reality with me, the lionesses that circled, and my imagination all came together to form a new life, real on the page. Most of my diaries were destroyed in the fire. My words melted, my version of events erased. As they say, history belongs to the victors. But history is constantly revised. New victors will rise.

Now Adam is perfectly still on the chair, I'm sure he's asleep, and I want to place a blanket over him, and kiss him goodnight. I look closely at his face. The skin is looser, but I know every bump and curve as well as I always did. The man who took me to galleries and fed me oysters for the very first time, who made me feel less like the circus freak I'd always known I was deep down. I decide to risk the kiss. My long eyelashes always used to brush his cheek. He called them butterfly kisses. As I leave, I whisper 'I love you.' He doesn't stir, but the tears still fall.

Adam

Adam had three missed calls. His brother, Michael. He texted rapidly with one hand, the other on the steering wheel, the gears automatic, freeing him to multi-task in a way Megan would have told him off for.

Can't talk now, busy at work.

Mere seconds later a beep indicated a most likely furious response. Ignoring it, Adam focussed on the road ahead. If Michael knew he'd driven back to Yorkshire, when he downright refused to return to either of the neighbouring Cotswolds villages where his mother and his brother and brother's partner Rich all lived, he'd never hear the end of it. Last time he'd answered his call, he'd regretted it.

'She blames herself for dragging you away from home that day. Come visit. Don't block us out. We miss you,' Michael had pleaded.

Emotional blackmail was always Michael's strong point. How could she blame herself? Adam had asked more than once. What sense does that make? Everyone knows that she hadn't dragged him anywhere. It was all just a terrible misunderstanding. Adam had tried to reason with his brother.

'Ah but Adam, you've stayed away so long, she thinks you must blame her.'

In some respects, Adam suspected Michael also

irrationally blamed himself. If he hadn't been away on yet another European jaunt — that he loftily referred to as a teaching sabbatical — perhaps Adam wouldn't have needed to go. There was an unspoken rule that their mother was more Michael's responsibility that Adams, but Adam knew that had always been unfair. Truth was, Adam couldn't face her; couldn't look into her eyes and lie to her. Even now, telling anyone the truth about Olivia was impossible. Avoidance tactics, the only way to keep moving forward. Sometimes he wondered how long it was possible to live like this. In London, it felt like he was getting away with it, right now, on the M1, driving home from Yorkshire, it felt utterly ridiculous.

He'd thought Megan's friends might be able to help him. Was he looking for their absolution? For anyone's absolution? Olivia had come into his dreams with hers, but he couldn't trust himself any more than he could trust Olivia. It was Megan's forgiveness he needed and would never have. His wife's friends had not only come to the funeral but helped to organise the wake, despite being strangely absent for the last few weeks of her too-short life.

Later, looking through her phone, her laptop, he'd found all of the emails, the texts. He'd known about just one, which Megan had denied knowledge of. To find so many, all sat there in her archive was painful. Such spite. Similar to ones she'd sent to him, or he thought she had, that year. At the time he'd been so angry. He didn't know then what he knew now. The guilt was eating him alive, causing him to doubt his own mental well-being. On a whim, he'd dressed for driving rather than for work. He'd called Elizabeth as he walked to his parking space underneath the building, and asked if he could visit her. He wondered if finally, they could talk about Megan, if she and the others also felt guilty for abandoning her.

Elizabeth had led him into her formal drawing room when he had arrived earlier that afternoon, rather than the kitchen or the television room he'd usually been hosted in at drinks parties for the couples. The others were already there, conferring. As he entered, they abruptly stopped. Bea leaped up from the armchair to embrace him in greeting. Antonia stood slowly, smoothing away creases on her bright blue knee-length skirt. She didn't quite kiss both his cheeks, but her breath touched them as she leaned into one side and then to the other. They asked about his work, his new home. Adam asked after their husbands, who he knew only superficially, despite shared evenings and holidays, on which they'd passed time talking about nothing much to please their wives. So much easier to pretend to be friends with the spouse of your wife's friends than make new friends of your own, whose spouses would potentially be shunned by your own.

'Vile messages, so personal, they could only be from her, she was the only one who knew. Of course now I know she was seriously unwell, Adam, but who she became, the person who said those things, that wasn't Megan.' Elizabeth had dispensed with small talk as they sat awkwardly around the coffee table, ignoring the prettily arranged biscuits, allowing the tea to stew in the pot.

'Don't blame yourself, Adam,' Antonia had said. 'None of this is your fault, she was ill.'

Whilst in death they magnanimously forgave Megan's final vicious acts, their stiff postures and polite smiles built a wall around them keeping out untidy deaths, damaged minds and the Devil's own licking flames. Adam wanted to correct them, defend Megan, but it was too late for that now. The lies were ingrained in every pore. The afternoon was an utter disaster and over the painful hour and twenty minutes he endured he asked himself thirty times at least what else he could have possibly expected. They'd patted his leg, and cocked their heads in sympathy. The meeting only crushed his weakened heart, as he continued to allow them to believe his original fiction, protecting Olivia despite everything. He repeated the script like the well-worn mantra of someone in a catatonic state, but he knew there was no end to the chant, no relief in the words; Sisyphus endlessly pushing the boulder up the hill only to watch it roll down again. His own punishment for hubris, thinking he knew better than Megan, and better than Olivia.

One thing he could see clearly that Olivia had seen all along though: these women were quite dreadful, except Bea, who he believed had truly loved Megan, yet today she had remained insipid at best. Her mouth, unlike the set, pursed lines on her friends' faces, was downturned all afternoon, a quiver in her lips, her regret palpable. The others wept crocodile tears from heavily made-up eyes full of woe. They made it clear that this was to be a single visit, their debt to the dead paid. Tomorrow, normal service resumed. Adam observed them carefully, wondering who had taken his wife's place in the centre of their circle. Who hosted book club now? He didn't ask.

As they said their goodbyes, he felt almost pushed out of the door, the three women a blockade on the porch, re-entry not an option. Then Bea stepped forward and hugged him without saying a word, holding him tight. His body responded, arms wrapped around her, his wife's oldest and best friend, not that it had counted for much in the end. She'd been as blind as Adam, and she knew it.

His phone started ringing again cutting through the news as he accepted its interruption by touching the control screen of the car's audio system. This time, Peter. Again, not likely to be good, but this one he couldn't avoid. No small talk, straight to it. Adam attempted to beat him past the post.

'Look, I can explain—'

But Peter's voice was stronger, and he cut him off. 'What the fuck?'

Adam sighed, and waited for him to go on.

'You run off, pissed as a skunk on your first night out with the team, like a fucking pussy, no goodbye, spilling your drink all over Leanne, and then don't turn up on Monday! What the actual fuck? Are you an intern wanting the sack? James texted, said you were probably on a three-day hangover. He was joking but the man is, as I said to you, a cunt, he'll have you out, and I'll look like a right tit for having your back, you total fucking piece of shit.' He'd finally finished.

Adam had been expecting this and knew that he deserved it. Another poor judgement. This morning it had seemed so important to go back there. He'd driven past the charred wreck, the graveyard, the church where he'd married and later buried Megan. He didn't bother to take the detour to see her old family home, which they had sold for not enough when her father died, up to his neck in debt unbeknownst to anyone. His cheerful veneer had been full proof, and he'd have rather died than talk about something as vulgar as money. And in the end, of course, he did. Adam had,

101

however, stopped at the livery yard, which he'd sold for a great deal, and which, until recently, had funded his getaway lifestyle.

'I'm sorry. It was an emergency. Had to go back to Yorkshire. Loose ends. Estate agents. I should have let the office know, out of the habit. I'll fix it.'

Peter hung up with little more than a grunt, and with little indication of being appeased. He'd get over it, Adam thought.

A ten-hour round trip had provided ample time to think, and whilst a good portion of that was muddied with the car crash of his life, he was onto something at work, and would prove himself wrong about being ready for the scrapheap. He'd prove everyone wrong. He had been stupid to let himself loose his focus as he drowned in a temporary surge in memories and visions of Olivia. Perhaps he'd been overwhelmed with the new job, and the new start. But this was the wake-up jolt he needed, and he didn't plan to let it happen again. He had to let go, for good.

Had he been guilty of arrogance, of ignorance, of neglect? Yes, indeed. Had he misjudged the people he believed he knew best? Every time. Could he have prevented the fatal blows? Almost certainly. He'd never forgive himself, and that was his punishment. There was no peace to be found, except in death he presumed, and so seeking it in Yorkshire, in reason, in therapeutic *sharing* of all things, with women he hadn't shared more than a bottle of wine with prior to today, was a complete waste of time and energy.

He had been foolish, acting on a whim — ill-rested and tortured by the haunting memories all weekend — and desperate for salvation. He half wondered if he'd had some

102

sort of short-lived episode this past weekend, but he pushed that unhelpful thought away, just as he'd pushed away the daylight by keeping the blinds down, and pushed away anyone who'd tried to call or text by turning off his phone and putting it in a drawer.

The summer rain slowed the traffic, and the long journey became longer. A Radio 4 play chattered in the background, punctuated by low-budget sound effects. The closer he got to London, the more his mood improved. This enchanted city was like a sanctuary for the wounded, shadows everywhere concealing scars. Shaken initially by the rediscovered note, unused to so much daily stress, he had allowed himself to wobble. Resolved, he was driving back to a place of stability. He would throw that damned suit away, instead of according it the power to remind him of the blood on his hands. And then he would pour a glass of wine for Lucy, and kiss her firm belly underneath his crisp white sheets.

It was after eight when he pulled into the gated driveway of his block, and deftly swung onto the narrow ramp to find his underground parking space. From exiting the elevator on the forty-second floor, he could see Lucy leaning against his front door. His paced quickened, fear mounting that he'd got his times wrong, sure they'd arranged a late date, her arrival time set for eight thirty, thirteen minutes from now. More angry, disappointed women were not on tonight's agenda, but he set his face in the correct shape: remorseful and ready to make a rapid apology, not caring if he was in the wrong or not.

He was right to be nervous, he thought, her face looked different. Neither the smooth calm of her slumber, nor the pretty animated version she usually greeted him with. Worry

103

in her eyes, her mouth set straight, tense, as if otherwise it might wobble, and betray her lack of composure.

'Where have you been?' she demanded.

An unexpected challenge, and Adam was unprepared. He hadn't planned to lie about taking the day off work and going to Yorkshire, but nor had he expected to be asked about it. Telling Lucy about Yorkshire would have meant talking about his dead wife, or worse still, Olivia. Telling Lucy about Yorkshire without telling her about the whole sordid mess would have involved lying to her, which he didn't want to do. Not beyond omission at any rate.

The night should have unfolded predictably, Lucy kissing him hello, and quickly starting to regale him with tales about her day, funny stories of dreadful PR types, or something she'd read in the free newspaper that tickled her. When it came to his, she'd ask how it was, and he'd reply, 'Uneventful, compared to yours.' Adam realised too late that he should have postponed the date once he decided to drive to Yorkshire. He was in no state to defend himself and he had no news worthy enough or appropriate to report.

Lucy repeated her question.

He paused a moment too long, and now a lie was expected.

Adam delivered, 'Work. Then to see old an old friend. Am I late? I thought we said–'

'You're lying.'

Adam entered the door code and they silently made their way into the dim light of the flat. Lucy threw her bag on the floor and Adam switched on the lights. Definitely angry, Adam thought. Her face was contorted, and the down lights exaggerated her frown lines. He'd never noticed them before.

She stared him out. Utterly at a loss, Adam reached for her. She shrugged him off.

'Where have you been?' A third time.

'How did you get into the block?' Adam countered, realising he sounded accusatory, his defences kicking in. 'Why are you interrogating me, Luce?' It took just a moment for Adam to realise his choice of words and his evasion of the question were an unwise strategy.

'I walked in with a neighbour, why does it matter? Look,' she sighed. 'You don't owe me anything, Adam, I know that, but I thought we were honest with each other, and I thought this was going somewhere, and now, I don't know, because suddenly you've become very mysterious. You crept out early last time I saw you without even saying goodbye!'

'You know I had a ridiculously early meeting on Thursday. I didn't want to disturb you — you looked so peaceful,' Adam countered, not skipping a beat, but Lucy hadn't finished.

'I've hardly heard from you since, and you haven't written more than two words in a text. And where were you all this weekend? I thought we'd at least FaceTime, but—'

'Hold on,' Adam interrupted, learning nothing, 'You said *you* were busy all weekend! I didn't expect to hear from you. My phone's been off, mostly. I needed to focus on work.'

'But I texted you, tried to call for a catch up. Like a *normal person*. And you've pretty much blanked me. Now it's Monday, and you're not dressed for work but for some unfathomable reason won't tell me where you've been. Surely you can understand this doesn't look great?'

Her voice was becoming shrill, and Adam really didn't care for it. He needed to end this conversation and get things back to that place he'd been longing for as the hours on the motorway dragged on and on. His mind worked quickly. The housemates.

'Your housemates! They've put ideas into your head. They don't like me. They don't trust me because I'm not a vegan right?'

Humour, it transpired, was also the wrong strategy. Lucy seethed. She stared at him.

'Adam, just tell me where you've been.' She sighed again.

Perhaps, Adam thought, she had genuinely expected a reasonable explanation, and Adam's reaction was suggestive of the fact that it was unlikely to come. She bent to pick up her bag as Adam continued to search for what had motivated this easy-going girl to turn so suddenly possessive.

Adam Wished that rather than swinging her bag over her shoulder and walking out the door, she would instead casually throw her light blazer over a kitchen stool, as she usually would. He stepped towards her, and opened his mouth to start to explain as his mind worked over time, constructing a plausible account of his actions, one so good it would explain away the lies.

He'd worked all weekend. He had been planning to go into the office all day today, but some urgent loose-ends came to his attention in Yorkshire. The old friend he mentioned is actually a solicitor back home and had a rare opening in his diary. He simply hadn't wanted to talk about it to be honest, just wanted to leave that behind, and have a lovely evening, in the moment, with her.

Why hadn't he just said that in the first place? He wished he hadn't been so afraid of her questions, especially as Lucy, until tonight, rarely had any.

But Lucy wasn't leaving, she was unfolding a piece of paper she'd taken from her bag. Her eyes were glistening with tears threatening to overflow, which she determinedly held back. She bit her bottom lip, but Adam could still detect a slight quiver. She was pale; she looked frightened. He'd misjudged her fear and rising panic for anger. Torn from a notebook, the paper was familiar. She pushed it towards him, and he leaned over the kitchen island to see the handwritten words in that unmistakeable scrawl.

Ever think he's too good to be true, Lucy? I heard you say so on the phone to a friend. Maybe you're right. Does he talk about his past? Don't you ever wonder what he's hiding? Ask him where he was today. He'll lie, he's quite good at that. Be careful, Lucy, as the women in his life tend to get hurt.
From a concerned friend

Part Two

Christmas, 2017
The one before last

Olivia

'So, you're just going to give up?'

Megan was getting on my nerves as we worked together to prepare for their annual pre-Christmas gathering, a cinnamon candle sweetening the air, convincing us it was time to feel festive. She'd waved me off almost three months ago, dabbing at her eyes, wishing me well, promising she'd miss me. I'd hardly heard from her since.

'Of course not,' I snapped, getting the cheese from the fridge and placing it on a board to get it to room temperature. 'But it didn't work out there. My work was too modern, I think. They're stuck in the nineties. People still play The Strokes in bars. I'll continue working from here, like I was before.'

'Oh, I used to love The Strokes,' she said, chopping fruit and mixing it into large jugs.

I pulled a face. I hated those nineties bands, it was the only thing that had irritated me about Adam and Megan, until that point. Terrible dinner party music choices. Now, since I'd arrived back a couple of weeks ago, hiding my tail between my legs, Megan was starting to find new ways to irk me, and Adam seemed to be avoiding me. I was utterly deflated. I'd been looking forward to being back after my disastrous trip.

'Something must have happened,' she continued. 'I thought you were happy there. You can tell me. Man trouble?' She winked.

She had no idea. I'd been to New York, thinking I'd finally be amongst my own kind. Artists, hipsters, weirdos. I was going to eat street food and live in a loft apartment decorated with meaningful graffiti instead of subtle tones of paint and tasteful wallpaper. I was going to have friends, a collection of humans beyond our trio. I wanted to introduce them to Adam and Megan, who'd be in awe of me and my life, for once. It wasn't as easy as I'd thought, coming from my small village existence in Yorkshire.

I did live in a shared loft apartment. My flatmate and I had a misunderstanding so I slept rough for a night; the bitch had changed the lock. She had been a total drama queen. Just before that, the department and I had struggled to see eye to eye on my work. They had asked me to leave, though I hadn't told anyone that minor detail. Anyway, the street food gave me diarrhoea and I couldn't keep up with the dialect, consisting mainly of slang that made no sense to me.

'Nothing happened. Just wasn't for me.'

I didn't want to talk about it. For once she didn't push it. She'd been distracted since I'd returned, and not at all like the Megan who'd help me choose my New York flat scrolling through hundreds of indistinguishable grubby boxes on endless websites, or the Megan who had upgraded me to business class, our little secret she'd said. I didn't tell Adam, though I couldn't imagine why it was a secret. I had been sure he would have been glad to help. My Megan, the old Megan, was beguiling and attentive. The new Megan was preoccupied, easily irritated, and not so polished, somehow.

We always spent Christmas together, but this year something wasn't right. Still, the show must go on and the party was still scheduled for tonight. I noticed that a snowflake-shaped wooden decoration had fallen from the eight-foot tree in the corner of the kitchen and replaced it onto a sturdy branch. The tree was fat and emanated that familiar festive smell, just like the other even larger tree in the living room. It stood firm in a gold-painted bucket of water.

I took some glasses from the cupboard and placed them on the island ready for the guests, as large quantities of Winter Pimm's was glugged into jugs by Megan. I noticed she poured herself one and drank it all quickly, her back to me, surreptitious. I'd heard Adam ask her if it was wise to drink so much the other night, given what she was taking. I'd been immediately stricken, thinking she was ill. She'd snarled back at him that they were only sleeping pills. I felt sorry for Adam, always so caring, and Megan now not as much as before. I didn't know why.

She quickly lost interest in finding out more about my problems in New York, and started ordering me about to get the final details for the party ready. I fetched the mince pies from the larder and put the oven on so we could warm them. I removed the cloves from the ham before carving it for her and fanned the slices onto a large serving plate. As I made myself useful, Megan ran upstairs in a flustered fashion, complaining, mainly to herself, how she hadn't had a minute to herself all day, and wondering out loud where Adam had got to.

'Could you light the fire, Olivia?' she shouted down, an afterthought in a demanding tone.

I was starting to feel like fucking Cinderella. No wonder I was the only one who'd offered to help if this was how she now spoke to people. Even Adam had gone out.

It wasn't until the party was in full swing that I understood why she was so tetchy. She thought she was whispering as she confided in Bea. I didn't mean to eavesdrop, but I'd been getting some air, sat on the swinging seat at the bottom of the garden, wrapped up in one of Adam's old coats, seeking quiet and making plans, away from the room full of voices speaking over one another all desperate to be heard, though not by me. The words had whizzed by me and travelled over me, but were not aimed in my direction.

Bored and with a headache threatening to come on, I'd retreated to the kitchen, and given in to the pull of the silence of the night outside. I was swinging, my boots grazing the rectangle of pebbles the structure stood on at the end of the stepping stones peppering the lawn. My phone was a small bright light in the darkness, until the patio lights suddenly flicked on, a spotlight that finished before the grass began. Megan and Bea clattered and clinked through the kitchen patio doors and loudly pulled the heavy wrought-iron patio chairs out from under the ornate little white table in the centre of the patio, sitting down, and splashing wine into glasses.

'Bea, I don't know what to do. He's so distant at the moment,' she said. 'He's stopped asking about moving to London, but instead of trying to make a go of it here, he just spends all of his time there without me.'

This was the first I had heard about him trying to persuade her to move. Until now, it had been a fantasy, wishful thinking, nothing more than a pipedream. He wasn't serious, surely. What about me? Would he just up and leave with her? I listened to her continue with mounting dread.

'I feel like I'm having to do everything alone, but the more I nag him, the less I see him. He tells me I don't need to do it all, to leave it, to stop worrying, but how can I? I have responsibilities here. I thought we both did.'

Bea was typically useless, placating her with meaningless comfort words and pouring more wine, so that their conversation became repetitive and would be soon forgotten. Megan was right though, Adam was distant. He had been away a lot since he'd picked me up from the airport two weeks ago. Before Megan and Bea had disturbed me, I'd been searching for exhibitions that I might interest Adam with, get back into our irregular routine I loved so much. I still harboured hope that everything would slot back into place, and life would return to the way it was before I left. It hadn't so far.

Bea was smoking and Megan, to my horror, occasionally took the cigarette from her fingers and inhaled it herself before passing it back. I felt oddly let down. Megan was too poised to smoke. I stilled the swing and myself, not even the smallest creak allowed to escape from little used metal chains, and they didn't notice I was there. Megan continued to deliver her woeful tale but they'd mastered the concept of whispering now, and I couldn't make out what they were saying. Bea stroked her hair, and embraced her.

'I just wish we could go back to how things were,' Megan said more loudly as she pulled away. 'Adam's not making the money he wants to, and the yard is struggling. I'm sure we'll get it back on track, but it's not helping, you know?'

The perfect exterior I'd never dared to penetrate started

to crack. Megan, smoking, drinking too much and too often, and now uncouth enough to talk about money problems. I really don't like the notion of money problems. Until now, my own lack of cash hadn't been an issue, and Megan and Adam had always been so generous. Now I see why she'd kept the upgrade to business a secret from Adam. I'd been back just two weeks, but in that short time it was clear to see a lot had changed in the last few months. Even in the last few minutes, I'd learnt a lot. I'd gone away, and they'd lost their way.

'Didn't you sell your parent's home a couple of years ago? Will that not tide you over?' Bea asked.

Megan sighed deeply. 'Turns out my father wasn't quite as on top of things as we'd thought. He had paid out a fortune for Mum's care home. The house had been re-mortgaged. The yard had been eating away at his funds for a while, and all he wanted was to keep investing in it, make it work. It was his life's big love, Bea.'

Sympathetic murmurings ensued.

'And if I moved to London, what would I do? Adam says I should sell the yard, the horses, the school, and the little black book of clients Dad collected over the years. He says its reputation and assets are worth more on paper than we can ever make at it. He thinks I'm making myself ill. The sleeping pills aren't working, I just can't turn my mind off at night.'

My poor Megan was falling apart. Bea, lacking imagination, started to suggest practical solutions. She worked as a freelance marketing consultant and I imagined this was what she'd be like at work, where they probably claimed that no idea was a bad idea. Megan made

116

appreciative noises but she didn't sound inspired. Her ideas were all rubbish. Calming pillow spray. More pills. Counselling. A holiday, just the two of them to rekindle the romance.

'I know we need to spend more time just the two of us, but it's difficult right now. We're going to have to rent out the granny flat. I put an ad out already.'

I dropped my phone in shock but it landed softly on the grass verge to my left, where the pebbles ended. I couldn't allow them to rent out the granny flat. I'd hoped they would offer it to me. I'd been waiting for them to bring it up since I arrived back. They would have too, I'm sure, except for now they wanted to give it to the highest bidder. I had expected them to allow me to stay in it for favours. I already help out so much, and now, I could see, I was going to have to do a whole lot more to help put the broken pieces of their neglected life back together. It was all I had.

'Oh, good idea!' Bea exclaimed incorrectly, all attempts at whispering now discarded. 'I know someone who's looking actually, an intern at the office. She's over from Canada, staying with an old aunt at the moment, which doesn't sound much fun.'

Megan took a number down. And they chatted on. I heard my name shortly before they adopted a more conspiring tone and volume.

'No, of course I'm happy she's back around. I'd missed her. Though I do think our kitchen is going to get a bit crowded with a lodger popping in as well!' They laughed.

Very funny. Implying I'm always around, in the way. I knew she didn't mean it really but it still hurt. She quickly rectified the misunderstanding.

117

'No, no, you know me, I love a full house. Always have! Adam and I just need to find a way to carve out some time, just the two of us.' She sipped nothing from her empty glass.

Realising they'd polished off the bottle they'd brought out with them, they moved to go in.

'It's bloody freezing anyway,' they muttered, in sync.

Before the party ended, but after most people had gone, I took Megan aside as she opened more wine. She was a little drunk but in a better mood than earlier. Now was the time to change her mind: pick me instead. The last thing she needed was a stranger around, that would only add to her stress, and to her problems with Adam, who would probably never be seen again if he had to put up with sharing his space with a lodger, granny flat or not. Megan was right, it would be better if things could revert to the way they had been before. Before I went away. The happy trio.

She listened to my suggestion, which I was embarrassed to have to make unprompted. I sucked it up, after all, I kindly thought, Megan was tired, anxious and drunk. If her mind wasn't full of husband troubles and fears about money, she would have thought of inviting me to live in the granny flat herself. She said she'd talk to Adam, but I convinced her otherwise.

'Let's surprise him. He'll be so relieved not to have a stranger in the house. Major brownie points for organising it too,' I'd urged.

If she suspected I must have been listening in earlier, she didn't mention it. As I say, she wasn't as switched on as she should have been. I offered to clean the house in return saving her the money she spent on a jolly Polish woman, who religiously listened to sports radio as she slowly cleaned the house top to bottom, twice a week. I could easily fit that in around my work. It was a bargain, I'm sure the granny flat wouldn't have gone for more than two days' cheap labour. Luckily, our relationship was founded on respect and love, so it didn't bother me to clean for them, as it might have for Bea, Antonia or Elizabeth. Their relationships were based on status and showmanship. If they fell on hard times, they'd struggle to find the humility needed to ask for help. I was deliriously happy to be the one to find Megan and Adam a solution. I felt useful, and that felt good.

'You're a lovely person, Livvy,' Megan said, as she handed me the keys.

I moved into the granny flat the next day: no time like the present. I saw Adam's car pull up in the distance from my window, and so I slipped my shoes on, and walked through the garden to the main house. I couldn't wait to see the look on his face. But as I neared the French doors of the kitchen, I heard raised voices, and retreated. I guessed she hadn't told him yet, if they were arguing already. Thank goodness I came back, I thought, and how useful I'm able to stay so close. Their other friends are too self-obsessed to see how much this perfect couple are starting to come undone. It mattered more to me than any of them. In fact, it mattered more than anything. If they fell apart, so would I.

Adam

Adam didn't understand Megan. Last year she had wholeheartedly encouraged Olivia to leave the country. She had voiced her concerns loudly and repeatedly. Olivia had become too attached to Adam, and Adam was encouraging it. Megan found it easy to have difficult conversations, so usually everyone knew where they stood, but Adam was lost now. He'd denied Megan's accusations that he too was to blame for Olivia's increasing possessiveness, and she'd raised a knowing eyebrow. She wasn't stupid, the opposite, and she played her hand with skill and determination.

With Olivia gone, they'd reunited to blame their drifting apart on the strain her constant presence had started to create, amongst other things. He'd even thought he was making some progress with his campaign to relocate, but even with Olivia gone there was a great deal of work to do to get Megan to relinquish the responsibilities her father had bequeathed to his only, treasured daughter. Loyalty was something she'd always had in spades. Adam admired that, in fact he welcomed it with open arms, after all, he was the main beneficiary. But now her loyalty put her in a stale mate against herself, and against their union. Loyalty to her father's legacy, and now to Olivia.

Adam missed Olivia when she went to New York, but as the weeks had passed, he'd realised — profoundly he'd thought — he'd actually missed his wife more. Olivia's absence freed up space in the house Adam had forgotten existed, and it felt big. Perhaps too big for the two of them, he thought, as he fantasised about modern two-bed flats with views of the Thames. Fantasising powered guilt; Olivia expected, maybe even needed, them to stay there. They couldn't blame her for it was Adam and Megan who had made her so dependent on them, through a feeling of obligation, then love, and now habit too.

With Olivia so entwined in the threads of their lives, they divided their attentions. It had felt natural to do so, enriching their home and keeping them interesting. There was always something to talk about with Olivia around, even if it was how to persuade another friend why they shouldn't be offended by her latest faux pas. They laughed about these things, their strange yet captivating Olivia, but he couldn't deny that her absence was providing a sense of calm he'd forgotten he liked.

Adam also remembered how much he and Megan had liked each other, especially when it was just the two of them, and with shame confessed to himself that he hadn't made a great deal of effort to spend time with her. He'd probably spent more time with Olivia alone than he had Megan in recent times. Committed to rectify the situation, win his wife back, and in time convince her to build their life, part two, with him, in London, Adam got to work on a new start.

Out of practice, his efforts were raised to meet the deficit in the skills that used to hold Megan's attention and draw out her laugh, and her touch, but his attentions had gone unrequited. Megan went to bed early after the mandatory bottle of wine, and was asleep before he climbed under the sheets. His hands were pushed away, sleepily, yet firmly. He bought tickets to a show, but she was too tired to go, and in the end he and Peter sat awkwardly through the long performance of Faust until the interval, and then gave up and went to the pub for a couple of hours.

Adam found that somewhere along the journey into middle age his once long ribbon of patience had unravelled leaving a little frayed stump. His attempts at reviving his marriage met with little success and it didn't take too long before he started to feel exiled. The original remorse he had felt upon realising that for the last few years, Olivia had benefitted from his attentions far more than Megan had, was turning into resentment towards Megan, who had left such a gaping hole when she'd stopped giving a damn about him, that he'd had no choice. With Olivia gone, he started to wonder how long Megan had been this distant, his heart heavy because he couldn't answer his own question.

'Maybe it's just too little too late,' she'd sadly told him when she refused his offer of a weekend away, and he'd asked why. His questioning had been laced with animosity. He knew he sounded childish, exasperated as to why she couldn't just switch back to old Megan, as he switched back to old Adam. The only logical conclusion was that it was her fault. If it was so hard for her to recover her old self, it must be her that had changed. Old Adam had been resting just beneath the surface layer, and he'd gone to the effort to peel it away and wake himself up, while Megan reinforced the stitching and added more layers. They were impenetrable. Stunned at the resignation in her response, he'd asked her if she wanted to divorce.

'Of course not! But after years marriage, plodding along, I can't just suddenly pretend to be twenty-one and newly in love. We're happy enough, Adam. Why is it never enough?'

Adam didn't know why it was never enough. It used to be. Truth be told, he was bored. He'd hoped Megan would want to try something new, as he did, but she wanted everything to stay the same. She saw her friends less frequently too, Adam had noticed. When questioned, she said that she sometimes preferred a little quiet time.

His dazzling wife, host with the most, was shrinking. He asked himself if the truth about Megan and Adam, the couple who always laughed hardest together, had turned into a show for the benefit of their audience. With the audience gone, there was no point in continuing the performance.

Adam didn't like to fail, and he wasn't ready to give up on finding the answer to the problem in his home. One thing he did know: the answer wasn't Olivia living in their granny flat at the bottom of the garden. But now, just as Christmas approached, that's where she was.

Avoiding the difficult conversations she used to be a master of, Megan hid behind their infrequent guests, her work, her *incessant pottering*. Now with Olivia back and showing little interest in pursuing any opportunities away from the home, they never had any time alone. Time that Megan was afraid Adam would spend listing his arguments for a move and a fresh start, trying to persuade her to sell her beloved yard for the small fortune they needed to fund the lifestyle they craved. Or worse, time she was afraid he would spend trying to rekindle the romance, nibbling at her neck, cold hands feeling for her bra.

Adam wondered if Megan would ever soften again, so that he could find a way back, for both of them. She didn't, and instead, he found them doing an encore of the act of their lives for Olivia.

The threesome fell back into old habits. Megan pushed Adam out into the cold, and straight into Olivia's embrace. Meanwhile, Olivia and Megan became close again, Megan full of warmth when Olivia was basking in her light, but the fire went out when Olivia paid Adam attention instead. It was becoming a strange relationship, Megan and Olivia thick like thieves one moment, and then Megan bridling at the mess Olivia would leave, or the money they could be bringing in if they'd rented out the granny flat.

Adam didn't know what she wanted, but he found himself defending Olivia when Megan complained, feeling sorry for her, so unaware of the mess she'd inadvertently walked into, yet when she and Megan were huddled together sharing secrets, he hated it. He felt exposed. He didn't want them to talk about him. The version of himself he kept for Olivia was untainted, and he wanted it to stay that way. He, like everyone else, wanted to be adored by someone. Anyone. Megan mocked him.

'Darling, you're far too old to be anything but a bore to her. Stop monopolising her time! I'm sure she's got other things to do than accompany you on your little cultural jaunts.'

Megan didn't know then, he'd thought, how many were Olivia's own idea, and he didn't want any of Megan's irritation at his extra-curricular travel being directed at Olivia, and thereby limiting it, apparently for Olivia's own good. On the one hand, Megan enabled her dependence by offering her the flat, and on the other made the case that she needed to find friends her own age; build a life of her own. Adam was determined to find a way back to Megan, but in the meantime, he needed something in between the bad news about money and the bad news at home and the endless silences to keep him sane.

'Hey you.' Olivia's hands gently covered his eyes. 'Guess who?'

'Rhianna?'

'Ha. Ha. Ha. Nope, someone much cooler. Better singer too.'

Adam swivelled around in his chair, to face Olivia. She was wearing paint-splattered clothes. She'd essentially turned the granny flat into her art studio. He didn't dare go in in case he accidentally gave away his hatred of mess and disorder, which he knew without seeing was what awaited behind her closed door. He liked to pretend to be cool about it. He wanted Olivia to think of him as still embodying a youthful zest for life. Megan teased him about it, and told him that he'd never convince anyone.

'Do you want to come to Harrogate with me tomorrow? I need to get some supplies.' Adam did want to. He wanted to get out of the house, and forget the frosty atmosphere.

'I'd love to,' he started.

Olivia grinned widely, and began to suggest a time, an itinerary, lunch at Betty's.

'But I can't,' Adam finished, interrupting. 'Megan and I are going to Peter's for dinner and I've a load of paperwork to finish before we set off. He's finally returning the favour before the year is actually over.'

Joking, lightening the mood, hoping to erase the frown growing on Olivia's forehead. It didn't work. Olivia's invitation from Peter was conspicuous in its absence.

'The day after. Sunday. We can go then.'

Success, the frown melted.

'Excellent!' she said. 'And on Monday, Megan and I are going last-minute Christmas shopping, so lucky me. Lots to look forward to. I'll get on with my work tomorrow, in peace, whilst you're both out having fun.' Olivia was still smiling, and Adam pretended not to hear a bitter tinge to her words.

He was trying to be a better man. In action and in thought. He surprised Megan the following day with flowers. She was pleased and put them in her favourite vase. He heard her telling Olivia that maybe romance wasn't dead after all, and although she sighed a little as she said it, he could tell that he'd elevated his current standing in the house. He didn't hear Olivia quip that hopefully they weren't a sign of guilt.

They'd left Olivia in the kitchen, raiding the fridge when they headed out for dinner.

'I've run out of everything in the flat,' she'd said, without apology.

Megan had bristled a little, but Adam had taken her hand, and the little practised gesture had distracted her, as he guided her from the room and called goodbye to Olivia, asking her to make sure she locked the patio doors when she went back to the flat.

When they returned later that night, Megan suggested a nightcap in the kitchen. Adam hesitated. Megan had drunk two large glasses while she got ready, and had started to slur as she messily ate her cheesecake, dropping crumbs down her white silk blouse, which earlier had looked so chic. Her intake was steadily increasing, but her tolerance was not. It perturbed him. He knew that she'd started to take Xanax occasionally, despite her efforts at concealing it behind rows of tiny glass containers of expensive face creams. He wondered if the mix made her worse. On the other hand, she was in a good mood, and her hand had squeezed his thigh more than once in the back of the taxi.

'Let's, why not? After all, it's Saturday night.'

Megan zig-zagged through the hall towards the kitchen, kicking off her shoes as she went, padding in nude tights, as Adam hung his coat by the door. Her scream was high pitched and loud, morphing quickly from anguish to anger.

'Shit. Shit, shit, shit.' He heard as he ran through.

Megan was sitting on the chair clutching her foot. Blood had soaked through her tights and was staining her hands.

'My bloody foot!'

Adam saw the beautiful vase she'd chosen to house her flowers in was in pieces on the floor. A large puddle of water drowning sad-looking stems and petals. Shards of glass lurking. He hadn't heard the crash.

'What did you do?' he asked, accusingly.

'What did I do?' She snatched the paper towel from his outstretched hand as he attempted to avoid stepping in the perilous pool. 'I stepped in a load of broken glass, which, I assume, Olivia left behind.'

'It's not as bad as it looks,' he said, removing her tights. He put her hand on the paper towels and pressed it firmly. 'Just keep the pressure on,' he advised.

'Did you hear me?' Megan demanded.

He had heard her, and was, he thought, wisely ignoring her preposterous claim. Megan was drunk, she'd knocked it over herself. That was bad enough without trying to blame someone else.

'I'm sure it was an accident,' he said, carefully not

naming the culprit. Absurd to assume Olivia's culpability. Had she broken the vase, she'd be mortified. The least she would have done is clear it up.

'If it was an accident then why didn't she clean it up, leave a note? Hmm?' Megan glared at him, dropping the paper towel on the floor.

He picked the bloody rag up and tore a new one from the roll next to him, still kneeling on the tiles, brushing up the final few glistening fragments. He tried to take a breath and swallow his words but they were too quick for him.

'Megan, exactly. She didn't do this, you did. You're drunk.'

She threw the second towel to the floor in rage. Adam noticed that the bleeding had stopped. The cuts were not deep. 'I think I'd notice if I smashed an enormous vase, Adam.' Her tone was more sneer than anger.

It was unpleasant to his ear.

'Megan, you didn't notice that you'd pranged your car the other day. You didn't notice that you'd spilt red wine on the sofa, either. I'm not sure these pills are good for you, not if you keep drinking to this level.' He'd said it.

Her face crumpled, but she blinked back the tears.

'I'm sorry,' he continued. 'I should have said something. I saw the Xanax, I know you're not getting along with the sleeping pills. You drank a lot tonight, in fact most nights. I'm not having a go at you, love, I'm just worried.'

Adam was a little drunk too, he realised, as he unsteadily got to his feet, and pulled a chair close to Megan's, before sitting in it and taking her hands. She looked him in the eye. Hers were glassy, pupils large. She was pensive, unspeaking. Her eyes gently closed and slowly reopened. He waited for her to say something.

'I didn't smash the vase, she did it.' Her eyes moved more quickly than her head, which then slowly followed her gaze out of the window up to the illuminated window of the granny flat, through which Olivia's silhouette was visible.

Olivia

Megan cancelled Christmas but I still spent it with them. She said she wasn't up to the usual big dinner, too much stress at work, too little sleep, but she told me she couldn't imagine not having me there. Even during the hard times, deep connections like ours endured. That was a comforting thought, but everything else was pretty awful. We didn't even have a starter. Adam said none of it mattered. His brother, his partner, and his mother could sort themselves out for once. It was possibly the worst Christmas ever up until that point in my life. The atmosphere was dreadful, and it was dull. Megan spent most of it drunk, declaring it civilised to drink all day because it was Christmas, even though Christmas was cancelled.

The rooms that had always been so warm even when the air outside was cold had lowered in temperature. Their doors shut on my face. Behind them recriminations were rife. I tried to bury my hurt feelings. I had to remind myself that it wasn't personal, or even aimed at me. I became very discreet, but I couldn't abandon them now. They needed someone to confide in, and sometimes they needed someone just to be with, easily, without being chided. Although they put their happy faces on when I was in the room, I sensed tension all the time. I avoided occasions where they were together. It was awkward. Instead, I sought out opportunities to spend time with them separately. Megan had very little energy and expelled what she did have on shouting at her accountant over the phone, arguing with Adam, and downing wine. Naturally Adam and I found refuge in each other. He's so caring, he worries the atmosphere isn't fit for me. He tells me he wouldn't blame me if I renegade on our agreement on the flat, moved into one of the artists' residencies we'd seen. He joked even he didn't want to be here some of the time. I didn't laugh. I didn't leave.

I found her Xanax when I was cleaning for her. In my diary, I wrote a sad little vignette next to a sketch of Megan slumped over a bottle. In it she lacked excuses for her self-destructive behaviour, so I edited it, creating reasons, mystery, and malice. It made for a much better story, and gave her character a deeper sadness, as opposed to the boring and predictable reality of her middle class, self-indulgent unravelling. Creating villains and victims is fun.

Megan doesn't know how lucky she is, yet she is throwing it all away. If I had what she had, I'd be more careful. I wouldn't want to make it too easy for anyone to steal it. Her attention span was decreasing. Torn, I was in two minds. I wanted to rescue her from herself and bring the sensational siren I loved so much back. Jarring with that feeling a disgust was rising up. Anger, because she was supposed to be perfect. She made her home my sanctum, and now she was chasing Adam away, spoiling every happy moment, and putting me on edge. Despite it all, there was still nowhere I'd rather be.

In February, we had snow. It covered the ground evenly, and half of each tree. The sky was as white as the thick crunchy floor, the evergreens were hidden in soft, wet, white clouds, and the spindly black branches were the only contrast in the bleak backdrop. Bracing winds turned our faces red and made tears fall from our wind-whipped eyes. Never enough layers to keep the cold from freezing our bones, but too many to ever feel comfortable, skin daring to sweat despite our body's refusal to warm. It was a cold, cold, winter, for sure.

I worked hard to try to make Megan happy. I delighted in snow days, sat by the log burner in the snug, under blankets, drinking hot chocolate. Calls were made to stable girls who lived by the livery yard, and could still walk to work: bring the horses in, give them extra blankets and plenty of sugar beet to eat. For a change, Adam spent a lot of time at home, the combination of skiing season ensuring a quiet time at the office, and perilous ice and slush providing an indisputable excuse to avoid the office, and other people. I buried my increasing suspicions that I might be in the way to one side; the three of us almost felt like a unit again. Inconvenience be damned, old people with temperamental old heaters — get a blanket. I adore the snow. They called it *The Beast from The East*. I called it heaven.

As spring snuck in, pushing the rapidly weakening winter out, the shield of ice thawed too quickly, and I struggled to keep track of the shifting dynamic between us. Adam and Megan were 'trying', they said — to each other, to their nosey friends, sometimes to me. They started to plan a holiday, just the two of them. My efforts as counsellor, confidante, and peacekeeper had not been in vain, though they had been unappreciated. I quietly fumed as they poured over villas, their backs to me. I hadn't been on a proper holiday in a long time, and I could really do with a break too.

Besides, without company, without me, they'd probably just end up killing each other. I planted the seed first with Megan, who was more sympathetic to my solitary existence. Adam would take me away later in the year, he'd said. I wanted to go away now. In the end, we compromised. A group holiday in which couples could spend some time doing their own thing, but in which everyone was included.

There was plenty of space in Bea's seaside getaway cottage in Silverdale for everyone. Physically, anyway. Six bedrooms were given out to the four couples, Bea's oversized son, and Antonia's twins. I, as the only one who didn't have a prior claim to a room, or a partner or twin to share with, took the foldaway bed in the study. I didn't mind, not that it would have mattered if I did, as no one asked. The study housed a beautiful leather-topped desk, with an antique green leather captain's chair. I swivelled in it as I wrote my notes and created sketch after sketch. The study was downstairs, next to the kitchen at the back of the house with views of the beach beyond. In my more generous moods, I wondered if Bea wanted to provide the only artist in our group with the room with a view. And a desk to work at.

The kitchen window framed the sea, which seemed to go on forever. I painted it, bold greens muddying perfect blue hues. I painted myself, Adam, and Megan on the seabed, our watery graves beneath layers of textured acrylics, known only to me. In book club, our ladies would hypothesise, in art classes, students would infer meaning. I, on the other hand, wondered what had been painted over, scribbled out, rewritten and hidden; what the true meaning was, and what the artist wanted you to see. Were the two ever the same? I delighted in knowing that in my own work the truths were hidden, revealed only to those who looked hard enough, and even then, some remained elusive. As with life, the top visible layers were a delicate façade consisting of pretence, lies, and our desperate imaginations. My work, art, and diaries were no different.

It was a quiet couple of weeks in Silverdale, punctuated with late-night hyena laughter. Secret cigarettes were smoked by the back porch, whispers about husbands never to be told, as if the stench didn't give their deceit a voice of its own. My routine was out of sync with everyone else. They preferred late nights and late mornings, hangovers suffered bravely. I was an early riser, and like early nights in general. I don't drink. Schedules out of sync worked well, giving me respite from the women's dull chatter about their lives, which seemed alien compared to my own.

Antonia and her husband Daniel fussed over their over-indulged, late-in-life badly behaved three-year-old little girls, who were always dressed in twinsets with pastel-coloured bows, which they tugged at and lost. Dressing them smartly was a futile exercise in convincing anyone that they had any control over their offspring, doted on, desired yet denied to them for so long until science finally delivered.

The girls were early risers too, so my morning routine sometimes collided with Antonia's, but we barely exchanged a word. She busy wiping food from faces and floors, preparing stacks of Tupperware boxes full of mush, and endlessly washing and folding miniature outfits soiled and changed several times a day. Me, I was just taking up too much space in the kitchen, painting the view from yet another angle. Antonia would tut loudly as she squeezed past me or rudely piled my materials into a corner of the table to make room for her own monotonous activities.

The other child, if you could call him that, was a huge oaf of a man-boy, who took an irrational pride in his teenage status, as if staying alive for sixteen years, no matter how uneventfully, was an achievement in itself. From the little I saw and heard of Josh, he moved very little and took fewer risks, apart from potentially getting repetitive strain injury from texting and shooting bad guys on the screen in his room. He belonged to Bea, just Bea. His father was a late twenties fling, now fulfilling his role with monthly transfers wired from LA. Josh called Bea's partner Patrick, not Dad, not Stepdad. Patrick didn't seem to care.

Josh made friends during a visit here last summer and so, rising at lunchtime, he'd leave a trail of toast crumbs before disappearing to hang out at a bus stop with a similar bunch of awkward, unruly teens, with terrible haircuts and poorly judged attempts at facial hair. I walked past them once. He pretended not to know me when I called out. I took a different route for my afternoon walks from then on. When his gaming console stopped working later that day, naturally I'd hoped he'd find himself forced to interact with the group, me even, perhaps realising there was more to life, actually noticing the beauty around him. But he didn't. He sulked, a child again, his teenage stature diminished. I carefully returned the screwdriver to the shed, and the broken console, unchanged from the outside, remained a mystery.

Bea, Elizabeth, and Antonia were nicer than usual, inviting me when they took walks, or asking for my help to prepare dinner. In return I bit my tongue when their inane chatter provoked the anger hidden inside. The men, apart from Adam, generally ignored me. Typical. There's a theory that women pay more attention to other women when those other women are admired by men; they see them through that masculine lens. Clearly, I was not a threat. I bored them a little, as they bored me. I listened as Adam took poor advice on his marriage. He was urged to spend money on jewels.

'Just throw some money at the situation, mate,' they joked. Or perhaps not.

One night, Bea admired Elizabeth's bracelet.

'A birthday gift from Tom.' Her husband, a man who could afford precious gems.

Megan's most precious stones circled her ring finger, the question was a huge solitaire, the promise lined with tiny diamonds, and the eternity, thick with stones on a platinum band, the kind they could afford after the first decade of marriage. She would remove them when it was her turn to wash the pots after dinner, carefully placing them on the window ledge, always in view. They all wore expensive cashmere scarves for windy beach walks, and didn't give a thought to the value of their adornments.

I'd do mental calculations, having a good sense of price tag. Google is my friend. I wondered if they were all living beyond their means with secret cash flow problems tucked away behind the platinum cards, assets, and an over-riding sense of entitlement accompanied by an unerring belief that it would all be okay in the end, as it always was for people like them. My patience began to thin as the days wore on, and their conversations sounded more like letters to Father Christmas. I want, I want, I want. You have so much, I wanted to scream. I have nothing, yet it's enough. All I want is to keep hold of the little I have: the people I love.

Bea didn't even notice at first when one of her pretty

pearl earrings fell down the plughole. That's how little their things mattered. Elizabeth, however, sobbed and sobbed when she discovered a cavernous gold well in her gem-studded bracelet, where a large emerald should have been. At over £8,000 for the bracelet — Elizabeth had whispered with an air of scandal when she had first showed it off, loudly enough for everyone to hear — and one fifth of the jewels now missing, that's a pretty devastating loss. We searched everywhere, except in my washbag, where it sat, a lesson learned against greed and taking things for granted.

Megan told Elizabeth something similar had happened to her one of her mother's sapphire solitaire earrings given to her as something blue and something old on her wedding day. She shared the name of a good jeweller, who'd sourced a new stone and fixed it for her, though she still stares down at the carpet as she walks through her home, hoping to catch the glint of the sentimental stone nestled between the strands of yarn. She never will, though. Does she care? Not really, because everything is so easily replaced and paid for. Losses forgotten.

I tread softly through the world, leaving the lightest of footprints, day to day. I allow others to lead, I don't take over conversations, or make other people feel small or stupid. I feel grateful for what I have, and I'm careful not to risk losing it. But sometimes, just very occasionally, I make a small difference: a slight payback, or a small keepsake. Consequences tiny, justices fleeting. The world, for a moment, seems just a little bit fairer, and my calm is restored.

Not everything in life is fair though, is it? I had come back from New York and devoted an enormous amount of time to helping Megan and Adam tackle the rough patch. I'd saved them from embarking on a make-or-break holiday that surely would have broken them. When I heard Elizabeth ask Megan how things were, I'd expected some light praise at the very least. Instead, she stuck a knife into my back and her friends twisted it round and round.

'Olivia is always there. It's hard for us to talk. It's actually been a godsend having this holiday, where we can go off on our own once in a while. I swear, she's my shadow.'

'Well, we've been trying to encourage her to give you some space.'

That hurt. I thought they'd been making an effort with less disingenuous motives when they'd suggested walks where I could find some lovely views, or invited me to watch a film with them when Adam and Megan had gone out for dinner. I hadn't been stupid enough to think they actually liked me, not really, but I'd imagined they could see what I brought to the table. How much Megan and Adam needed me.

'We were surprised you didn't go on your own,' Bea said. 'Happily surprised to have you, of course.'

I remained seated on my captain's chair, my study door ajar. The kitchen door was not quite closed as they talked behind it.

'Don't ask. In the end Liv totally guilt tripped us,' Megan, the traitor, said.

Antonia took her turn with the knife in my back.

'Megan, you mustn't keep being so nice. You and Adam need time just the two of you. We don't like to say anything, but doesn't it bother you, having her living in the garden, monopolising you? Monopolising Adam? She's supposed to be in New York — or at least somewhere, working, building her career, rather than sitting in that little flat all day. Reclaim your marriage, sweetie! It would be good for her too, you know?'

What would she know about what would be good for me? She couldn't give a damn, anyway. I always knew Antonia hated me but I didn't expect Megan to use that twisted knife to tear out my broken heart.

'You're right,' she said, two words to change everything.

The last week of the holiday passed slowly after that. Memories made, shared history produced, and my spirit crushed. Adam and Megan seemed to be getting on a little better. Yet again, my thinking paid off, but I went without thanks. Megan had drunk less than usual. They argued only once. As we packed up the cars, I indulged myself in fantasy. Megan hadn't meant it, she was just going along with the pack for an easy life. Days had passed since she'd made those nasty comments and nothing had been said about my living arrangement.

The days have been getting longer since we arrived back from our holiday, and routines have been restored. I've made myself useful, and I've managed to keep Megan distracted. So far, my endeavours have been successful: still nothing had been mentioned about the granny flat. I've started to relax again. Megan's started to drink again. She needs me more than ever, and she's not foolish enough to think otherwise. Away from her clique, she sees that it's me, not them, who is always there for her and Adam.

We had the first barbecue of the year in the middle of April, the weather unseasonably warm reaching the high twenties, and Megan and I laughed until it hurt. She was a little woozy, with drink and Xanax, and other stuff to boot, but frankly, now I'd become accustomed to this alternative version of Megan, I found I liked it. Her edges softened, her mind became pliable. I'd thought hard about what she'd said back in Silverdale following our holiday, but as she succumbed to my influence, I felt my anger dissipate. Eventually, I decided I was prepared to forgive her.

Now it was possible to sit outside in the evening sun wearing just a shirt, feet bare, sandals kicked off to feel grass between toes. Our existences merged more in the garden that falls between the big old house and my new little flat. Purple irises appeared in the street's displays that the council half-heartedly maintain, in the misguided hope that our nearest town may one day relive its 2013 Britain in Bloom victory, for which town border signs still sing. Luckily, they don't add the date on the winning plaques, which sit proudly below the passive aggressive so-called welcomes to careful drivers, bookending our tiny village.

I continued to put up with Megan and Adam's tedious friends, and I only occasionally allowed my impish side to reveal small frustrations, accidentally allowing sarcasm to roll off my tongue, or precious possessions to roll into my bag. I never mentioned her cruel betrayal in Silverdale. Then, one day she did, as we tidied away the remainders of lunch.

'You must be very cramped in the flat with all your art materials,' she pretended to say casually.

I froze. Lulled into a false sense of security I hadn't predicted this. I did not have an answer. I put my coffee cup in her dishwasher.

'Not really,' I said, grasping for something to stop the tide from coming. 'That reminds me though, I need to go and pick up a new canvas from town. I'll see you later.'

Was Adam in on this? She had waited until he was out to broach the subject, so I assumed not. But then she brought him in on it. Later that night, I'd returned and was painting in the garden, enjoying the gentle evening breeze on my bare arms. Their French doors were open, and they moved into my view to sit at the table. They were huddled together, looking at a laptop. I tiptoed over and peered from a safe distance. Their backs faced me, as did their screen. Properties filled the screen. I knew what this was, and soon, I surmised, it was going to be an ambush. They knew I couldn't afford rent if I stayed focussed on my art, which they'd always wholeheartedly supported. Now I could imagine them 'encouraging' me to get a 'proper' job — in a supermarket or an office — sucking the last bits of joy from my small existence.

Where had it gone so wrong? What had I done wrong? I was baffled. First spurring me on to leave for the opportunity in New York, then nearly choosing a lodger over me for the granny flat, and now trying to get rid of me for a third time, after everything I had done for them. I had no idea she disliked me spending so much time here, or with Adam. Perhaps that was naive, but I don't see the world in exactly the same way that others seem to. My lines are fluid, roles and relationships not stuck in closed boxes, labelled clearly with permanent marker pen on those dreadful shop stickers that refuse to peel off, even after a long old hot-water soak.

I'd been lonely all my life. I've read this is typical in artists. We struggle to play along to what are considered normal social cues. At school, they'd once assessed me to see if I belonged somewhere on the Asperger's spectrum. I didn't, but you get the picture. I didn't even belong there, with the other freaks. So belonging with the Sykes had become very important to me. I'd been led to believe I was welcome. I spent more and more time in that kitchen, drumming my fingers on the marble counters, doodling on a notepad meant for shopping lists, watching her cook and drink. But it turned out I was in the way: unwanted, but tolerated. Their vacuous, mean-spirited hanger-on friends had finally succeeded in turning them against me. Or at least Megan. And now Megan was going to work on Adam.

'She's too reliant on us,' Megan told Adam.

Adam nodded. 'Yes, you're right.'

I was appalled at how little convincing he took. I hoped this was just for a quiet life.

'She needs space. And so do we,' Megan said, pretending this anything other than pure self-interest. Her words, his agreement, their plot to cast me aside. The first time they encouraged me to leave, I told myself I was paranoid for thinking perhaps they wanted rid of me, but the conversation I overheard in Silverdale, and now this. There was no coincidence, I was right. I'd served my purpose, whatever that was, my utility spent, my role in their happiness overlooked. Was I ever really wanted here? It had felt so real. But you don't toss the people you love aside like this, so what else could I conclude?

My stomach contracted, my head spun. It isn't a lack of pride keeping me here. Momentarily, I thought about packing a bag and leaving without saying goodbye. I could give them space and a reason to miss me. But where to I honestly didn't know. My roots had taken hold, and starting over felt impossible. For years, all three of us, I'd thought, had nurtured this precious relationship. To suddenly be confronted by my own foolishness was awful. I felt physically sick.

I was in limbo for two weeks avoiding them and refusing them the opening they craved. I snapped at her when we briefly passed, and she asked me what had got into me, her cheery and caring window dressing now veiling only very thinly the unscrupulous sly smile that I suppose had been there all along. I wondered how she really saw me, and why she had bothered with me at all. Perhaps I was like the feature wallpaper that seemed like a good idea at the time, until you realise it clashes dreadfully with the subtle creamy tones made more interesting by their expensive sounding Farrow and Ball names. Slipper Satin. Dimpse. Wimborne White. Antonia, Elizabeth, Bea.

I simmered, and seethed, all the while unsure of what to do. Adam, always astute, was concerned at my sullenness, further blackening the mood in their well-lit, ambient rooms. He persuaded me to take a walk with him, and I knew what was coming. He reached for my hand as we walked by the River Wharfe on a breezy Saturday, sun hidden by clouds. He squeezed it. As much as I craved his touch, that warm reassurance that we were connected, I felt unsure of him now, wondering if he was as much of a charlatan as she. I didn't want to believe it. I pulled my hand away. I couldn't let him do it.

'I'm going back to New York,' I told him.

'What?' He was as taken aback as I was. I hadn't quite expected to say it but it was the first thing that came to mind. My thinking caught up quickly, time could be bought.

'Yes, October. So you might want to look for a lodger after summer.'

His face looked so relieved at not having to perform the awkward task assigned to him by *Her Majesty* that I wanted to punch it. Visions of blood pouring from his nose appeared in my head, and I kept them for later. I had no intention of returning to that ugly, dirty city. By October, I'd need them to have changed their mind. My hand touched the note I'd intended to leave for him before I'd overheard Wednesday's brutal conversation, since then I'd kept it, feeling peevish, feeling stupid. Inevitably, the punishment went unnoticed and I wondered if he'd care if he never received another note. I had always believed my notes had brought him pleasure, and he'd whisper in my ear as he hugged me hello 'Thank you for my note, you're so wonderfully sweet, darling Olivia.' Now I felt patronised, and above that angry, because I wanted nothing more than to believe in him again.

From the moment May's book club kicked off, my sensitivities were heightened, alert to duplicity, seeking out Judas.

'Xavier got exactly what she deserved, if you ask me,' Antonia quipped, simplifying that month's complex story down to something stupid, like karma. Presumably a tactic to quickly move on from Simone de Beauvoir's novel, *She Came to Stay*, to more grounded topics, like how they might go about wreaking revenge on any woman brave enough to turn the head of their husbands. Much more fun for them than actual literary review. I sighed, ready for another wasted evening. I'd read it, and researched it online, and was ready to impress with my knowledge of how de Beauvoir had based

Xavier on not one, but two, of Sartre's lovers.

'Well quite,' Bea agreed. 'Gruesome way to end, though. Françoise does not pull her punches.'

Megan poured more wine. Elizabeth lifted her half-empty glass, stretching out her arm, gently touching Megan's knee to indicate the need for a top-up.

'I think,' Elizabeth began carefully, 'that the really interesting point is that Françoise invited Xavier into their marriage in the first place.'

Her eyes locked with Megan's. The others murmured agreement. I flushed a deep scarlet and my heart beat a fraction more quickly than I like it to. I knew they thought of me as a third wheel, but it's really not the same at all.

'So if we invite trouble in, then it's on us to rid ourselves of it. Take back control girls! Winners fight dirty!' Megan laughed. They all did.

As the night wore on, my desolation increased. I went to make tea, the only non-drinker of the group. I left the living room door ajar, and the kitchen door wide open, glutton for punishment for the pain that listening in to private conversations could cause me. I wasn't to be disappointed. As the kettle noisily boiled, and laughter and clinking disguised words and broke up sentences, a few phrases fluttered past.

'Perhaps she'll go...' Bea seemed to say. 'Megan, you could hint that it's getting late.'

'I really must tell you this but not in front of Olivia!' I heard Antonia say.

And as the song of the boiling water began its decrescendo, Megan finally said, 'Let me see what I can do, girls.'

'Wait, Megan, I'll go — I'll plant the seed,' Elizabeth again. 'We all know you're too sweet for your own good. You'll suggest she leaves and end up putting her on the mortgage.' Bitch.

She sauntered into the kitchen, glass in one hand, lipstick on her teeth. Like a leader of the pack, ready to take me down. She stood too close to me, and touched my hand, which I moved away to pop my teabag in the cup resting on the counter.

'Olivia, sweetie, I'm thinking of a cup of tea myself, before I go home, it's getting so late, I need to sober up, and get to bed soon. What about you, you look—'

Her sentence was interrupted by her own inadvertent blood-curdling scream. I swear I could hear the skin bubble and blister as the boiling water splashed all over her arm. I withdrew the kettle. Pale skin turned an angry red, as blotches blew up into blisters and rapidly pulled away as peel. What a raw, offensive-looking mess.

'Olivia! What are you doing?' Antonia rushed over, roughly pushed me away, as she pulled Elizabeth's arm towards the sink, quickly turning the cold on, as the commotion drew the rest of them into the kitchen, like a dramatic magnet.

'It was an accident,' I told them.

They bustled, they panicked, and within minutes we were outside, Antonia making accusations, Elizabeth quietly crying, as Bea fumbled for her keys and Megan looked bewildered. They were arguing, acting as if I wasn't there, as usual. Unable to stand it for a moment longer, I finally told Antonia something I'd longed to tell her for years.

'Fuck you.'

Without warning, Megan hit me, hard across the cheek. And then suddenly, he was there, truly my knight in shining armour, and I refuse to apologise for the cliché. He stood between us, he held me. Adam was the one person willing to defend me, protect me, and see the best in me. The only person I could trust. His anger at Megan was palpable. His horror at their accusations revealing what I'd known all along: it was I who needed protecting, the antelope cowering amongst the lionesses. They're beautiful, strong, powerful, whilst the antelope is weak, desperate and awkward. There's no contest; we all flock to admire big cats — the kings and queens of the jungle. When you watch the chase narrated with an anthropomorphism lens, do you want the lionesses to starve and die, or the antelope to be torn from limb to limb, eaten alive? Adam backed me, an unexpected but welcome twist in what had been a fretful, few weeks. My doubts about Adam's true feelings erased, I knew now someone like me couldn't afford to lose someone like him.

May's book club had been a revelation and, as Megan said herself, winners play dirty. I needed to up my game. Megan wasn't yet as malleable to my offensive as I'd started to think she was. If I couldn't manage to get us back to the way we were then we needed to change the game, and I had to win it.

Adam

He'd spent Saturday night in London with Olivia, and she'd tearfully thanked him for his support on that dreadful Thursday night just gone. Adam had felt her hurt deep within his own chest, and sensed her overwhelming gratitude at being believed.

'You're the only person who seems to like me at the moment,' she'd said, and Adam knew in his heart she wasn't fishing.

'I don't just like you, Olivia, I love you. We both do. It's just a blip, we'll figure it out, I promise.'

Back at home, a few degrees colder than London's insulated walls, both literally and metaphorically, Adam found himself daydreaming with intense frequency about the pace of life he craved, far away from the building strain of his home life. More than two decades and not an itch and now it was coming apart at the seams. Before, Megan wouldn't have questioned him paying for a hotel in London for the two of them if it made life easier for him. Now he wasn't so sure, as memories of her hissing in the dark three nights ago repeated on him.

'You chose her over me, instinctively! You couldn't possibly have known what had happened. When did you stop trusting me? When did we become strangers? How could you?'

So he had lied. Not outright, but by omission. The day

trip had been planned a while, both Adam and Olivia delighted by Giacometti's spindly sculptures, currently on display at the Tate Modern for a few short months. Megan was attending an eventing trial all that weekend leaving Friday afternoon to ensure that she and the team were ready early Saturday morning to walk the course. As usual, she had urged him not to bother coming, which he rarely did anyway as horses really weren't his thing.

'I think a bit of time apart will do us good, you go to London as planned.'

Throughout their marriage, Adam had rarely questioned his wife. In the pecking order he knew his place, he'd never forgotten his good luck in finding himself secure above his station. He'd ignored niggling doubts as to the sincerity of her girlish laugh as she'd teased Olivia good-naturedly. He'd refused to see any real malice in that old-school group of apparently — according to Megan — sweet, friendly women who'd so intimidated him at their lavish house parties years ago, as he strove to impress them enough so they'd urge Megan to say yes: to another date, to a late-night coffee, to a weekend away, until death do us part.

All it had taken was one slap, and as he looked into her eyes, he saw a different person. Her increasing reliance on narcotics and booze was enticing something unknown within out from its hiding place. The flute coaxing the snake out of the pretty woven basket. Had violence always lurked? Those funny school stories of pranks and high-jinks she had always told so well, having him in stitches, took on new sinister meaning. Peter used to joke that she was out of his league, and she'd eat him alive. Star struck until now Adam hadn't given much thought to the fact that the elusive popular girls, he'd never known up close — but rather, observed from afar — tended to keep their position of authority through a reign of terror.

Yet, he had been by Megan's side for a long time, a lot of good times, and Adam chastised himself for his wilful blindness to imperfection and his current penchant for melodrama. Megan not being perfect, perhaps even having the capacity for cruelty shocked him, but what horrified him more was the naivety he'd displayed in believing in such implausible fiction about another human being for so long. He'd never considered himself a typical guy, lacking in observation skills, head buried in work, assumptions gently propping up a happy home, as the pieces that didn't fit the picture were ignored, unnoticed.

Until this last couple of years, Adam actually felt rather smug about his marriage built on friendship, tenderness, love. Not for Adam and Megan the secret rolling of eyes or frustrations shared with friends over beers, but instead genuine communication, good and regular — if a tad predictable — sex, and for Adam at least, a sense that he really couldn't do any better. Adam wasn't the sort of guy they laughed at on far-fetched American films, when some stooge discovers his partner of several decades is actually a spy, a vampire, or a psychopath. It seemed he'd not been paying attention. Megan seemed to remember the last few years very differently. The word neglected had been overused, the rhythm of its syllables like nails on a chalkboard.

He knew it was unfair to demand perfection and to resent his wife's less flattering recollections of their life, but he couldn't help it. He felt stupid, rejected, and uncertain of his future, and he didn't like it. He shouldn't blame Megan for this sudden overwhelming sense of loss, but he did. The loud voice in his mind that had told him not to let Olivia infiltrate so absolutely when she'd first demanded re-entry on a full VIP season ticket, no areas barred, had shrunk to a whisper. It was nice having someone around who didn't despise him half the time.

Megan, usually sanguine, assured in her role, and content with her reflection in Adam's eyes, knew she'd toppled. Now she limped and hesitated. Her irritation at feeling insecure made her feel tense, and subsequently she alternated between ignoring Adam and annoying him in the couple of days that followed the slap. Adam may have felt unworthy of his wife sometimes, but he surprised himself by feeling quite disenchanted by her sudden dissonance. It didn't suit her. Or maybe it didn't suit him.

No one was there to notice his absence that Saturday night, and when Megan returned after a long drive home on Sunday night, she went straight upstairs. He followed her, and she didn't turn away as he kissed her hello, giving Adam hope that maybe she wanted to mend and make up. It seemed to Adam a foolish idea to re-open old wounds, so he smiled as her and offered to run her a bath. She'd let her hand brush his arm as she passed him in the bathroom doorway.

'There's something I need to talk to you about. About Olivia. About the talk she and I had on Friday? Later?'

He'd nodded, trepidation in his eyes, willing this mess to disappear. 'I'll go and fetch you a drink,' he found himself saying, forgetting his promise to himself to try to stop encouraging everyday intake of spirits and wine. It was so embedded in their lives.

Take a bath, pour a drink. Cook a meal, open the wine.

Megan didn't argue, and instead nodded. He headed down the landing and turned the corner onto the staircase. He abruptly stopped, startled, finding Olivia stood still on the stairs, holding a drink. He'd seen her walk down towards the granny flat on their return, but evidentially she'd changed her mind about staying there.

'I thought she'd want this upstairs. I came to see how it went,' she'd said, in response to the curious look in his eyes. 'She said we'd have a chat tonight, so I came over when I heard the car. I called out but there was no answer. Thought I'd bring this to her. Peace offering.'

He quietly told her that Megan was taking a bath, and he was going to get an early night. She duly left, handing him the gin and tonic. She looked a little put out, but said nothing. Adam took the drink to Megan. Later came, but Megan, sleepy from her long bath, was gently snoring, still in her fluffy robe. Adam had looked at Megan, peaceful in this moment, her skin smooth, rather than creased with worry. He was determined to shake off this feeling of betrayal, as if Megan had purposely duped him, pretending to be so flawless. He reminded himself there'd been arguments before, that in the past they'd both said things they later regretted that likely dented the perfect shapes they'd cut out for each other. This was no different, it was just now, in the moment, still raw.

When Friday night came around, the atmosphere had not improved despite the glimmer of hope that Sunday evening had briefly offered. Megan had been distant again and hadn't got around to updating him on her conversation with Olivia.

She'd been quiet and broadly agreeable, if not a little docile, going to bed early, rising late, and napping in between. Coward that he assumed he must be, Adam couldn't cope with more confrontation and so he'd left it there, trying to convince himself that no news was good news, and the whole episode would blow over in time.

The dinner had been scheduled for weeks, and Adam wasn't prepared to let Peter down at short notice. He'd been ready to dig his heels in should Megan advise against an audience, but she too was committed to the show of normality, and even more committed to their good, kind friend, even if not, at this precise moment, to her treacherous husband, who she could no longer even be bothered to argue with.

It seemed to Adam that the fight had gone out of her, yet he hesitated to ask her about it, hesitated indefinitely. She'd told him too casually that her therapist had changed her dose today. The subtext was blame. He imagined her retelling of events would paint a different picture to the one that haunted him: neglected wife, stressful job, unsupportive husband. Even if it were true, Adam doubted devouring pills was the long-term solution.

For well over twenty years they'd honoured their monthly kitchen suppers with Peter and that wasn't about to change. The first one was just months after their winter wedding. Peter's best man speech had sealed the deal, his place at their table never questioned, as Megan embraced him warmly and whispered, 'thank you'. They didn't know that Peter would never marry and complete their hopes of perfect symmetry but even then, they knew it didn't matter. Megan adored her new husband's oldest friend, and he never felt or acted like a gooseberry.

For the past few years Olivia had joined them, at first at Megan's behest but over the years, Adam had come to appreciate the dynamic too. Spellbound from a young age at the beauty of maths and its influence on every part of life, he'd studied our all-too-human reliance on symmetry and habit for survival. Symmetry was economical, habit expends less energy. Bees use hexagons rather than organic shapes to improve efficiency. There was reason powering our ordered, harmonious existences. It was simply in our nature. What Adam didn't consider was the other side of well-worn routines was how easily observed they were — how vulnerable they made you to robbers and thieves. Great efforts made to build safe nests, so inviting to nearby cuckoos.

Naturally Adam and Megan were disappointed in Peter's lack of interest in Olivia, and as was her way, she took it personally and was, at best, blunt with Peter if not downright rude. Peter took about as much interest in social etiquette as Olivia, who didn't appreciate Peter's tone when he'd teasingly tell her she was 'simply impertinent', calling her out over her scurrilous remarks.

Adam and Megan had always told their friends that they found Olivia's manner wonderfully amusing, a breath of fresh air in their world crammed full of deference and obsequious mild-mannered diplomatic exchanges. They'd often privately comment upon what they saw to be a shocking level of intolerance for the virtue of candour as their oldest, most cherished friends criticised Olivia, and tried awkwardly to gloss over her brusque opinions, as if they were a social blemish everyone ought to politely pretend, they hadn't noticed. Neither cared to admit, even to themselves, that her absence had brought with it an easing of tension, and after the New York interlude, her return had heightened their senses to the disquiet she brought to every room.

Peter arrived at seven o'clock by taxi, and as he walked down the hallway bellowed his compliments to the chef, the aromas delighting him even from a distance. He brought good wine, and they all drank it apart from Olivia, who silently laid the table, only occasionally glaring at Peter, who topped up everyone else's wine as he retold old stories, pouring cold water on the heated atmosphere. In the kitchen, a large Le Creuset casserole pan, bright orange, sat on the wide, eight-ring hob, paella rice steaming, and plump langoustines delicately balanced on top, with mussel shells, clams, and white fleshy squid pieces protruding from the rice. Megan carefully carried the hot and heavy pan to the table as they all took their seats, and Peter announced before tasting it that Megan's cooking could never be surpassed.

'I live for our Friday-night suppers, my dears, and even Olivia glaring at me couldn't stop me from coming here like clockwork,' he chuckled, cheekily.

Olivia bristled, but said nothing. Adam noted that Megan smiled, where usually she might have laughed. He wondered if it wasn't such a bad thing for her to show Olivia that they were on her side, especially after recent events. Olivia did have a rather stern resting face, but Adam doubted being constantly reminded of the fact was doing her self-esteem any good, hence most likely increasing the chances of her responding in a prickly manner, and proving hastily made assumptions correct. Adam changed the subject quickly, and

155

started to describe the sculpture exhibition they'd been to on Saturday.

'The only problem with the Tate is that it's in bloody London, and is full of bloody Londoners!' Peter quipped, not in the habit of feigning interest, but loving an excuse to return to his favourite topic of why the north was much nicer than the south.

Familiar banter between the old friends naturally ensued, Megan always siding with Peter, play-mocking their soft southern counterpart.

'Technically I'm from the Midlands,' Adam would inevitably reply, and their well-trodden conversational pathway would lead them to safer grounds.

'I love London. The hotel on Saturday was divine,' Olivia quietly interrupted. The sound of Megan's fork hitting the floor punctuated the new silence. Sat next to Olivia, she didn't turn to reply but instead she looked straight across at Adam.

'We couldn't face the journey home, just found a cheap place nearby, much easier in the end, did I not mention it?' Adam cleared his throat, and Peter looked, uncharacteristically and feverishly, for a social queue. He might not have taken to Olivia, but these three were not usually in the habit of strange exchanges, loaded with unspoken resentment.

'No, you didn't mention it.' Megan poured herself more wine — a 2010 Pomerol, Peter's evening offering.

'A very good vintage,' he'd told them, 'let's drink the lot before we move onto the plonk I got from the supermarket on the way here.' He laughed, knowing they'd polish off at least three over the course of the night.

'I'm sorry, I forgot, we weren't going to mention it—' Olivia began but Adam quickly cut her off.

'Not so much that, I probably just thought after a rough, few days, and with your new boy not getting placed at the trial, the last thing you'd want is to have us banging on about what a nice time we'd had.' Adam's voice was unsteady, too quick.

Megan simply nodded, conscious of poor Peter's discomfort. 'Of course, don't worry. It was an unprecedented poor performance at the weekend, I was quite miserable. I'm not sure my rider had enough experience for the level of competition, and the Charlie is still young, and can't carry a weak rider — lesson learned.' She was babbling, and her voice was too high, and too cheerful, yet strangely robotic. 'Has everyone had enough of mains? I've pudding, and cheese, to come.'

With the clatter of dishes and the sound of water running the silence was quickly eroded with building chatter. But something hung in the air between Adam and Megan, and her arched eyebrow questioned his choice for the second time in as many weeks, her forced smiles failing to cover the hurt in her eyes.

Hours later, still sat around the table, conversations were becoming more animated and Megan's words were becoming more slurred. She sloshed more wine into her glass, filling it almost to the top — unseemly, Adam judged, even if they were now only drinking the dregs of Waitrose's own-brand Bordeaux.

'Poor Elizzy, her arm! What a mess,' she was saying. Adam gave her a pointed look: don't bring this up, not now, he tried to telepathically tell her. Incoherent now, and oblivious to his facial signals and his soft shin-kick beneath the table.

'Of course, she's quite horrible sometimes, always gossiping. And she can be very clumsy. Still...' She'd drained the glass, and was reaching for a new bottle.

'I think you've probably had enough, don't you?' Adam tried to disguise his irritation, to not be the patronising husband — a role he'd never needed to try on before. Megan had always self-policed impeccably. Before this year anyway.

'Of course, I haven't been myself recently, no wonder I'm making fucking shit decisions at the yard. Mind you we've not won a thing in months.'

Adam winced. Peter looked amused, and a tad surprised. Drunk Megan was funny — and prude Adam even funnier — to their baffled guest. Her wistful look was abruptly replaced with a demented look of joy.

'Do you remember, Adam, the time we rode horses on the beach, and we thought it was so romantic, but then that old nag tossed you off?' She cackled, snorted at her own innuendo, and threw her head back with such force that her chair fell backwards, and she narrowly avoided cracking her head on the kitchen tiles by some instinctive pull that allowed her to tuck her chin in and prevent her skull from meeting the floor.

'Jesus! Megan! Are you ok?'

She was still laughing as Peter and Adam helped her to her feet, Adam aghast.

'I'd better help Megan to bed, Peter, I'm sorry mate.'

'Ah, well it was a *very* good vintage,' Peter good-naturedly teased as he slipped his jacket on, and tapped a couple of times on his phone, quickly finding the local taxi number.

As he sat in the back, a drunken sleep was kept at bay by thoughts of the curious scene he'd left behind. From Peter's perspective, it was entirely unremarkable to witness Olivia attempting to play the two off against each other, looking for weaknesses, a nasty habit he often noticed, but the happy couple appeared oblivious to. However, for her to succeed was astonishing.

In general, Peter's views on the doomed nature of most marriages were proven right with time. He didn't like being right. He hated to see good friends stoop with the strain of sullied love. But it was a sad fact, and he had always believed he was better off out of that game. Adam and Megan were different though, the one couple he thought would make it to the end, which was the only reason he'd agreed to be best man. Asked often due to his brilliant storytelling and exquisite comedic timing, back in those days of fervent knot-tying, he'd refused on the grounds of having no experience and nothing good to say about the institution. Yet he'd been as bewitched by Megan as Adam had been, still was, and genuinely didn't think he could bear to see either of them suffer.

Meanwhile, Adam lay next to his snoring wife, drool anchoring her red wine-stained lips to the white pillowcase, wondering what signs and clues he must have missed to enable her, so quickly and without warning, to unravel so spectacularly. Because, Adam thought, that's not how it works. Wives aren't perfectly poised one moment, and unstable wreckages the next. They'd been set against each other in December, he thinking it a poor decision to have Olivia in the flat, Megan arguing for it. Now he was stood by

Olivia, as Megan irrationally pushed them both away. Full circle, opposing sides once again. It didn't used to be this way.

She'd slapped Olivia, and that had made him pay attention, but how many more subtle shows of that temper had he happily overlooked? He'd turned a blind eye to the anxiety medication, trusting that doctors knew best. But had things got out of hand now? It was utterly unfathomable that Megan should be classed as an addict of any kind, but without a shred of doubt, she was overdoing everything to a critical point. She'd admitted she was struggling with work, which would undoubtedly be getting to her. She moaned constantly about his absences. Had wine been transformed from middle-class social prop to a way to cope with life's increasing disappointments, as they aged, their bodies changing, and bitter resentment growing?

They were closer to fifty than forty. Adam inwardly sighed at the dreadful realisation that the hope and buoyancy of their youth was becoming almost mythical, so far it seemed from today's reality. It was turning out, against Adam's preferred perspective that midlife was here, it had been for a while, and a crisis was looming.

Olivia

'We need to talk.'

No pleasant conversation ever began this way, but that's how Megan and I began, that Friday morning after book club, and the day before my trip to London with Adam, my cheek still red from the slap she'd delivered that night before.

'I can't go away this weekend and work with this ugly affair hanging over us.'

'Well, we couldn't have that,' I sniffed. My feelings were a little hurt that her main goal was to gain another trophy for her display, rather than mend our broken relationship. How did we go from such a warm, happy threesome to this well-worn dance of jealousy, in-fighting, bittersweet female competition? I'd thought we were above all that.

Despite my loyalty, my efforts to be the best I could for both of them, she was ready to sacrifice me like a lamb to the slaughter, or to a one-bedroom flat above a grotty shop. Whatever. I never intended to be a threat to her or her precious marriage. Instead of looking closer to home for reasons why he was never here, she wanted to point the finger at me. She thought he'd choose her, he always had, he almost did. I was preparing myself to be thrown out. I had no plan, no comeback, and then she planted the seed of doubt herself, in that one simple act of violence.

Of course, it didn't take much persuasion that the book group clique could be wrong in their interpretation that night.

He always saw their evident dislike of me, and was suspicious of their snobbish agendas, favouring my clumsy, quirky honesty, even if it wasn't to everyone's taste. He always stuck up for me. She used to as well. The conspiring, good old-fashioned schoolgirl meanness, as if I hadn't had enough of that my whole life as it was, was devastating. I was reeling that she should believe the cat choir of book club over me, the one she was closest to, the only person who loved her truly in that group. Those women had only a superficial love for Megan, and if at any moment she couldn't fulfil her role as the polished, horsey, pearl-wearing, shiny-haired domestic goddess, they'd ditch her without thinking twice, never looking back. Not me, though, I was here for good.

'Don't be like that, sweetie, you know what I mean. I'll be worried about you, about us. I have been for a while, actually.' She touched my arm, tears in her eyes.

Despite my new, not to mention justified, cynicism of Megan's feelings towards me, my heart surged. She'd been worried about me for a while.

'I first noticed it in Silverdale,' she continued.

Hope soared: Megan had seen up close how excluded I was, the disdain in their comments, their easy dismissal of my views, my feelings. She had realised I'd been keeping it to myself to protect her, stoically, and she was going to apologise, explain she had got everything wrong, and that my neediness was clearly a direct result of a sustained campaign against me. Now she understood, she'd banish the wicked witches forever more and keep me close.

'Perhaps, if I'm honest, I'd noticed it long before, but I didn't want to admit it to myself. I buried my head in the sand.'

For those few moments, it was too good to be true. Finally, to not be alone in my perspective, I was temporarily elated. So this was what it felt like to be normal, not to be the only one who saw things my way, to not constantly need to question my every thought in case I was wrong though, I knew deep down, I wasn't. My perspective wasn't distorted, the world was. Then she said the words that ruined everything.

'You need help.'

I stared at her, confused.

'You steal things, you break things on purpose, you lie. I know you've always found it hard to fit in, had your fair share of difficulties, and I know my oldest friends and you, well, you jar a little.'

An understatement, and shockingly poor attempt to demonstrate diplomacy following the character assignation she was in the midst of delivering, blow by blow.

'But this isn't the solution,' she calmly told me. 'I think you're looking for small ways to get back at them, at me, for whatever wrongs you think you've suffered at the hands of others, but your insecurity is getting the better of you. You don't need to hurt them, they don't mean to hurt you. And you don't need to hurt me either. Tell me, was it an accident, or did you lose your temper? I'll believe you, whatever you say, and I'll help you, but I need to ask.'

As I said, no pleasant conversations ever began with those four words, we need to talk. I wanted to return her slap and I wanted to run away, but I took a breath instead.

'I do not steal and lie. I don't know what you're talking about. And of course, I didn't hurt Elizabeth on purpose. It.

Was. An. Accident,' I spat my last four words at her, glaring, unblinking. Furious.

She sighed. She looked tired. A small silence.

'Olivia, what is this?' Her mother's missing sapphire solitaire sat in her palm. She placed it on the kitchen counter.

'Oh, you found it then? Jolly good,' I said, looking into her watery eyes. Poker face.

'It was in your trinket box on your bedroom windowsill.' She looked at me straight, no hint of shame for snooping.

'What were you doing in my flat? Rooting through my things?' Hysteria was rising in my throat.

'Your flat?' she asked, incredulous that I should feel entitled to privacy in the place I rent from her, paying her in kind.

I didn't bother to respond, not that she gave me much opportunity to before continuing her righteous speech.

'I wasn't rooting. I was looking for the bracelet you borrowed. I wanted it, and you were out. I really didn't think you'd mind, as we *all* come and go here as we please, don't we? Besides that's hardly the pertinent point right now.'

She was lying about the bracelet. She never wears it, and she has hundreds of others. She was snooping. The fucking audacity! And while she stands there accusing me of lying. I'm not a liar, I just have a different frame of reference.

'It doesn't matter,' she continued, holding my stare, boldly. 'You took it, because you're jealous — and you have nothing to be jealous of — you'll have your own beautiful things one day. You're angry at the world and for some reason you have these odd inclinations. You collect things, you write everything down, you study people obsessively. I love you, Olivia, but I've seen it now and I can't un-see it.

164

It's clear that you have a good heart: you're fun, you're kind, you are so good to us, but you must see that you can't go on like this. It needs to stop. The three of us should talk, because right now, there's a lot of animosity in this house, and you seem to be putting yourself at the centre of it. And you shouldn't. We shouldn't have dragged you into our mess either. It wasn't fair. I'm so sorry for slapping you, but we need to put our cards on the table, we need to be honest, all of us.'

She thought I was a sociopath. Or a lunatic. Or both. Maybe they're the same thing. Luckily, whatever else I was, I was clever, and I could think fast. This conversation was getting out of hand. I'd been caught off guard. Stupidly, I'd thought she was reaching out, but this was a threat. To give her credit, though, she was being rather reasonable seeing as she considered me a thief and a liar. But she was going to tell him I was mad, or bad, untrustworthy, and then it was game over. She expected me to corroborate her version of events to get her off the hook for her little cat fight display so I could hang myself in the process. Then together they'd eject me from my home, one way or another.

Despite residue warmth in my belly for her — the only person who would confront an apparent thief and nutcase, and then offer a way out rather than frogmarching me to the front door, or worse, the police — I had to quickly weigh it up. Yes, she could simply say I wasn't the person they thought I was, parade my betrayal, get a mob together, and burn me out. But this way, in offering sympathy and support she could negate the crazed image she'd painted over Adam's perfectly poised portrait of his wife.

I'm not paranoid, I'm astute. I know how her mind

works, and despite her protestations of my oddities, we're not so different. She hadn't told him yet, otherwise they'd have approached me together, unified. That much was clear. She wasn't sure, not one hundred per cent sure anyway. That's the problem when you spend half your days and nights in a pill and booze-induced fugue. Maybe she was convinced about the earring but everything else was hunch. Her fine brain was a tad addled, but she wasn't stupid. After book club, she wasn't sure he'd believe her over me, and although that would have killed her, she knew that she needed me to admit guilt.

'I didn't steal anything. I found your sapphire on Thursday night. I should have given it to you straight away, but everyone was arguing over bloody Simone de Beauvoir, and then...' I tailed off quietly before continuing, 'I was going to. I forgot.' A well-timed tear fell onto my cheek. 'I honestly don't know why you're accusing me.'

She wasn't buying it.

'Please don't spread these lies about me.' My sobs were loud and messy now, hiccups punctuated my words in the wrong parts of my sentences, making me shrill and staccato. 'It's hard enough, everyone hates me so much already. They'll believe you, even though it's not true. He'll hate me.' Now my sobs were real, because this idea I couldn't bear. 'You attacked me, for sticking up for myself,' I continued, now on a roll, sniffing violently, my own story taking shape, becoming real. 'They're bloody awful, all of them, I can't help being different, I thought you were different, but you're not. I suppose you don't want me around anymore?' But Adam did, we both knew that, he wouldn't see me turned out onto the street. 'They've poisoned you against me, accusing me no doubt, you're seeing a pattern that isn't there. Accidents happen, people lose things. I found the stone underneath the sofa when I was cleaning up a spilt drink, and I meant to give it to you, I thought you'd be so pleased! But then book club turned nasty, I heard them talking about getting rid of me, and then you hit me! And now, rather than saying sorry, you're accusing me of terrible things I would never do. What do I want with your precious jewellery? I just want to be able to be myself without being made into a pariah or a victim. I thought I belonged here.'

My speech was deserving of a standing ovation. She looked crestfallen as she automatically embraced me, unable to stomach pain of any kind in anyone. She had been so sure of herself at the outset, had it all figured out. But nothing is straightforward. Context is everything. She could still see in me that innocent she'd wanted to mould. She could still see the good. She was questioning herself. I could see it in the crease on her forehead, the way her eyes darted to avoid mine as she pulled back from me, my sobs subsiding.

'Shush, shush, it's okay. I'm sorry. Maybe I've got it wrong. I don't know.' She wasn't convinced, or convincing. 'There's just so many coincidences, and you've been acting so strangely lately. I won't say anything to anyone, for now. You must understand why I thought as I did.'

I nodded, benevolently, forgiving.

'But please, Olivia, make an effort to mend things with everyone. Just be a little more malleable, tolerant.'

'I will try harder.' We hugged again, stiffly this time.

'Can we put the book club incident behind us, now? I shouldn't have lashed out. I'm sorry. We'll all try harder.'

She desperately wanted to believe the best of me, for the

nastiness to dissipate. So did I. But it was those four words, we need to talk, and everything that had followed in the subsequent few minutes had made that impossible. She couldn't take back her recriminations. The trust was gone, and I knew that despite her promises, she would take her allegations to Adam.

She was away for the weekend, after that Friday, as were we, giving me the first play. I couldn't stop her from talking to her husband, but I was pretty sure I could stop him from believing her accusations. After all, he chose me in the book club debacle, and her testimony was becoming decreasingly credible the more it appeared she relied on self-medication. I was also cheered by the fact that Adam had silently defied her by choosing to take me to London for the night, when she clearly thought I should be punished, or worse, ignored. You'd have thought she was the one with third-degree burns.

Adam needed to be shown once and for all that Megan was unreliable, and that her mindset was marred. She drank too much and by now, despite her efforts of concealing it, we all knew she was hoovering up prescription pills. The dosage was low on the ones I'd seen at the back of the cupboard. She needed better ones, but as doctors can be so fusty about such things, I'd already been providing supplements throughout the days we spent together, ever since I discovered her tendency to forget who was most important to her as I listened to her almost deny me a home, sat in the garden smoking with Bea.

I'd taken control of the situation, blunting her wits a little at a time, planting the seed of suspicion in Adam that Megan couldn't be trusted, and making myself indispensable to her. Megan was generally more compliant these days and, until now, her dazed state had made it easy for me to have my fair share of influence about what goes on around here. Her meekness had been lovely at times, sadly I now needed a dumbed-down version of the new Megan. One less likely to cast aspersions against me, or at least likely to forget to. I made a mental note to see what I could do about that. The web can be a dark place. You really wouldn't be able to trust a word she said, soon.

We'd gone to London on Saturday afternoon. The train was overcrowded and the sandwiches were stale. We'd sat in companionable silence, me staring out of the window. He'd asked how I was, tenderly. I'd told him I was fine, but that I was worried about her. He'd furrowed his brow, gently smiled, touched by my kindness, even as I was victimised by pack of she-wolves.

'She's under a lot of stress. She never would have lashed out like that if she hadn't been in a bad place. She didn't mean it,' he'd agreed.

He defended her, of course, but in doing so he told me he was ready to believe she wasn't stable. Poor, mad, middle-aged Megan. Once a vibrant young woman but now a wine-soaked old crackpot. It could happen to anyone, though he was clearly taken aback that it might well be happening to him, and his perfect prize. Lucky for him, he still had me. I could see him thinking the very same thing, and he squeezed my hand.

Giacometti's sculptures were amazing. One of the viewer's notes cards told us that his post-war sculptures captured the tone of loneliness and melancholy potent in the existentialist world of philosophy that inspired him. I knew

169

how he felt. But for a blissful twenty-four-hours, wrapped up in the city whirlwind and each other, I forgot just how low I'd been feeling. I knew he'd purposely not mentioned that we were staying overnight to Megan, although at some point she'd known and forgotten.

Adam was quiet in response to my enthusiasm, and I felt we completed the exhibition more quickly than I would have liked. I didn't get to read all the cards, and we didn't, as we had on previous visits, need to take a short break for a coffee because we'd spent so long gushing over shared opinions. I'd hoped that as we exited the exhibition space, we might go to one of our favourite spots, The Laughing Gravy, for dinner, or cut all the way across town to The Café du Marche, maybe calling into the Barbican on the way, as we had done a few months ago, but Adam had work to catch up on, so we ordered room service instead.

I heard her car pull up on Sunday evening from the flat where I'd safely ensconced myself. I was curled up on the sofa, looking at the postcards of my favourite sculptures that I'd bought from the Tate's gift shop and listening for her arrival. I meandered over and let myself into the kitchen, calling out quietly so that no one could hear me. I went to fix drinks. I listened from the stairs, poised to take a step up should I be caught, drink in hand. As I had suspected, she had no intention of keeping her thoughts to herself. She told him they'd need to talk. About me. And she thinks I'm the liar? I could push that conversation back a day at least, I thought, as I dropped a little white tablet into her drink, and mixed it well. In the end, Adam administered the medicine and I knew it was very unlikely that they'd have a chance to talk.

In the days that followed I helped her keep up her new and improved treatment regime, switching her pills for my more effective meds as I cleaned the en suite, and adding extra doses when I brewed her tea or fetched her wine. I'd been too cautious with my previous efforts, not understanding the intensity of her emotions, which despite being dulled kept rearing their ugly head above the parapet taking aim at my comfortable life. I updated my diary, recording her mental decline. It made for grim reading.

Megan had been distracted as we'd headed towards Friday's ritual supper with pompous Peter. She slept a lot during the day, but little at night. Her memory was faulty. She complained how little sense it made, vowing to talk to her doctor.

'I've been under so much stress, Olivia, the business is struggling. The team are losing everything. I just feel so ill all the time. Things here haven't been great.' She gestured loosely, eyes wide, gazing around her beautiful home, adorned with photos of her beautiful life and her beautiful husband. Some people mess everything up, no matter how lucky they are.

'Go back to the doctor,' I'd said, knowing he was useless.

'I will,' she'd resolved.

I spent more time than ever by her side, looking after her. I brought her things to eat and drink. I ensured she got some sleep, even if it was during the day rather than at night. Friday night supper came but no great revelations had been announced.

It had been easy to find and procure the right meds for Megan. Benzodiazepines are the G&T of middle class neurosis by all online accounts. I'd recently discovered through a colourful forum for unhappy, drugged-up women with healthy credit cards designed to facilitate borderline legal abuse of anxiety meds that if standard benzos weren't doing the trick, you could miss a few baby steps and jump straight to clonazepam, a good twenty times the strength. They look identical, though, all part of the same family. These women never shut up online. If you ask me, most of them are already addicts, but in a very civilised, dignified way. No forgetting to brush your hair, or losing your job (if they're unfortunate enough in marriage to have one) with these little babies. More a slowing down, both physically and mentally.

I thought her permanent wistful look suited her, her slowing movements were calming. She was still graceful like a ballerina, but a weak one, in need of a good meal. The increasingly fragile Megan was a breath of fresh air: quiet, absent, and completely lacking in violence or denunciations. At this rate, I'd probably save her marriage. I'm sure Adam would prefer this feminine creature to the neurotic psycho she'd shown signs of becoming before her meds had been optimised. Perhaps for once, he could play the starring role in his own home, rather than supporting actor for the lady of the house.

I'd been looking forward to Friday's supper, unusually, as I loathe Peter even more than he loathes me. However, he's Adam's most trusted friend, and therefore the perfect witness to Megan's erratic behaviour should Adam question himself or pretend it isn't as bad as it seems. Megan's drinking and her increasing reliance on sleeping pills and anxiety meds will surely render her a basket case, to be humoured maybe, but hardly to be relied upon. I, on the other hand, intend to be very reliable. Cardinal.

While we waited for Peter to arrive, and Megan put the finishing touches to her famous paella, I upped her dose and handed her the glass of wine. The rest she did for herself, too drowsy to handle the wine, then too drunk to know when to stop. In vino veritas, she proved me right, the accident with Elizabeth's arm still a worrying issue for her at the top of her befuddled mind.

She'd mentioned earlier in the week how groggy she was feeling, how no matter how well she slept, she felt so tired. I was careful with my doses; I didn't want to render her physically ill, I just needed her to keep a low profile, my very own unreliable narrator contrasting against my sober, straightforward counterpart.

Late into the evening, she slurred and waved her arms, hobbling along, intermittently laughing painfully as she recalled her fall, and unceremoniously felt for bruises on her own bottom, creasing her skirt and laddering her tights. Adam carried her upstairs, said his goodbyes, and muttered to himself about what a disaster the night had been.

It was a roaring success.

Adam

Seven months into the year and Adam was starting to resign himself to the fact that 2018 was a really shitty year and there was nothing he could do about it. He was staring at his screen in the home study, trying to predict the latest fallout as politic negotiations continued to stagnate, and trade deals his trade relied upon failed to be brokered. The last few months had seen a remarkable economic upward turn, despite the farce that Brexit had become, and always been, in Adam's opinion, though he wasn't paid to have political views, just to make money out of whatever dire circumstances his glorious leaders and fellow citizens created through their hard-won right to vote. Yet he was failing to concentrate on work.

Instead, he procrastinated, staring at multiple screens in his home office, waiting for Megan to return from the MRI scan that could destroy their lives, her life, most importantly. Yet, he couldn't help but think that a tangible problem could provide an explanation for his wife's drastically altered, frankly frightening, behaviour. Just so long as it could be fixed. Then Adam was sure everything else could be. The rock in Adam's stomach, the beating of his heart, the pain burrowing beneath his eyes told a different story.

'Don't let there be anything wrong with Megan, not my Megan.'

Yet, if not something that had a name, a set of treatments, and a good prognosis, then what? Adam hated to contemplate it, so he continued to stare at his screen, scrolling idly through news stories that didn't affect him. This was a new hobby of his, and not one that was helping his sorry performance against this month's targets. For once it was easier to worry himself sick about work, his floundering profits and the long-term impact of leaving the EU than it was to worry about anything else in his life. He'd once seen a t-shirt on a market stall made from cheap, thin cotton, adorned with the slogan, *Marriage. Because your shitty day doesn't have to end at work.* He thought of it now, sighing deeply. Home used to be his haven. Megan, his salvation.

Typically, these days, Adam allowed his mind to wander and reminisce, this time not too far, just back to the previous summer, when he'd first suggested a fresh start to Megan. They'd toasted their success, teased each other about how old they were getting, and so fast, and generally felt quite content, as far as things go. Megan had said she'd think about it, but now he saw she hadn't intended to seriously consider a move.

Megan's business was struggling, her eventing team was becoming less successful, and that wasn't helping her to drum up or retain existing clients, who'd previously revelled in being part of the yard that boasted so many trophies. Her drinking was obscene, he assumed related to the pressure at work. He felt that they'd forgotten how to communicate. He was still confused about her lashing out violently, and since then, maybe before to a lesser extent, living in a trance.

Adam was grateful to have Olivia. Peter didn't know what he was talking about when he suggested over a pint that perhaps she was part of the problem, rather than the solution.

Peter did not give up on his gentle anti-Olivia campaign, and shortly after May's supper club, suggested that Olivia hadn't been too helpful that evening, a theme he favoured, much to Adam's increasing irritation.

'Just be careful, Adam,' he'd said. The mere suggestion that Olivia could be dangerous was so outrageous that for the first time in over thirty years of friendship that Adam raised his voice.

'She is very fucking helpful, actually. The only person who is still here, every day, making sure Megan's okay.'

Peter had backed down, he knew when he was beat, and his bond with Adam was far more important than making a point. Olivia had continued to surprise him with her magnanimous attitude despite the fact she seems to be the preferred punch bag, half the time.

'I love her, I love both of you so much. I just want to help,' Olivia had told him, sweetly.

She'd left him a little card later, a childish one that played a whistle to the tune of Bobby McFerrin's *Don't Worry Be Happy*, her scrawl inside simply saying:

No need to worry, I'm here, and I always will be. I promise. Never forget that.

It had made him laugh, an unfamiliar sound. She'd been a rock these last few weeks, which he felt guilty about on so many levels. How dare he seek solace in her, when all of his efforts should be helping his wife find herself again? But he couldn't help but bask in the relief she offered, those simple moments, that unconditional love and support, in the midst of the anguish that pervaded any room he shared with Megan.

Olivia was a marvel to Adam. As he found relief in his relationship with Olivia, Megan seemed to distance herself further from everyone, batting away outreached hands with stony stares during her more focussed moments, though more usually by seeming to look right through you. Olivia, also, had found herself at more of a loose end lately. She was rarely included in the girls' get-togethers since the book club incident, but they also had become a rarity in themselves, as Megan neglected her gang-leader role in favour of lying in lukewarm baths, and sleeping too much. Olivia looked to Adam for company more often than before, and he didn't resist her.

He was only human, he'd remind himself, and he needed the human touch, love, even laughter for heaven's sake, as did his dear Olivia. He was truly convinced that they were two lost souls, adrift, hanging onto each other for life. Their mutual support and combined scaffolding holding up Megan's crumbling foundations were surely the only things that gave any of them a chance at getting through this intact, including his beautiful wife. He loved Megan and Olivia, in different ways, and despite earlier fall-outs the very idea of needing to choose between them, or ever take sides, was not only ludicrous, but impossible, and simply, he refused.

Not that Megan demanded much at the moment, she seemed to only want to be left alone. They all did. Adam was unsurprised, but still irked by the absence of Megan's so-called oldest, best friends, who increasingly stayed away. Thinking about it, as far as he'd noticed, lately those little poisonous gatherings had stopped altogether so no wonder he hadn't seen the clique. Whilst this was no problem for him, he worried about Megan's isolation. She'd never been alone;

she was always surrounded. Yet, he'd even cancelled June's supper club, blaming work, unable to face another catastrophe.

'I have to work twice as hard and long, for half the reward right now', he'd persuaded Peter.

'You can't blame *everything* on Brexit, anyway, things are pretty stable now, mate, you know that, — or don't you? Because your returns — or lack of — might just be user-error!'

They had joked, but Peter had acquiesced, still audibly hurt and desperately worried about Megan, something Adam simply couldn't deal with on top of everything else. Peter was well able to take care of his own emotions. As Adam had ended the call, he'd felt terrible, but he was becoming accustomed to that. Apart from when he and Olivia stole a little time away from it all, allowed themselves to just relax, and forget the complications.

Adam sat back in his chair, he sipped his tea and spat the cold brown liquid over his keyboard. He'd been here, almost paralysed, for longer than he'd realised. Disgusting stuff, cold tea, Adam thought. Almost as bad as warm milk. Funny how temperature transformed utility. Warm wife, cold wife. As he started to wipe up the mess with tissues that started to tear immediately, he heard the key turn in the front door.

'Megan!'

He ran down the stairs, his urgency deeply jarring with the delicate removal of her shoes, open-toe sandals in white with a tiny, pointy heel. He'd heard her refer to them as kitten heels, which made no sense to him. She slowly turned to him, her face puzzled by his presence, as if calculating the time of day, questioning herself. What's wrong with this picture, she seemed to think. Adam scrambled to explain, so they could quickly get to the point.

'I left work at lunchtime — I wanted to be here when you got home.' His voice had calmed, softened, and her face followed.

She hadn't let him go with her, telling him he'd only make her more anxious. Megan looked too thin despite dressing in tailored clothing, a stark contrast to her crocs, dressing gown and legging combo she'd taken to living in, at least when in the house, over the last month or two. Her hair was styled as she used to wear it, rather than pulled back from her face, her current preferred look. She looked less pale than usual, and Adam realised she'd made up her fine-boned face. War paint for when you're expecting the worst. It made sense, he thought, to show you've got what it takes to fight. He embraced her, a sudden rush of love bringing tears to his eyes before he swallowed them whole. How could he have been so selfish, how could he feel sorry for himself, when Megan could be ill.

'I'm not ill.' She said the words quietly, as she stepped back and tilted her head to catch his gaze. 'Not physically, anyway.'

Adam's relief was palpable but brief, all too quickly replaced by the fear of the unknown.

'That's wonderful — but what then? You've lost weight, you're not yourself. Are you depressed? Is it me? Have I done something?'

As was Megan's habit of late, from her lacklustre demeanour, the feeling of being too weighed down by tiredness to argue, to care, she swiftly found energy reserves made of pure irritation with her husband's name on them.

'It isn't always about you.' And with a quick glare, she swivelled on her bare foot, and stomped into the kitchen, somehow without making a sound, weightless on the thick, luxurious, shaggy runner rug. Adam took a breath. He did not want this exchange to spiral into yet another argument. God knows they'd had enough of those lately.

'I'm sorry, I know that. I just don't understand. It's all happened so quickly. What did the doctor say?'

Adam was starting to realise that his experience in these matters was almost as limited as his bachelor best friend's. How perfectly easy his relationships with women had always been, teaching him nothing about how to communicate with a fuming wife, who'd suddenly transformed from a witty, bright beauty queen to a short-tempered shell of her former self.

He'd believed in his own good luck, but there was a real woman beneath the illusion she'd run out of energy to maintain. Despite his constant state of bafflement at the speed of which her entire persona and attitude seemed to have changed, he genuinely wanted to understand so he could help fix it. She was making him miserable, but herself too. She must want to get to the bottom of it, he couldn't conceive of any other possible desire. His problem-solving experience was at work, where 'Inspiration Ideas Innovation' was written on the top of notepads and post-it notes.

'Could it be hormonal?' he asked, thinking on his feet.

A plate that he'd left drying by the side of the sink after a snack crashed by his right foot, shards bouncing across the stone tiles they'd once chosen together as they'd transformed their house into their home.

'I'm not having early menopause, I'm not losing my

fucking mind, but there isn't a single fucking person that believes as word I say!'

Adam visibly shuddered at the raw, uncontained hostility within her. Her anger, her face so full of instant hatred. She seethed, and then almost as if she were a balloon that had been silently popped, she deflated, and once again there seemed to be nothing left of her. She collapsed to the floor and hugged her knees. The urgency in Adam to fix Megan was suddenly absorbed by his need to not make it any worse. He stepped around the broken plate gingerly, and made his way to his wife, bending at the knees, which loudly clicked as he went to sit with her on the floor.

'You used to say I needed oiling when that happened, remember?' He talked to her like he might to a child, but now the burst of anger within had withered, she didn't seem to mind.

'Dr Lewis thinks I'm self-medicating. With alcohol. And pills. I'm not, Adam, I promise. I haven't needed to refill in weeks. I can't explain the tiredness, the bags, I have no energy. I can't concentrate at work. The girls, they said I said things… I didn't, I don't remember. I feel like I'm going mad, Adam, I wouldn't say those things. But they all say I did. They said I'd emailed Lizzy, told her to pass on some pretty vile things. I didn't, why would I? I wanted to see them. Now Lizzy won't take my calls.' She started to cry silent tears.

Adam stroked her hair. Despite his best efforts, the fixer in his DNA won out, it was too obvious a solution.

'Let's check your sent items. That'll put your mind at rest.'

She told him she had, there was nothing there. 'I started

to wonder, after the…' She delicately paused '…the accident, with Lizzy's arm, perhaps she wanted to, well, detach herself, and take the others with her, because I wouldn't go along with their version of events. I talked to Olivia, I took her word, and I told them it was an accident.'

At that moment, the patio door creaked open, and Olivia stood before them, taking in the scene with undisguised horror. 'I'm so sorry. I'll go, I'll come back later.' She exited quickly, more loudly than she'd entered.

Megan had barely seemed to notice. Adam was more perplexed than ever. That night his wife had quite clearly sided with Elizabeth over Olivia. Megan saw the disbelief in the crinkles between his eyes.

'After I'd spoken with Olivia, we were chatting on a group WhatsApp Bea had set up. They said perhaps it would be best if Olivia didn't join us for a while. I defended her, Adam. She's been so kind when I've been so low. I shouldn't have ever believed she could do such a thing, any of the things I thought she had done.'

Adam didn't know what she meant, but before he could ask, she started to cry yet she continued to explain.

'I must be such a terrible person, when the people who love me the most are the ones I accuse to save face with Bea, Lizzy, Antonia, who as soon as things get tough — Liv was right — they just, just…' Megan's cries were loud, and pained.

'Hush.' Adam, started to lift Megan to her feet. She weighed nothing. 'Why don't you lie down? I'll bring you a camomile tea, have a nap, we'll get through this together, I promise. I love you, and you're right, we're lucky to have Olivia. After your nap, why don't I get her to go see you?'

Megan nodded, weakly. Both too afraid to dig any deeper. Could Megan be mentally ill? Were her so-called friends bullying her? A couple of months ago the very idea would have been inconceivable, to anyone.

As Megan dozed, Adam started on some detective work, realising that in order to be useful, he needed the facts, and he was not getting a great deal of sense out of his exhausted, potentially insane, wife. First, he opened the wine fridge. It was almost empty, and yet the delivery from the posh village wine shop had arrived just a week ago. Seeing as they'd not entertained, or drank more than a glass together over dinner since then, and he was trying to abstain in a half-hearted attempt to lose a subtly increasing middle-age spread, that was some going for Megan.

He checked the recycling bin, and laughing back at him were oodles of bottles now empty of their expensive contents. Worse still, there were bottles of cheap supermarket wine in there too. Next, he'd be checking the shed for empty cartons of paint stripper, he wryly thought, before checking himself for the seriousness of his predicament. How had he not noticed his wife was downing two bottles a day? How was she still standing when she brushed her teeth? There's not a chance she had time to drink that much without him noticing in the evenings, so not only was she hungover at work, she may also be topping up. Which would explain why her cherished father's legacy seemed to be going down the pan.

Adam knew that the current status quo was to treat alcohol abuse as a disease, but he was struggling to see it that way. He imagined men with dirty fingernails drinking cheap cider, oblivious to the rain, as they staggered from park bench to doorway. Not his wife, who just a short time ago would refuse a third glass for fear of forgetting herself. She'd always been able to make the right choice before, and Adam couldn't see any reason why she couldn't now. There was no tragedy here, though she seemed to be creating the beginnings of one. Beneath this growing bitterness, plain irritation at an inconvenient twist in otherwise perfect lives, Adam knew it was more complex than he allowed for, that, apparently, this sort of thing could happen to anyone. Though it hadn't happened to him, had it? He would not have bet on being the more together, in control, one of their pair.

Feeling a perverse sense of pride as the evening drew in, he avoided the temptation to open one of the last remaining bottles of his favourite Saint-Émilion Grand Cru (at least she'd left the 2000 vintage alone, for now, he thought), as he logged onto her laptop. He'd always trusted his wife implicitly, but after two bottles of wine it was perfectly possible to forget sending an email, and the following day, after two bottles of wine, it was perfectly possible to not see the offending item in your sent items. She trusted him too, so there was no need to log into her Gmail account.

Clicking straight onto sent items, he saw she was right. The last item she'd sent from her personal email was over two weeks ago, a message to a friend in Australia. Without meaning to, he opened it and read it. She hadn't confided in it, or confessed. Nothing untrue, but everything sugar coated and the sad bits glossed over. He opened her archive items and the email he was searching for jumped out at him, the subject line holding no punches, impossible not to see. An attack on each of her friends one by one, and then on their husbands, and most hurtful of all, and attack on him, complete condemnation of her own husband. Adam exhaled deeply, his pulse quickened to an alarming rate.

As he'd started to read the opening, a passionate defence of Olivia, still unsure of how Megan could have claimed not to have authored this message, he'd almost felt a surge of pride for Megan choosing the underdog over her security blanket of her oldest friends and their apparent unbreakable bond; the kind of friends who'd help you bury the body. That feeling can't have lasted more than seconds until he saw what this really was: an attack, not a defence, and one built on paranoia.

He'd made his strong wife insecure and jealous. Adam knew he'd been the cause of some frustrations, but he'd also believed that's all they were: natural irritations in a long marriage in which some disappointments must be endured as life taught that not all postgraduate dreams and ambitions would fall into laps so easily. He had not known that burning beneath her elegant manners, her kind smile, those light touches of his arm as she passed, the giggle as he tickled her feet when they lay on the sofa, was a fury waiting to catch a flame should life not deliver on its promises.

Adam didn't know if she was ill, drunk, or both when she wrote the hateful words. Regardless, Adam's position started to harden to anger, a response designed to keep overwhelming sadness at bay. He asked himself, over and over, now with a much-needed glass of red in hand, could alcohol or depression really create such feelings from nothing? No, they'd already be there, but now they've been unlocked.

He'd been torn between waking Megan to confront her and leaving her alone to sleep, but then Olivia arrived.

'Is everything okay?' she asked, awkwardly referring to the earlier scene she had interrupted.

Adam stopped short of confiding all to Olivia about what he had read, and what he'd discovered. This wasn't her burden to shoulder. Right now, he needed Olivia on Megan's side, for whatever happened, whatever she said or did, everyone needed someone, and he was beginning to fear he might not be that person, not any more.

However, he did ask Olivia if she had noticed Megan drinking more, but she'd just shrugged and told him that everyone always seemed to have a drink in hand in this house, except for her, so she'd stopped paying attention. Adam awkwardly set down his second large glass of wine.

'She just seems to be very angry with everyone right now, except perhaps you,' Adam told Olivia, who simply smiled.

She said, 'It's okay, I can go up. Perhaps a little girl talk is what she needs.'

Adam didn't protest, feeling weak and miserable. Olivia made a tray up with cocoa, and a biscuit that would inevitably remain untouched, and climbed the stairs leaving Adam alone with his thoughts. When she returned only ten minutes later, she looked sad, and told Adam she'd not been able to chat, such was Megan's exhaustion, so she'd let her sleep. With that, exhausted himself, Adam simply told Olivia how much he loved her, how grateful he was, and held her close, not letting her see the tear slide down his cheek.

Olivia

They all drink far too much anyway, I'd told myself as I'd tipped bottle after bottle of overpriced plonk down the sink over the course of the last weeks. I carefully disposed of the bottles in the recycling bin just outside the kitchen door so as not to alarm Megan, who more often than not now received rare guests in the living room where she could sink into the enormous corner sofa. Before she used to always be in the kitchen, a blur of activity, even when she had a house full. Pouring more wine, finishing off a casserole, watering her windowsill herb garden.

Adam was right, she was drinking more, but not that much more. She wasn't eating much, and she was taking far too many sleeping pills, alongside mood-altering pills, a rather wonderful cocktail of standard anti-anxiety, low dosage depression meds, and a selection of Internet-sourced benzodiazepines. And not just at night either, so her sleeping patterns were muddled, as was her mind. Yet she'd deny it all if asked, wanting to point out the almost full packets of pills she hid from the world.

I'd pour her extra-large glasses of wine, refill them often, she barely noticed. Yet habit kept her hand reaching for a full glass that never seemed to deplete, sipping it, and wondering why she always felt like half a person. I was amazed that neither of them had commented on the rapidly bankrupt wine fridge until now, but then again, its expensive dark glass front had probably been designed to conceal rather than publicise the bad habits of the wealthy drinkers.

Megan had confided in me about her conversations with the ever-unhelpful Dr Lewis, who must be truly baffled by her unexplained symptoms and complete denial of self-medication. Since she turned on me, first colluding to exclude me, then striking me across the face, she'd changed. I'd helped her to become more introspective. She always assumed that problems came from the outside, and that she, her husband, her friends, must be in the right. Now she was starting to see that she wasn't as perfect as she thought. She could also see that ever since she started to feel unwell, and wasn't her usual dazzling self, I was the only one of the girls still here, loyal.

Elizabeth is a bully and a bitch, and so are the others. Everything in that email was fair comment, and if Megan was more astute, she'd have seen it too. I've had her email password saved on my own laptop for a while now, easily cracking the code Sykes1996; her wedding anniversary and married name, not very savvy or secure in this day and age. I liked to see the email chains between Megan and her friends, from which I was more often than not banished, find out which were the latest events and secrets I'd be prohibited from sharing in.

Originally it was like picking a scab and watching it bleed. It hurt, and only made me feel worse, but I couldn't help myself. Rubbernecking at my own wreckage. Now my snooping had a greater purpose, providing insight with which I could be Megan's true voice, the one I knew was in there somewhere, beneath that phoney guise. Write the truth Megan: our truth. Finally, tell them what we really think of them, I'd say to myself, as I composed an email for her. I overheard her on the phone to Bea, who, from the side of the conversation I could hear was clearly confronting her.

'Bea, I wouldn't say that. And I've never said a bad word about your son, I wouldn't. I don't even think those things. Why didn't Elizabeth call?' Silence followed by, 'Oh, I see.' I guess Elizabeth was reported as being too upset to call.

Megan should put less stock on being liked by everyone. Bea's son is stupid. Elizabeth is the jealous type. Antonia does have a double chin. Megan should have told them long ago. Bunch of hangers-on that they are. But she couldn't understand where the texts and the emails and the rumours of cattiness overheard were coming from.

'I don't want to say anything out of turn,' I began, shortly after she'd disconnected the call, as we started to lay the table in the garden, having decided to enjoy the warm summer evening. Megan looked at me, urging me to go on. Even my opinion was more desirable than the mystery before us. 'Elizabeth says things sometimes, when you're out of the room, and she thinks I'm not listening. She whispers catty comments, about you. She calls you 'Queen Bee'. I think she's jealous. Maybe, since the...' I pause, for effect, awkward, embarrassed about past accusations, but kindly trying to brush over it, '... the *accident*, she wants to split the group. She hates me, and you stick up for me, I know you do, and I think maybe she just wants to turn them against you. I've always appreciated that, by the way.' I touched her arm gently.

Megan was aghast. Even in her groggy state, she couldn't fathom it. She said so. 'It's unfathomable, Olivia.

189

We've been friends for thirty years! It can't be. It really can't. We all say silly catty things sometimes, I'm sure she didn't mean it.'

The seed was planted. I left it there. I'd water it later with the last of the wine.

'You're right. I'm reading too much into it. It just doesn't make any sense though.'

It really didn't, and a shrewder version of Megan would have certainly looked for more obvious answers. Adam was looking for answers when I saw him last night. Earlier, they'd been in chaos in the kitchen. They looked distraught but united, and although I closed the patio doors behind me, leaving them to each other, it felt that they were the ones putting up barriers.

'Bad day,' he said, when I asked him. He was sat in his armchair in the living room, and Megan was nowhere to be seen. Peace had been restored. She'd been to the doctor, I was informed fairly curtly. He clearly wasn't in the mood to share any more. Adam was in the living room drinking the last bottle of red, and looked ravaged. I hoped he planned to restock the wine fridge; I was planning on pouring that for Megan later this week.

'Shall I take her a glass?' I asked. He put his hand on the bottle, in a propriety manner, as I reached towards it. 'No, cocoa is better, for today,' he instructed. So he'd finally noticed the empty wine fridge, and by the looks of her laptop by his side and his pallid complexion, perhaps he'd been snooping in her emails too. He didn't mention it, and when he asked about the wine, I dutifully denied her excess, at least to my unjudging, innocent eyes. I made the cocoa, and dropped in a couple of ground-down pills. When I took it to her, she was sat up in bed.

'How are you?' I asked her.

She smiled, and patted the bed. 'Just had a very long nap and I'm about to get up and be a bit more useful. Look at me,' she said. 'What a mess! I'm so sorry, we should be downstairs, music on, chatting away, and I'm behaving like an invalid, and you, my carer, of all people!'

I don't think she meant it offensively, but I still prickled.

'Now, let's forget all about me, and have a proper chat. Tell me how you are. How is that project going, the one you started in Silverdale?' She really was quite chipper, bizarrely, but then again, she'd eschewed my company and my offerings for the last two days, detoxing and resting ahead of her big mysterious appointment she'd had today. 'So kind of you to make me a hot drink, how about I drink it, then I'll get up, and we could watch a movie or something?'

I'd nodded enthusiastically, of course. She sipped the cocoa, ignored the biscuit, and not long afterwards was sliding down the pillow, as her eyelids started to droop.

'Night, night, sweet dreams' I told her, as I took the tray, and quietly closed the door, returning downstairs to Adam.

He was in no mood to talk. Although he attempted to avoid my gaze, I made sure he could see the unconditional adoration in my eyes, all for him. He needed it, craved it, after seeing those damning words, perhaps even starting to believe he was a useless disappointment. Their relationship was not atypical. I'd always thought compared to other stories I'd hear there were worse marriages. I had no desire to harm theirs. But I had every intention to preserve my own life, and my own relationships. I'm not selfish, I don't wish to destroy what anyone else has, I just want to keep what's

191

rightfully mine. That has to come first. I'm not being unreasonable.

Later that night, I reflected on everything that had happened recently. After all the turmoil of seeing myself as unwanted, I'd focussed all my energy on reinstating myself as useful. I may have manipulated conditions slightly to foster utility, but that's just the basic principles of supply and demand. Sometimes you need to create a market for your product. Nobody needed a smartphone until they sold them to us. Megan and Adam needed me, just as much, perhaps even more, than I needed them. Adam hadn't seen Peter in a while, cancelling the sacred supper, and Megan had been cast aside for bad behaviour.

I recorded it in my diary. Adam, Megan and me: the unholy trinity. Their characters were really starting to take wonderful shape in my prose. They truly were coming to life. As summer progressed, I thought I was getting somewhere. Adam was home more, Megan had stopped her incessant accusations, and I was central to both of them once more. I admit they probably weren't at their happiest, but at least we were together, time unspoiled by invasive intruders. I did my best to stay positive, and to make them smile once in a while. I watched closely, paying attention to every detail, conscientious as always, concerned that I should succeed in my project to save the three of us from imploding. I must have missed something, despite my diligence, because then, one day in August, Adam dropped the bombshell.

Adam

'I'm sorry, mate, it won't be for long,' Adam said as he unzipped his small, brown leather holdall on which his initials were imprinted beneath the Purdey stamp, in Peter's second spare room — the first he had converted into a home gym. The room was empty, save for a king-size bed made up in white and grey stripes and a large chest of drawers. Fitted wardrobe doors were mirrors that made the large square space seem twice the size. He looked out of the window admiring the penthouse view of the manicured gardens, a quiet haven in Ilkley. One of a handful of Peter's neat, masculine homes, dotted around his favourite countries and cities.

'I hope not, Adam, quite frankly.' Peter produced a half-smile, woefully shaking his head. 'Megan needs you.'

Adam wasn't so sure. He'd tried to help, but she refused to be helped. She wouldn't even admit there was a problem, denying her daytime consumption of fine wines through slurred words, her eyes roaming, and pupils dilated. No further enlightened by the MRI results, Adam and Megan had talked.

'Is it delayed grief for your father? Is it stress at work? Perhaps you should throw out the wine, the pills, and see?'

But to no avail. Megan promised she'd refrain, yet the bottles mounted up, her condition deteriorated. Adam couldn't keep tabs on her day and night, due to work, but

Olivia had continued to be their guardian angel, reporting back that she'd persuaded her to have tea or cocoa instead of wine. Assuring him that as far as she knew, Megan wasn't refilling her prescriptions. But she'd always add, how would she know? Megan became increasingly erratic all the same.

Adam called the office of her doctor. 'It seems nothing is working. She doesn't sleep, despite sleeping pills, she drinks despite denying she does. I feel I'm letting her down. I can't manage.'

Prompted by insider knowledge and disappointed that he didn't yet have full transparency with his client, in August, Dr Lewis suggested a short stay in rehab. She'd refused and said simply that she was needed at home and at work. It was impossible. She had angrily questioned Adam. They'd fought.

'Dr Lewis seemed to have a very similar view of me as you do Adam. I don't suppose the two of you are in cahoots now? Two men solving the problematic woman in the way by putting her in a straightjacket.'

Adam couldn't deny it, promising her he'd done it out of love, and mostly out of desperation. 'It's not about a straightjacket!' he'd pleaded. 'It's just giving you the space and professional help you need to get well. Something I'm failing miserably at.'

Megan had looked into his eyes and, without emotion, said she couldn't trust him. He'd lost his temper then, and they'd thrown their angry words across the room at each other. She'd told him to leave if he couldn't believe her when she promised she wasn't drinking, she wasn't self-medicating, and she hadn't authored cruel emails and texts, and alienated her closest friends.

'How can I believe you with a recycling bin full of empty bottles just outside? You're clearly under the influence of something right now! And what about the vicious texts you sent me last week? Look, it's still here on my phone!'

She denied it again.

He lost his temper. 'You're looking for conspiracy theories everywhere when the simplest solution is that you drink, you forget, you deny!'

Adam knew he had a duty to his wife. In sickness and in health. Nobody tells you how difficult it can be to nurse a sick person who insists they are not sick, and pushes you away, again and again. Those summer weeks and months had dragged as Megan had deteriorated, her walls built too thick and high for him to reach her. Olivia provided the only respite from the constant strain of work and his wife. He'd put on a brave face for her, wishing for just those few moments to be free from the constant buzz in his mind of the problems drowning him. Even Megan made an effort in her company as far as he could see. Frankly, he had started to avoid being in the same room as his wife. Confrontation wasn't his friend.

'I just need a break, Peter, we both do. A bit of space. It will do us good, and I'll go back, refreshed, ready to try my damnedest to get her the help she needs. It's a cliché, but unless she wants to accept help, there's very little I can do.'

Peter grunted, and Adam wasn't sure if in agreement or dismissal. In Peter's eyes Megan could do no wrong. Adam simply hoped that her anger and disappointment in him were symptoms that would disappear with the right treatment, but he knew that the damage she was doing would run deep. He loathed the idea of his marriage crumbling.

'I will try,' he said, as much to himself as to Peter.

Two weeks later, he was already feeling more positive, vindicated that his idea of space was the right one. He'd spoken to Megan, who was reasonable on the phone, if a little cool. He'd become accustomed to the slur to the point that he had stopped commenting on it. They said they'd talk again next week. Neither was ready to put an end date on the separation, in fact, neither was prepared to mention it. An eavesdropper could be forgiven for thinking that Adam was simply away with work.

'I'm sorry,' he'd said, as they prepared to hang up.

'Me too,' Megan had answered sadly.

Adam had arranged to pick Olivia up and take her for dinner. Did it feel wrong to be dining out with Olivia without Megan — instead of Megan — he asked himself? Perhaps, yes, but she was doing so much for Megan, and she might have insight. He owed her, if nothing else. Adam's stomach rumbled, hunger mixed with anxiety. Without Megan's cooking and with Peter's fridge empty aside from dangerously old condiments, he wasn't quite so chubby now, that middle age spread burned off, revealing a not unattractive flat stomach. Muscle definition was lacking, but Adam was pleased.

He wondered if Megan would notice if he went home. Sadly, he assumed not, her eyes hadn't focussed on him in a long time. He couldn't remember the last time she'd been awake as he undressed for bed, let alone the last time they'd had sex. That he could live with, after so many years of marriage his expectations weren't that high. He missed the conversation though, the feeling of being heard, and understood. It was little wonder he craved time with Olivia, the only other person he could really talk to, and relax with.

Peter was good company, but if Adam was really honest with himself, despite doing him a great favour by allowing him to stay, his little digs at Olivia, his opinions on his relationship with her, and his ardent commitment to the myth of Megan's unblemished record of perfect wife was beginning to irk him, not least as he knew if anyone should be a staunch member of the Megan fan club, it should be him. Peter's faith was showing him up, and Peter's opinions on Olivia only added to his sense of guilt. Maybe Megan was right, perhaps he really wasn't a very good husband.

Olivia was closing the gate behind her as he pulled over on the street, eschewing the driveway. The night sky was only just closing in, as the late August days squeezed out the last of summer. She jumped into the passenger seat.

'You've been neglecting me.' She stuck her bottom lip out and looked up at him through her long lashes.

She was dressed differently, still all in black, but a more grown-up ensemble compared to her usual baggy, bohemian style. Her top was low-cut, provocative, almost. He didn't like it. Embarrassed he looked away. She looked self-conscious. Next to the frighteningly self-assured women he was surrounded by, Olivia's lack of cultured style was refreshing. Adam enjoyed her natural, simple look. Unaffected, she seemed carefree, and that was infectious. Her eyes were heavily made up, and even Adam could see despite her lack of practice, she was quite the expert, clearly bringing her artist's hand to task. He'd prefer the swimming deep blues, blended with the smoky grey on one of her canvases rather than on her youthful skin. The make-up aged her.

'I'm sorry. I've missed you.' His hand reached over the gear wheel and squeezed her knee, as she fastened her seat belt.

Olivia sighed deeply.

'Tough week?' he asked, smiling. With his stalemate with Megan, constant digs from Peter, and work giving him hell, Adam wasn't sure he could cope with a downbeat Olivia too.

'Yes. Since you left, she's been a mess. I've been busy trying to keep her eating. She's frail. I don't think she's coping well at work either.' She turned to look at his profile as he stared ahead at the road.

He glanced sideways, seeing that she was making little effort to conceal her resentment. He stifled his own, not at Olivia, but Megan. The last thing they needed was to lose more business at the yard. Her father had been everything to her, and she'd worked so hard to maintain his livery business when she inherited it. Adam found it extraordinary that Megan would continue to risk the yard's success, especially when she fought him so hard to keep it and stay put, rather than selling and moving forward, away.

No wonder Olivia was hostile. He'd bailed, and she hadn't. After everything, she hadn't given up on Megan. Adam couldn't blame her annoyance, but he couldn't solve this right now either. It wasn't Olivia's job to look after Megan, but in all fairness, nor was it his. She was making dangerous choices, despite his pleas, despite medical intervention.

'I'll go to see her. This can't be easy for you. This must be getting in the way of your projects, your life, planning your move. This isn't your concern. Maybe you could bring your travel plans forward, get away from all of this? Spend a few weeks seeing some of the States before you start in October.'

Wrong choice of words. The fury in her eyes was unmistakeable. In fact, it reminded him of the way Megan's eyes had frequently started to cloud over, as she transitioned from sleeping zombie to tear-your-head-off zombie. But unlike Megan, she didn't raise her voice, she just quietly and calmly replied.

'It is my concern, even more so as it's no longer yours. She's still seeing her doctor, though. She went yesterday. Not sure he's helping, in case you're interested.'

Guilt winded him, taking the air from his lungs. Yet, he felt as though he was the only one seeing clearly. His oldest friend believed he was shirking his responsibilities, and now even Olivia, his most staunch champion seemed to feel the same way. Adam was more convinced every day that he didn't understand females at all. If it weren't such a depressing tangled mess, it would amuse him that he'd clearly gotten away without a clue for so long; without anyone, himself included, noticing. They, and he, were noticing now though.

Where was the Olivia who adored him, and who wasn't fooled by the hairspray and perfume brigade? How had she suddenly painted Megan as victim, rather than perpetrator of this mess? She'd seen with her own eyes. They'd comforted each other. Adam hadn't formed the thoughts fully in his head, he didn't dare, but if he was truly honest, he'd started to see Olivia as his. He'd started to imagine a world in which their increasingly dysfunctional trio became two. In the moments before sleep would wash over him, as he lay in bed, his mind painted pictures of the two of them, a flat, the walls full and alive with her artworks. She'd make a success of New York this time, and when she came home, buoyant and with firm foundations beneath her, they'd flourish together. They'd make frequent trips to galleries and live a simple life. A fresh start. He'd been hankering after one for long enough, but he now saw the one he'd desired might not have been the right one. Adam's dismay at the changes in Megan's character had dissipated and reformed into an acceptance. Had she changed, or was it always an act, no longer a sustainable performance under the weight of midlife stress and middle-class addictions? Perhaps she'd just evolved, eroded, her mind and body adapting to new perspectives, new challenges and a new time of life. Still, he would try, he owed that, to everyone it seemed. Olivia was quiet over dinner.

'How are you feeling, Olivia?' he asked.

'Guilty. Confused,' she answered.

Dumbfounded, Adam asked her what she thought she had to be guilty about.

'I don't know how to put this without sounding horrible, especially knowing how sad she is.'

Adam reached for her hand, so smooth, so pale, giving her permission to go on.

'I just thought, well, I thought if you decided to leave her, we'd still be together in the end, but now it's happened, I don't think that's the case. I think you're looking for a completely fresh start, no ties back to your old life, bad memories, and you can do that, just extricate yourself, I know you can. I just can't, not permanently. So, I think I'm going to lose you too.'

She opened her mouth to speak again, but Adam silenced

her with a gentle touch of his finger on her lips.

'Don't say another word. Of course you won't lose me! How could you think such a thing? I promise, whatever happens, you're not going to be forgotten. I promise.'

The thoughts he'd had about their future were suddenly clear to him, and yet in refusing them a voice even in his own mind, he'd failed to comprehend the enormity of what was required of him. He had experienced a cacophony of emotions over losing Megan, first metaphorically, then more recently, losing her tangibly, potentially for good, at least the Megan of old, but he hadn't allowed himself to consider his relationship with Olivia. He saw now, that he'd been afraid she would see him in a new light suddenly, a wife-deserter, no longer the hero he liked to play, and then shut him out. A thought so unbearable it had been barricaded to the depths of his self-protecting mind.

He'd allowed Olivia to feel abandoned, this whole time not daring to think of their future out of sheer cowardice for the answers he might find in the corners of his mind, or worse still, escaping from her mouth. And whilst he sought peace in her company, she continued to try to pick up the pieces without demanding any answers about what was going to happen to them.

She must begrudge her role, and Megan. Hell, she must begrudge him too. Yet still, Adam realised, Olivia must feel it was her duty to care for Megan right now, regardless of what the future held for any of them. He couldn't allow her to sacrifice her opportunity in New York, yet feeling so simultaneously trapped yet insecure about their future he realised she might be too afraid to stretch her wings.

'Just give me a few weeks to figure out what to do. Do

you trust me, Olivia? Can you hold on a little longer, and let me fix this?'

Olivia nodded, focussing hard on the plate of food in front of her. A rare steak, a rare treat. Despite the magnitude of the conversation, she looked to be savouring every bite.

She took her time chewing and swallowing before she replied, 'Of course.'

Adam saw her eyes well. There were too many tears these days, and as he looked at Olivia, always thinking of others before herself, he inwardly cursed Megan for ruining everything, and leading them to a place where any of this was possible. Adam had never imagined, at the beginning, that he and Olivia would together need to save or desert Megan. It was supposed to be he and Megan who looked after Olivia. Yet, even now, as the impossible unfolded before his eyes, it took on a natural, almost inevitable light.

'Leave it with me. I'm sure things will look very different in a few weeks.'

Olivia

Adam was right, things did look very different a few weeks later, though no thanks to him. Despite his promises, he spent more time in London. He rarely rang. No more dinners were scheduled. As I predicted, without his marital anchor he was floating away, directionless. I was unpleasantly surprised. It hurt my feelings to realise how much persuasion he would need to retain our close bond.

'I'm sorry, Liv,' he casually said, 'but it'll be worth it in the end.'

Cryptic evasion was his finest new skill. I knew what he was up to. Hardly took a genius to work it out. With Megan too weak to protest he was setting up a new life in the city, and either he'd take her along out of guilt, or he'd cut his ties and go alone. It was clear, whatever he claimed, that I wasn't currently in mind for this new adventure. He still assumed I was heading back to New York.

'I don't have to go to New York,' I told him.

'You must,' he replied, 'I won't be the reason you don't find the success you so deserve.'

I am not blind, nor stupid. I know he is only thinking of me. He talks of time as if it will be endless. As if any time at all living and working far from him wouldn't feel like forever. He thinks everything will stay the same. I know that if I let him drift away from me now, I'll never hold his heart in my hands again. I need him to stay here, just a little longer.

Our ties are not as strong as I thought, the stitching needs reinforcing, and that takes time and effort. As usual, the effort will be exclusively on my part. I decided the first step was to bring him home to Megan, the second step would be to persuade Megan to leave, by choice or by recommendation from her long-suffering husband.

I arrived at Megan's precious yard on Wednesday, at about five o'clock. Megan had come home at four, and we'd shared a pot of Earl Grey tea before I made my excuses, leaving her to snooze. Before her father died and she took charge Megan had taken me to visit the old family pile a few times, when we fancied a nice wholesome day out in the countryside. I'd met her father; she adored him. His face was stern, his body rigid. He looked old at first sight, the colour drained from him. He seemed to be entirely in black and white against the lush greens, deep muddy browns, and golden hay. In the picture in my mind, the sky is bright blue. He looks like he has been photoshopped, a sepia print cut out from a rare photograph taken decades ago and placed on a cheerful postcard from Yorkshire — the kind tourists buy from the ice cream parlours during summertime.

Megan had loaned me one of the older nags once or twice, fit for little other than cat food, but having been in the family for so long had become full members, and were used to keep the grass short and to teach nervous novices, just like me. I remember her mounting a dark beast of vast proportions with a neatly groomed mane and long eyelashes. Megan was fit and agile and didn't use the mounting block, instead gracefully slipping one leather-booted foot into the stirrup and effortlessly propelling her body upwards, slinging her other leg over, and gently seating herself on the thick, shiny brown saddle. I'd been rather less elegant, not abetted by my wellington boots, thick green rubber toes and tractor style soles awkwardly catching in the stirrup.

'If you like riding, you must get the proper gear, but there's really no point getting it first as it's frightfully expensive,' she'd commented.

I'd felt self-conscious, but didn't want to spoil her treat, so I'd meekly smiled. Her father had adjusted my stirrups for me, made me comfortable. He smiled a toothy grin, the literal personification of growing long in the tooth. I liked him a lot. My horse was cruelly named Beauty, cruel for she had tufty black hair peppered with whites, and a mottled nose, with a thin mane only just reaching her dipped back, and a bony old body, which barely responded to my touch. She ignored the squeeze of my legs around her girth if I wanted her to trot, and pretended not to feel the slight squeeze of my reins if I wanted her to stop. Despite their efforts to persuade me, I didn't take to riding; too many uncontrollable interdependencies, not enough stability. I liked art, my hand controlling the brush stroke. I liked to write, my pen creating my truth.

'She's fit as a fiddle, lass,' Megan's father had said.

It amused me that he adopted phrases from the local dialect but retained his family's plummy posh accent. It was endearing on him, where it might have seemed affected in most. I didn't doubt Beauty's health. She was better fed and watered than me. She was just old and grumpy, and didn't take to being told what to do by a neophyte.

Even before she took over the business, Megan worked alongside her father, and their clients. Although I got the sense that she worked when she felt like it, she often said, 'horses don't believe in weekends and ultimately I think we humans work for them, rather than the other way around'. And so, occasionally, back at the beginning before Adam and I discovered our shared interests, I'd accompany her to the yard on a Saturday or a Sunday, and instead of riding would spend some time with her father, helping to fill buckets of water or refill depleted hay balls in stables.

When the old man died, Megan was devastated, but utterly committed to honouring his work, his memory. She buried her grief quickly under the guise of a person with more important things to do. She started to take it all very seriously, and made it clear she couldn't really bring visitors any longer. She needed to command the respect of the team and the clients. She needed to focus. Her mother had died a year earlier after spending almost two in a home with early-onset dementia. The duty, Megan said, was hers, and hers alone.

Despite rarely visiting the yard, I still knew my way around. I knew what the horses ate, what they didn't eat. I understood the fields they went in at different times of year, and the blankets they wore in different weather. Occasionally I still visited, right up until recently, perhaps to see her off and wish her luck before an event. Adam and I might help with the last-minute grooming, horses being treated to the full beauty works: French plaits and hoof varnish. It was a ridiculous to observe — the antiquated uniforms of the riders, looking down from their prancing four-legged beauty queens.

I knew about one horse in particular. Prince Joseph was the proud name on his stable door, though he was known affectionately as Joey. Just three years old, standing tall and strong at over eighteen hands, a gleaming bay coat, accentuated by a long, thick black mane and a dancing tail. He'd cost a fortune, and Megan's clients, his owners, were some of her father's oldest.

'They're so loyal,' she'd told us, 'been with us for twenty years.'

Esteemed as his human parents were, Joey had little regards for their wishes. And despite being of excellent breeding (his father had won Badminton twice, apparently), he was described as capricious, a loose cannon, or, after throwing one of his riders, sometimes he was described in less endearing terms. He bit his stable door, he bit the hand that fed, and sometimes he kicked. I liked him. He was genuinely beautiful despite being a massive, smelly horse, and better still, he was wild at heart.

When I arrived, I watched from behind the feed shed in the corner of the yard, as a couple of stable hands carried tack to the tack room, where they'd painstakingly polish it until it shone. A couple of horses lazily chewed grass in the top field. Most looked out from behind their stable doors. The bottom field hadn't been weeded in months, and somehow that persistent pest, ragwort was in great supply, as it was every year the field was left to recover from the constant battering given to it by its equine residents.

'No matter what I do, the damn vermin weed returns!' I'd heard her say, year in, year out. It wasn't a bad bet to assume the field would be overrun, and it looked like I'd won it. Ragwort was an ugly yellow plant, inconspicuous enough to the untrained eye, but fatal to horses. I unlocked the gate to the field, and let it swing open, before quietly walking up to Joey's stable, and freeing him. The wild beast released.

'Be free,' I whispered to him as he happily trotted off

towards the field.

I discreetly made my way out of the yard, hood up, head down, unseen, I think. One of the last surviving public payphones was down the road, the elderly villagers campaigning with youthful vigour to prevent its removal citing poor mobile coverage and regularly being held hostage by poor weather during winter months. I called the yard, and told them I'd been passing on my afternoon walk with my dog, and heard an angry female voice shout at a horse for biting her. I told them I'd heard a scuffle of hooves on the concrete floor, and a voice shouting after him to bugger off. My afternoon route took me down the lane that backs onto the yard's bottom field, I explained. He seemed happy enough in there, eating away, but that the gate was swinging open. I'd hate for him to escape. They didn't thank me, the phone crashed down, left hanging rather than clicking down. No dial tone appeared, as I imagined them running as fast as they could to rescue Joey.

Two weeks later, and Megan hadn't returned to the livery yard, instead making garbled calls to her stable manager, an uptight plump girl in her late teens, rosy cheeked with comically short legs that stuck out as the rested on a horse's middle. She told me, she told the tinny, faraway voice at the end of the phone, and once I think I heard her tell someone at the front door and return with a parcel, so perhaps she also had started to tell delivery men too, that she was innocent of the crime she'd been accused of.

'I've been accused of something terrible. That's why I'm not at work you see. Of course it is nonsense, I'm sure it will all be sorted out soon.' She repeated herself over and over like a madwoman, gesturing at her stained legging and baggy T-shirt, even to the person on the end of the phone, her slobby attire presumably explained away by the grave injustice she had suffered. Sometimes despite the frequency of repeating these familiar words, she still managed to slur them.

True to her word, Megan wasn't drinking much. Her reduced intake made little difference, given the extra doses I dispersed. My remedies had all the depressive, stupid-inducing qualities of alcohol, but sadly none of the fun. Megan was by now genuinely anxious, unhappy and impaired through lack of proper sleep, a mixture of medication causing behaviours as well as reports of dreadful behaviours she didn't recall. Megan needed help. I continued to throw out bottles of expensive wine that arrived each month, despite Adam being away, in case he returned. Megan hadn't noticed.

She noticed very little these days. In some respects, I'd been tempted to leave her to make her own mistakes at work; she almost certainly would eventually, but patience isn't my greatest virtue. Megan didn't tell Adam about Joey, so I did. Three weeks since our dinner, three weeks since any sign of him. Two weeks since Joey almost died due to Megan's perceived carelessness. I knew they'd rescue him in time from greedily gobbling down the poisonous flowers. I'm not a monster.

I tried to persuade her to tell him what had happened, why she'd been strongly advised by her team to take some time off, even if she wouldn't tell me, which she wouldn't, much to my annoyance. I couldn't have seemed more dependable and trustworthy at this juncture, and yet I got fewer details than the delivery man on the doorstep. Perhaps she didn't quite believe herself anymore. Maybe she still had some pride. She was still angry with Adam, I could tell, though she refused to talk about it.

I knew he'd come back if he knew just how bad things were getting, and that seemed to be my only pathway to him, through her. I loathed that notion. Yet I was part of this particular set-up, this life chapter; he needed to come back, she needed to leave. I wasn't buying the 'needing some time to sort things out, then it will all be fine'. I wasn't born yesterday. No one walks away from that bat-shit crazy baggage only to start again with an oddball like me attached. He needs to stay here, and so do I. I don't think I'd fare well in the world he imagines he'd occupy in London, just as I didn't in New York.

I heard a car on the driveway, and key in the lock. I heard him close the door behind him, as I stood in the kitchen pouring water over the tea bags. He'd arrived without calling first. A surprise, but would it be welcomed? The pills I intended to crumble into one of the cups were on the counter. As he opened the door, I heard his steps heading towards the kitchen. No time, I quickly pocketed the pills as I poured my tea away and picked up Megan's walking towards the door to deliver. His footsteps stopped. I imagine that the glow of light in the living room, where Megan sat curled up, had forced a detour. They stopped talking as I entered. Megan hadn't risen to great her, and Adam hadn't slipped off his coat or bent down to remove his shoes.

'I'll leave you to it.'

They started to protest, but I insisted, and Adam hugged me, just before I bent down to kiss Megan. As I walked through the hallway, I noticed the return of the same bag he'd left with, back when the weather was still warm, and the evenings lighter. How quickly our seasons change from late summer to early autumn. How quickly everything can change. The important thing was that Adam was back. He knew she needed him, especially as her friends had deserted her. I'd written to them from Adam's email, asking them to give them some time and space, while Megan got the help she needed.

Now Adam is back, we can help her, and I can make sure this ends happily.

Adam

Megan was tidying up downstairs as Adam unpacked his bag. In the bedroom was a musty smell, and so despite the evening coolness, he opened a window and allowed the curtains to flutter in the breeze, revealing glimpses of the darkness hidden behind them. The superfluous throw cushions that usually took up half the bed during the daytime, only to be pointlessly rehomed onto the bed seat at the foot of the bed each night, were still propped up there. One had fallen off, perhaps kicked by a restless foot in the middle of the night, ignored, and stepped over in the days that followed. The bed sheets were creased, and there were smudges of make-up on the pillow. When Adam had first met Megan, and they'd agreed to share a home, and marry, he'd loved to mock her precise housekeeping etiquette.

'Women!' he and Peter would laugh, as Peter boasted of his practical bedroom free of calming lavender pillow sprays and useless cushions.

As a student, and subsequently as a young man, Adam had rebelled against his upbringing, shielded by lace curtains, protected by doilies, and structured with a military standard bed-changing schedule. Left to his own devices, he'd used his newfound freedom to let his sheets fester, and his bedside cups grow in number until they were growing new forms of wildlife. Megan arrived with her standards and rules which brought crisp matching sheets back into his life though, apparently, a much higher thread count, as his mother had commented to Megan on her maiden visit to their marital home. 'You've such wonderful taste, dear,' she'd said, smitten with his beautiful bride.

From then on, fresh scents he couldn't name filled his home, and their bedroom, with a feminine air. He pretended he didn't notice, and if asked, sniffed obtusely, and shrugged. He didn't think it becoming for a man to have strong feelings about such things. If anything, they should good naturedly gripe, as if they longed for the stark lines of a more masculine abode.

'Don't complain son,' his father had said. 'You don't want to end up back in some dirty bloke den. They never look like they do on the aftershave ads you know!'

His father was right, Adam had thought. He really did not want to end up in some dirty bloke's den, or even the more American movie bachelor pad that Peter maintained by paying a range of old ladies to wash, clean, iron and plump his expensive white sofa. This home they'd worked so hard for, that Megan had insisted be beautiful, that was what he wanted. Where had it gone?

He'd noticed the carpet needed to be vacuumed, and that there were dishes in the sink downstairs. The bed hadn't been changed possibly since he'd last lay in it, and the variety of scents, usually different in each room couldn't be detected. He didn't blame Megan, he really didn't think he was that kind of man. The home was a shared domain, not a woman's, and he had abandoned it. No, he didn't blame Megan anymore, at least not in this moment. He still didn't understand her neglect of herself — of everything — except her growing addictions, but he didn't blame her. In this moment, he simply missed her, and every small wonderful detail of goodness she had brought to his life, whilst he accepted it with a sense of entitlement and pretended not to notice.

Peter was right, she needed him. When he'd heard about the incident at the yard, he couldn't stay away another moment. He couldn't, or wouldn't, believe it was anything but an accident, but the prize horse was seriously ill, the owners were devastated and preparing to sue to cover mounting vet bills, and clearly, Megan had become a danger — to herself most of all. Adam was to blame. The signs had been there, but he ignored them, seeking solace in work. Then as she'd sank deeper, built her walls, instead of trying to knock them down, had he been too quick to put down his tools and run the other way, with safe, reliable Olivia. He'd been so disappointed with her friends, but he had been no better. In fact, he'd been much worse, for they had taken no vows of sickness and health.

Earlier, as he'd stood before her, he realised how he'd expected her to invite him to remove his jacket and sit by her on the sofa. Even now, he thought with shame, he was waiting for her to lead him to where she needed him. He could almost hear the ancient telling-off of parents and tutors alike, 'When will you take some initiative, Adam?' In the end, she'd wordlessly patted the seat, and he'd awkwardly sat, jacket still on, heavy shoes leaving marks in the carpet. She didn't comment.

'I'm sorry.' Megan had spoken softly. 'I don't know what's wrong with me. I love you, Adam.'

He hadn't known what to say, though an hour later, as he threw washing he hadn't bothered to do at Peter's into the overflowing basket on the landing outside their bedroom, he realised he could have said those exact same words. Instead, he had vainly said, 'Oh Megan!' and reached out to hug her.

She'd felt too thin, her delicate bones now protruding unattractively.

'Can I come home?' he'd asked, knowing the answer.

She'd nodded, weakly, and smiled. 'Let's work it out,' she'd said, more firmly now, outwardly appearing to take strength from their renewed bond.

'Please let's just be honest, if we're honest, we can work it out together,' he'd replied.

Now, thinking back to his words, he silently reprimanded himself for talking to her like she alone was in the wrong. She'd opened her mouth and inhaled as if preparing to speak. Adam felt he could read her mind, her readiness to proclaim her innocence, the impossible misunderstandings against all the evidence. He had known he couldn't take it tonight. It would wait until tomorrow. Tonight, he'd decided, no tears would be shed over self-medication, or worse, the poor, sick beast, the innocent victim of addiction. Being back in that familiar yet sullied home, seeing them both there and feeling the weight of what was to come had emotionally drained him, so he silenced her with a gentle kiss. He knew then, they were not beyond saving. She kissed him back, her fingers transformed from weak little spiders tickling gently against the shirt on his back to a more urgent, firm touch. Suddenly those forgotten reflexes of their marriage reappeared, effortlessly.

They kissed like teenagers, something they hadn't done for a very long time, even in happier times. Like many before them, over time, Megan and Adam had fallen into lazy predictable habits, which suited them both. But tonight, tongues touched, teeth gently tugged at lips, and his rough hands fumbled to find her braless breasts underneath her slouchy bed T-shirt. With passion came carelessness, and little attention to detail. In that moment, Adam didn't miss her silk underwear of past times, or complicated buttons on a well-structured dress. All he wanted, and it seemed to him she wanted, was skin on skin. To be one once more. Megan was alive as he entered her, ragged breath, eyes locked with his. They came quickly, with minimal fanfare, and then lay still for a moment on the sofa before they started to laugh.

'Well, I wasn't expecting that,' he'd joked.

Her head was on his shoulder, and her hands played with the hairs on his chest. No reply, but a sniff, quickly suppressed. Adam knew it was a foolish thought that had passed through his mind for mere moments that a quick shag would miraculously fix everything. As she'd stood, he saw her ribs, and as she bent to collect her clothes, he saw her belly was concave. Worst of all, when she rose and he saw her face, the glassy, sad look had returned, yet she offered him hope, as she smiled, and took his hand and kissed it. She picked up the still full cup of tea she'd been given earlier.

'I'll go clear up, meet you upstairs?' Which she'd said so casually that the seed of hope started to grow. Adam considered that this was the beginning of a reconnection that could lead to honesty, change, and getting back to the life they had before.

He could still hear her clearing up downstairs, he loved those familiar sounds. For the first time in quite some years he took it upon himself to strip the bed of its sheets. As Megan entered the room carrying two glasses of water for their bedside tables, she found him struggling to do up the tiny buttons on the fresh duvet cover with his oversized fingers, and without pausing went to him, and took over.

'Not quite the passionate return now, is it?' Adam said sheepishly, as she finished the job he'd started.

'Sometimes it's good to just be normal,' she'd replied, sleepily. They'd stripped once more, not bothering to slip on pyjamas, and fell asleep almost immediately fingers touching across the cold, clean sheet.

Adam woke up early the next day with a plan, and quietly made some calls, some excuses, and quickly organised the basic logistics with the help of a splattering of luck in availability, while he boiled the kettle and burnt the toast he planned to deliver to Megan in bed. Last night as he'd drifted in and out of sleep he'd half dreamt, half remembered a holiday he and Megan had been on together, many years ago.

It was long before Megan's mother became ill, and her father died, and she took on the enormous challenge of the yard at its pressures and stresses. In fact, it was so long ago, that his father was still happily smoking his cigars much to the disgust of his mother, no idea of the fate that would befall him before the first decade of the millennium was out. It had been before they'd become the kind of couple who neglected each other to focus on increasingly heavy burdens of the type they'd previously shouldered together, when they still had the security blanket of all four parents, and endless optimism.

That optimism creeping in caught Adam unawares but he grasped on to it all the same. The name of the village in Corfu they'd stayed in for their honeymoon was Nissaki. It was north-east on the island, a sleepy village with a handful of tavernas, little speedboats for hire, and clear blue-green waves gently crashing onto the pebbly beach. They'd stayed a long steep walk, or a short drive, away in a beautiful villa high up in the hills overlooking the sea, an infinity pool blurring the edges between the man-made and the deep blue wild unknown. They'd eaten in the same taverna by the sea every single night, having been utterly charmed by its elderly maternal proprietor, who heaped roughly served portions of the freshest grilled fish, caught that day, onto their plates.

He walked shoulder first into the bedroom to open the door, sloshing tea out of the cup on the tray and slightly dampening the toast. Megan was stirring, and as he entered, she pulled herself to sit up, brushing her tangled hair from her face. She looked almost fresh.

'I have a surprise, darling,' he announced.

Megan put up a small fight. Adam batted away concerns. Despite Megan's overall stewardship of home life, holidays had always been Adam's domain, conscientiously researching destinations, hotels, and booking the best restaurants in advance, insisting on the best table. He started to enjoy himself as she protested.

'Done that.'

'Check.'

'All sorted.'

'Anyway,' he said with a cheeky grin, 'I've booked it now, and we're flying to Corfu this afternoon. Same villa, same scorching temperatures in September. Let's hope the food at Mitsos' place is still as good.'

He'd sat on the edge of the bed and gently reassured her; everyone understands, he'd promised, he'd spoken to everyone, arranged everything. She didn't need to worry for a moment. They agreed, as they selected their clothes to pack, not to dwell on past arguments or the difficulties at the yard, but to focus on the future, on Megan kick starting the process of getting well.

'If we do that, everything else will follow, Megan,' he'd explained. Adam practised his best diplomacy choosing to force himself to, at least outwardly, believe his wife's testimony of taking her medication as prescribed. Rather than scrutinising the evidence, he called it their detox week: no alcohol, not even with dinner, early nights, and only absolutely necessary meds.

Adam said he'd pack her bag if she left out what she'd like to take on the bed. An old habit Adam had begun the first time he'd seen Megan attempt to fold a shirt. She'd happily agreed. Amongst piles of floaty dresses and colourful bikinis, she'd laid out her jars of lotion and serums, next to which was a small washbag. Inside just two small boxes: a packet labelled Zopiclone, and one half-empty packet of Xanax. No hoarding, nothing stronger. He hoped she wouldn't need them at all.

The sun was still shining when they'd arrived late afternoon, and they'd managed to hire a car and get to the villa in under an hour, stopping off for some essentials at a small village store. They'd looked around in wonder. Their view was as beautiful as they remembered, the furnishings of the villa still as outdated, but strangely no more so than before. As they unpacked, they chatted away about nothing in particular, commenting on the pretty bathroom tiles, remembering the unpleasant fact that toilet paper couldn't be flushed in Greece.

As they sat to enjoy a cold drink on the terrace, staring out at the sea, in comfortable silence, Megan almost tipped into worrying about home, the yard, Olivia, the others.

'Let's not talk about any of that,' Adam insisted.

'She's been a rock, Adam, she's been amazing. She's been there,' Megan had said.

Adam couldn't tell if it was pointed or not; he gave her the benefit of the doubt, then reminded himself silently that, to be fair, he hadn't. Adam steered the topic away from home. Megan, too, seemed happy to drop it. Undernourished, tired, and blurred around the edges, she clearly was not well, though, Adam noticed, a very slight brightness behind the eyes could be seen trying to burn through the cloudy glaze, which in the previous months had been completely snubbed out. You'd have to know how to look for it, how to see it, and he did.

Adam was an intelligent man, that he knew, but he liked the simple lens through which he observed the world and the behaviours of others. He reminded himself yet again that mental illness, addiction, whatever it was that Megan had, for that, he, along with Dr Lewis, could not fathom, were no longer understood to be cured by a week in the sun and some good old-fashioned constitutionals, more's the pity, he couldn't help but think. Despite this, he could feel his faith in a happy ending start to return.

Adam and Megan went down to the beach front taverna for dinner, Megan ate little beyond her starter but it was better than nothing, and in increasingly better spirits Adam finished off her main, which he'd insisted she ordered, if only not to offend the same maternal maître d' they recalled from their first trip. She looked much older, but then didn't they all

220

this year? She recognised them, and looked at them sadly when they ordered only the water, as if they'd lost their joy of life. Perhaps she saw that, for now, they had. They'd walked down the steep hill to the taverna, and after dinner, although it looked insurmountable to Adam, to his surprise Megan insisted that they walk back up it, not that they had much choice, taxis were a rarity in this sleepy village.

'You know what, Adam? I feel like my body has been asleep. Let's wake it up.'

With aching legs, they eventually fell into bed, hot and exhausted, and yet still found it in them to christen their first night back in Greece, back as they used to be. The sleep of the truly hard-worked is always more satisfying, and they slept in until eleven, much to their mutual shock. The heat of the day put Megan's enthusiasm for exercise on the back burner, as even in September, the midday sun beat down at over twenty-seven degrees. She lay by the pool, reading a tattered old novel she'd found in the villa, snoozing, occasionally dipping in to cool off, and Adam pottered around the gardens and read the news on his phone, unable to settle for long, innately restless on relaxing holidays. They chatted idly, mainly, until Megan sat up, and tapped Adam's arm, dangling from the sunbed next to hers for attention.

'I didn't take my sleeping meds last night Adam, I forgot,' she told him. 'I was genuinely so tired.'

A thought occurred in Adam's mind.

'Did Dr Lewis check whether they were okay to take with your other pills?'

'Of course, he prescribed the lot, and I only ever took the sleeping ones occasionally, but somehow, I was always tired, always awake at the wrong times, always felt, almost hungover, really, like I'd slept, but not well, you know?'

Adam did know, and suspected that Megan's hangovers were far from imagined. But if she's been functioning in a state of fugue, rendered forgetful due to the mix of chemicals and alcohol in her system, Adam started to see how she could genuinely not realise her own intake.

'Well, darling, if you start to feel better without them, and without the alcohol, we can go see Dr Lewis together when we're back, make sure it's all better managed.'

Megan's face involuntarily gave away the fact she felt patronised, but she rearranged it before it could be properly assessed. 'I truly am as baffled as you,' she said flatly, 'I wish you believed me, but—'

Adam interrupted her. 'I do! It's just hard to understand, I...' Lost for words he faltered, urgently clinging on to the closeness they'd started to re-establish. There was danger lurking at the end of every sentence, but he was determined to be stealthy enough to outwit it.

'I know you don't understand!' Megan's pitch was rising, but she took a deep breath, closed her eyes just for a few seconds. 'I don't either. Look, I agree, let's see Dr Lewis together when we get home. Mind you,' Her tone changed, teasing now. 'I'm not sure he has a clue either. I'm an enigma, darling, didn't you always say so?'

As she laughed, Adam smiled, happy to hear that laugh, but a little frightened at its maniacal tones. Her eyes remained open as the laugh continued, giving it an eerie quality, jarring with the mutual weariness that had permeated the last moments. He forcefully banished unwelcome words that crept into his confused mind: bipolar, personality disorder, manic depression. No. No. No. He looked at her, the

222

laughter had stopped, and she was simply admiring the flower that had bloomed right next to her sunbed, and smelling it. Her shoulders were turning brown already, and glistened with sun cream. She was, despite her diminished figure, thinner hair and fine lines around her pretty facial features, as exquisite as ever.

Apparently in agreement that there was a medical mystery without malice from Megan, with a vague plan of action for their return, both Adam and Megan simultaneously decided to draw a line under the topic and returned to easy conversations about where to place the sunbeds, what to eat for lunch, and what time to dine in the evenings. They tanned, they ate fresh, delicious food, and one day even took a speedboat out to explore the coves nearby halfway through the trip. They swam in the sea, splashing and kissing, and from a distance no one could have guessed they were a middle-aged couple with decades of marriage together, and complications deeper than the sea edge. Megan gained a little weight, her chewed fingernails regained a small amount of length, and she shaped them elegantly. Her hair had captured some of the shine from the tenacious sun.

Olivia

They fucked off to Greece! Unbelievable. I brought him home for us, and she took him away for herself. They've been plotting together, her claws have dug deep into his skin. Megan's feeling well, the romance has been rekindled and differences set aside. They're so content in themselves, they've finally decided to give a damn about me.

'When do you fly to New York?' they asked, and then they asked it again. They might as well have packed my bags. Though this time no offers of business class upgrades, and just as well as I'm not going, was never going. Their lack of interest in my plans has made it easy not to lie too hard. Last time we poured over flights and accommodation together, this year it's down to me alone. No change there then. It's now an unequivocal fact that the only way I can make my ending happy is for Adam to stay, and Megan to go. It's not enough to weaken her resolve to be rid of me. My efforts to make Adam happy will not be rewarded so long as she's here.

She's a warrior. A beautiful, shiny, indomitable, fucking warrior. When she greeted me, finally, a whole three days having passed since her return from their second bloody honeymoon, I knew she was preparing to move from a weakening defence position to full-blown attack. She was still thin, tired, slow, but she was getting better. Any fool could see. I'd been denied access, her treatment temporarily ceased even after her return as she refused my invitations for tea, coffee, or wine.

I'd tried to even the playing fields, she'd become less selfish, she grabbed less land, and she had stopped trying to push me away. Megan, finally, had needed me. They both had. She used to bulldoze her way through the world, carving out the path she craved, changing direction when it suited her, with her army standing strong behind her. It wasn't fair, I preferred the new Megan, the one I'd helped to create. But where was she now? Who was this shiny-haired, lipstick-donned bitch stood in the kitchen, not for one moment appreciating the fact that I'd been the only one left when the chips were down?

I had been furious when Adam told me he was whisking her away to Greece for a week, but I didn't let it show. I was right to distrust him, but screaming and sulking wasn't going to win this battle. He'd seen the real Megan, beneath her easily cracked exterior. He'd seen it, he'd been disgusted by it, and he'd promised a future for us. Just us. Then he'd changed his mind. And now, under the sun, she'd sown up that discarded apparel like a fancy-dress costume and the fool had forgotten the inner weakness that lay beneath. He was dazzled too easily; a magpie man.

Of course I knew she'd start to bloom in the sun, away from the useless Dr Lewis, and the meds, countless now in variety and number. Oh, dark web, how endlessly fruitful you have been. I hadn't realised she'd cast off that dry snaky skin so thoroughly. Her tanned skin stretched over protruding bones grotesquely, but she'd given some thought to her appearance for a change, and was wearing a loose fitting off-the-shoulder woollen dress, belted around her tiny waist, giving the illusion of catwalk slenderness, as opposed to the

225

recent heroin-not-so-chic look she'd been sporting in dirty, shapeless loungewear.

On her third day home, I was invited in but she refused my offer to help make dinner, and shunned the glass of wine. I noticed the rack was empty. In their absence, it had not been refilled, and I wouldn't put it past this new resolute version of the couple to have cancelled their monthly deliveries.

'I'm still suffering from terrible headaches, and I'm really not up to strength, but I know I'm on the mend. I am so lucky to have him! Who would have thought I needed a reset? Christ, before this year I hadn't even heard of stress.'

Well, that's just a stupid thing to say, I'd thought. What she meant to say, but daren't, especially in my company, is that she'd never been weak enough to succumb to it and it had never crossed her mind that she could.

'Not even in finals back at university! I've been so lucky, then, boom! They say it can happen to anyone, just like that. Bit of a minor breakdown, I think.' She'd been googling, no doubt, devouring self-help books. She was finding reason in the madness. Reset and go. I don't think so, Megan.

'I hear you shouldn't just come off medicine without seeing a doctor,' I warned her, honestly.

'Well, no, darling, but you see, I wasn't really on serious medication, it's just everyone assumed I was, because of the breakdown, you see, and now I'm getting better.'

The things we convince ourselves of. I'm sure before this year she'd never heard of a breakdown either. Now she was able to diagnose one and cure it, all with a brief trip abroad. Amazing, really.

'Of course, I'm sure I'd been neglecting myself. I never

did really grieve for Daddy when he died. We must all take better care of ourselves. And you, how are you, you've been so burdened with me, I feel terrible. How are you feeling? You look so well.'

That's another way of saying fat. My breasts oozed out of my top, and my stomach, if not breathing in and tensing, oozed out beneath them. I'd rather overeaten this last week. Boredom, loneliness, actual *real* depression caused by abandonment, rather than a fake breakdown.

'I'm fine. So you're really going to stop seeing your doctor?' I asked, full of concern.

'Well, we—' We, I noted: now she and Adam, not she and I, or Adam and I, 'did want to go together, sign things off, formally. I'm sure we'll get around to it. If I'm honest, I'm rather hoping we can forget about it all. I'm sure with the support I have, I can do this, fully. I'm going to call the yard tomorrow, see if I can take back control of that situation. A near tragedy, and a terrible one at that, but he seems to be responding to treatment, so hopefully we can move on. I know how to deal with these people and their blame tactics. I really lost it for a few weeks back there. And I really must call the girls, I don't know what the hell happened, I'm lost, but with a bit of perspective, I don't care about what's been said or not said. It's all about moving forward, Olivia. That's important to remember. We take ownership of the problems and from there we can positively solve them.'

On and on she went. I drifted into my own world. She needed only nods and the occasional 'hmm'. The self-help quotes were too excruciating to listen to attentively without either laughing or vomiting. So she'd seen the light, clearly. I'd failed to expose her. Adam was by her side, cheering her

227

on. I hadn't seen him yet, since their return. He'd dashed off to the office early each day, Megan had told me, having missed a week, and would be back late tonight, so I'd most likely miss him. Good work, point to Megan.

That night, as I tossed and turned, I thought about everything that had happened to me this year. After years of loyalty, she'd turned on me. I'd been violently attacked. I'd been called a liar. She'd tried to drive me away from the only people I loved, her included. I'd retaliated; who wouldn't? I'd tried to silence her cruel accusations, I tried to bring her back to me. When that didn't work, I tried to show him her true feeble innards to keep at least one of them, but he'd just walked away, from me too. I brought him back, to us, and they immediately abandoned me, and now we're back full circle, they forming it, me on the outside looking in.

He won't leave with me. She won't leave without him. I know she plans to oust me once and for all. It's a pretence, this solidarity, her love for me just part of her armoury, showing her gentle, loyal side co-existing with her sharp wit, her grace. I make her less superficial, I make her whole. Yet, for this, all I get is betrayal. Over and over again.

Throughout the next week, Megan continued to improve as my stockpile of medicine remained high, and Adam continued to be working too hard to spend any time with me, seemingly unconcerned with his false promises of mere weeks ago.

'I don't understand,' I'd said.

'I'm sorry,' he'd replied, not sounding the least bit sorry, 'I thought you did. Nothing needs to change now. Isn't that great? There's a long road ahead, but we'll get there. Thanks for all your help.'

I had done my bit and now I was being dismissed. Something needed to change, I was alert, waiting for my opportunity. The next week, on Thursday morning, as Megan and I baked some buns (her idea, I'm a terrible baker) the phone rang, and from the kitchen I overheard a call between Megan and Adam's mother. She scribbled a note down as she hung up, and returned to me.

'I don't know why she calls the landline at this time, she must know Adam's at work! Mind you, she's always that little but more needy when Michael's away.' she tutted and we returned to baking.

I made my excuses shortly after, telling her I was meeting a friend. She looked surprised at my plans, rather insultingly, and made a weak joke about secret trysts. If only she knew. I had things to do, but regardless I was glad to escape. After all, baking is bloody tedious. I exited via the front door, taking the note with me. It didn't say much.

> *Tests booked at hospital on Friday. Results due next Tuesday or Wednesday. Shouldn't be anything to worry about. At Bridge Friday evening so won't be able to call later. Call her over weekend?*

The old bat was starting to have increasingly frequent health scares. She always called from and to the landline regardless of other people's working schedules. She had never got to grips with the concept of mobile phones, and her own, Adam joked, lived in permanent hibernation in the bottom bits and bobs drawer of the kitchen, alongside broken torches and boxes of rusty drawing pins.

I returned to my flat, alone, angrily speculating that it might not be mine for much longer, now I was no longer of use, once again. I started to work up the courage to see if it was already listed online. I wouldn't put it past Megan, now her officious charm was reloaded.

A text from Megan arrived later hoping I'd had a nice afternoon. She told me that were both busy working all day tomorrow and that Adam had a meeting at four p.m. — of all times on a Friday — and then they were having dinner in the local pub. They knew I hated it in there, so they'd see me on Saturday. Both of them. They wanted to see my work, she'd lied. No doubt they'd been talking about me. I could picture it now, hear the malice in her voice, briefly lost but now found. They'd tell me they wanted to thank me for everything I'd done, so they'd pay for an upgrade again. Leaving tomorrow regardless of my own plans, no time like the present. My work would be laid out before them so they could gush at its brilliance, all the more reason for me to bugger off, thousands of miles from home.

Enough now. My decision is made. Megan must go, for good. The following day, I awoke with a plan. I spent the morning making sure I had everything I needed — of course I did, I'd done my research, and it's important to have a plan B. At ten past four. I called Adam's secretary to leave an urgent message.

Adam

He'd googled it. A nervous breakdown could take weeks or months to recover from, and in that time, the patient should be fully supported, avoid stress and establish a stable routine. Adam intended to make amends: he would police Megan's recovery. He cancelled the meetings that Peter had lined up for him in London. It would all have to wait until she was well again. She looked better every day, but looks were deceiving. Megan seemed happy to have him home. He thought Olivia would be happy too, the burden she'd shouldered now eased. She was free to get on with her life.

'This is my life.' Her tone was terse as she'd made her way out of the kitchen, into the garden.

Adam understood how much Olivia had given of herself to care for Megan, and to be there for him as well. Olivia had only ever wanted for things to return to normal. He knew she relied on them, otherwise friendless, alone, at least to all appearances. As a second-best scenario, she'd insisted that should they split, Adam wouldn't desert her, as Megan might, particularly if she remained unwell. He never would. What he didn't understand is why she seemed so on edge now she had what she wanted. Sat in the kitchen, nursing a cup of tea, Megan and Adam were puzzled by Olivia's recent, endless, sulk.

'She's always been insecure. I wonder if after being glued to your side these past weeks, she feels now you're on the mend you don't need her anymore. I expect she liked feeling useful,' Adam had put to Megan, as they discussed Olivia's strange attitude since they had returned.

'You're right. And we're really all she has, right now,' Megan replied.

'We should take more of an interest in her plans. Her work. I'll admit, I've not asked to view her latest project even once. I barely know anything about the move back to New York. I feel terrible.'

Megan touched Adam's hand, 'You've had a lot on your mind. I'll ask her to come over and show it. She's really taken the initiative this time with New York, she seems ready. I know she's nervous, especially as it didn't work out last year, but I think she's got more chance of finding happiness, meeting new people — maybe even a man — if she branches out.'

Adam tried to ignore the odd sense of discomfort he felt at the idea of Olivia bringing a man into their lives, taking his place as the one she adored the most.

They agreed that they'd invite her over on Saturday morning. In the meantime, Adam had one more day in the office to get through. He started to slack off around lunchtime that Friday. Between researching how to speed up Megan's recovery and avoid a second breakdown, Adam started a shortlist of restaurants and weekend getaways that he would shower his wife with. The cliché of overcompensating to alleviate guilt did not escape him.

A final meeting at four o'clock that didn't finish until after five meant that he missed the call. His secretary had left a note, and emailed, and texted him. It was clearly urgent.

Olivia

I woke up feeling nauseous on Saturday. My final move. Now was not the moment for self-doubt to creep in. Megan had already texted to say how excited she was to see my work. I noted the 'I' rather than 'we' and hoped that was a good sign. I went for a short walk to ease my nerves and reached the front door of their house at ten that morning. The door was unlocked and the house was quiet. I dropped my bag by the front door, still clutching my rolled work. No Radio 4 background noise floating from the kitchen, no sound at all. I wondered if Adam had spoken to his mother, if she'd denied leaving the message, and if Adam and Megan would be sat together, united, waiting to accuse me of meddling, bringing validation to poor broken-down Megan, giving them reason to push me out for good. As I walked into the kitchen, I stopped breathing altogether.

'Darling!' she exclaimed.

She was not sat at the island but was busy hanging a picture in the corner of the room. Adam wasn't there. It was one of my paintings. I'd given it to her months and months ago. I'd just assumed she hated it when it failed to grace her walls. I could see it would look good against the paint on her kitchen walls. It was called 'Borrowed Light' — the paint on the walls that is, not my painting. I would never be that pretentious. She blew me a kiss as she straightened it and stood back. She'd framed it. I was impressed. Shame it's all a little too late. Besides, I thought, she's probably hanging it out of guilt, getting ready to turn me into a long-gone memory, an anecdote to tell at the late-night suppers I'd no longer be invited to.

'I remembered about this piece when I got thinking about seeing your work this morning. I've been all over the place, and I'm so sorry! I actually framed it at the time, and it's been sitting there ever since.'

Lies.

We both looked at it. It was a portrait of the three of us, copied from a photograph I had taken with my phone of us all, a selfie, wrapped up warm on a freezing cold day trip to Malham Cove, when everyone was still taking time off after Christmas. I thought it was interesting to take the modern concept of a selfie and paint it. The composition was absurd. It broke every rule an artist is taught. My face was closest to the lens, too large, and Megan's too small, with Adam the only one looking like he had a normal-sized head, squished between a doll and a giant. My arm took up a whole corner portion, wider than my too-wide face, as it held the camera towards our jutting chins, upturned noses, and eyes, only millimetres from our hairlines.

It was ugly if you looked too closely. We stood back. From a short distance away, the overall effect was of happiness. The colours were warm. I'd called it, simply, *Days We Love*. At the time, Megan declared it beautiful, claimed she'd be rich one day, when I was at long last famous. I doubted she'd think the same about my new one. It was rushed and ill-conceived. You could tell I'd been preoccupied. I still was. I had to know. I asked where Adam was.

'Oh! It's a nightmare,' she started to explain.

His secretary had taken a message from his mother, and told him to drive to the Cotswolds urgently. She wasn't answering her phone, so he just jumped in the car straight away, full of worry. When he arrived after hours of awful Friday rush hour traffic, there was no answer at the door — she was out at Bridge. As he was trying to get hold of someone at the hospital, his mother just wandered up the driveway, oblivious to the panic she'd apparently caused. As they talked, it all became clear that there had been a mix-up. His mother explained that she had called the home line and spoken to Megan.

'Didn't Megan tell you?' she'd asked.

Adam had told her that yes, she had, so the message at the office had been all the more shocking. They'd feared she'd heard something from the doctor, or taken a turn. Confused, Adam's mother had racked her brains, sure that she hadn't called the office as well, and even if she had, she assured Adam that she wouldn't have told them anything other than not to worry. She'd been quite baffled, according to Adam.

'So all just a misunderstanding! I was so worried, so was Adam, so it's a blessed relief, but what an utter pain. I told him he must have a word with Jen. If she's muddling up family messages, what other mistakes could she have made? And of course with my mother suffering from dementia, well we're both worried it isn't Jen's mix-up at all, but perhaps his mother's. Anyway, as he's there now, he's going to stay for the day and see how she's doing, so I'm afraid he'll have to have second dibs on the unveiling of the masterpiece.'

As she patronised me, she feigned enthusiasm to see my

latest work. She unrolled it across the floor, for it was too large for the kitchen table, which was strewn with home life paraphernalia. Keys, post-it notes, a fruit bowl containing two rotting bananas, tweezers, a large glass jug containing dying cut flowers that had been there stewing in dirty water since before their little jaunt to Greece. Megan was still functioning at less than 60 per cent, I'd guess, and the house was still a mess. Her face was still drawn. Maybe she was withdrawing, but did not realise it, so whilst she felt better cognitively, and her motivation was growing, physically her body was drained. She was not as sharp, or as dazzling, as when she was at her best.

'Stunning, absolutely stunning.'

She insisted on the story behind it. It wasn't one I cared to share, so I made one up. She wasn't really listening anyway.

'Oh, I have a gift for you, from Duty Free, it's still in my bag,' she interrupted, eyes brightening for the first time since I started my spiel. Her turn to shine. Again.

She wandered out to the hallway. I waited. After five minutes, I lost patience with her dithering and followed her through. It took me a moment to work out what was going on in this picture. She was paler than a moment ago, her tan drained away, and she looked lopsided. She was gripping the banister with her right hand, knuckles turning blue, steadying herself. In her other hand was my diary: my memories and my future. The stupid bitch had rummaged through my imitation bag instead of her own genuine article. Identical only to the untrained eye. Megan really should have known better; she would have if she was her usual focussed self.

'How could you write these things?' she whimpered. 'It

fell out of the bag, the pages were open. I wish I hadn't seen it, I really do. It's all lies. Why would you say these things about us? It's so twisted. Adam would never, he would never do this. This isn't me. This isn't how it was! You're lying. After everything we've done for you. You're, you're—' I didn't need to know what she thought I was, so I interrupted.

'It's my truth. What would you know anyway? You've been in a stupor for months. How would you know what it was like for me?'

She was stepping backwards, twisting as if she might go up the stairs, for what reason I do not know. I reached for the diary to take it from her shaking hands. As she stepped back once more, she almost tripped over the little hallway telephone table, knocking off some of the clutter of magazines and newspapers, stacked for a recycling run.

'Give it back. You've no right to read it. No one does. It's just my story. It's not like I'm going to expose you both for what you are. Probably not, anyway.'

She put the diary behind her back.

'No, no, you are a liar. There's something wrong with you. Everyone said so, but I didn't believe them. These lies, they're hateful, vile, appalling, depraved...' She gagged, and swallowed. 'This is sick. How could you?' The diary was still in her hands behind her skinny frame. She was fidgeting. What did she think she was going to do with it? Make it fucking disappear?

'Give it back.' Not that it mattered, not anymore. What was left of her power to hurt me, to control everything, was about to be extinguished.

'What are you doing?' she asked, still fidgeting behind her back.

I was coming closer, I was reaching for something in my pocket.

'What's that?'

I didn't reply, I didn't need to. She could see what it was. She knew what was coming.

'No, please Olivia, what are you doing? Don't do this, please, Olivia, stop, we can sort this out, we can help you, no matter what you've written, or done, I'll get help for you, I'll—'

Before she could finish her sentence my syringe punctured her arm and her head lolled. I acted fast, cushioning her head from stairs. People do not sustain head injuries during afternoon bath time suicides.

Megan

My eye lids are heavy, as if they've been glued shut. My mind is full of fog. I can't see. Was I dreaming? I was looking at Olivia's painting. It was beautiful. Colours start swimming through the fog, I feel my body as if for the first time. I'm wet. I'm not cold but I'm not warm. I can't move. I'm nothing. It takes all my effort to open my eyes. Slowly. I'm in the bathroom, in the bath. I'm naked. There are no bubbles, I always have bubbles.

My head won't move but my eyes slowly open. I focus ahead, I raise my gaze. Olivia is sat on the chair at the end of the bath. What is she doing here? I try to speak but my usual mechanism to form words isn't effective. A visceral fear creeps in. I love Olivia, she loves me too. She's holding a syringe. I cannot move. I don't understand, other than I know that everything is wrong. My lips seem to be glued shut, but I prise them open with all my mental strength, of which there was little to begin with. I breathe in; the effort is immense, but still my throat refuses to release the words in my mind into the room.

She taps the syringe, professionally. She looks like she's playing doctors and nurses, as small children do, but her voice, when it comes, is that of a woman. She's not playing games anymore.

'Suxamethonium,' she says matter of fact. 'Causes paralysis, but it doesn't last very long, or stay in the system, and you've taken such a while to wake up, sleepy head, so you need another dose. Hold still.'

She giggles, childishly. It's unnerving. She stabs me in the arm. I feel nothing.

I try to speak again, I just about form the start of my sentence, croaking pathetically. 'What are—' my eyelids and mouth become dead weights. My eyes shut, my voice is gone, my lips will not move, but I know they are dry, somehow. My thoughts are jumbled as if I'm coming around from a general anaesthetic. Time has stopped, and I could be dreaming. Nothing is clear, and now everything is dark but even in the dark I see the evil words on the pages of her diary. I sense that Olivia is close to me, I think she may be crouching at the side of the bed. I hear the water ripple, perhaps she's running her hands through the water. Perhaps she is touching me.

'I'm sorry, I really am,' she says.

I feel like the fog is clearing in my mind, but it's still dark, and I'm perfectly still. I can't feel any pain, only fear. I can't see anything, but I can hear my heart thumping and my raspy rapid breath giving away my primal fear. The only clue that I am not entirely disembodied.

'You lied to me. You lured me in, convinced me to embrace your notions of what the world should be like. You tried to make me be more like you. Then you decided you'd had enough of me, and you tried to get rid of me. You were jealous because he loves me more than you. He left you. He'd be in London by now if it wasn't for me. But as soon as he came back, you abandoned me. You made him abandon me because he's bloody terrified of what his nutcase wife will do if he doesn't obey your every command. You don't care about anyone but yourself. You never listen. Well, you're listening now.'

I mentally flinched. I couldn't make any sense of what she was saying. I didn't recognise this version of events. I didn't recognise Olivia. I certainly didn't recognise my husband in this story, just as I hadn't in the pages of her fantasy diary, in which I didn't even recognise myself.

She paused, and then spoke more softly. 'I will not be sent away and forgotten about. Your disposable toy. So you have to leave. You have to.'

She was killing me.

I may be paralysed and numb, but I have never experienced any pain like this. The betrayal tears my soul apart, and breaks my heart into tiny little pieces. I desperately want to answer her. Why would she say these things about us? Why does she hate me? What I'd perceived as eccentricity I now saw for what it was. I'd ignored the warning signs. She wasn't insecure, she was controlling. She wasn't forthright, she was mean. She wasn't eccentric, she was a sociopath. But she was so warm to us so often, I never questioned her loyalty or love. She was psychotic. My mind is awake now: how could she, how could she, how could she?

Too late.

'You've been OD-ing on your Mother's Little Helpers for weeks.' She paused again, as if I would deny it.

I would, but I cannot even open my mouth.

'I've been helping you of course, with some extras. I just wanted to see beneath the front. I wanted him to see beneath too. It wasn't as pretty under there. Never is, I suppose.'

I had thought I was going mad. I had thought I was dying of a brain tumour. It broke the last of my sinking spirit when Adam didn't believe me. I'd never been so alone; I thought I could die. Just stop eating and fade away. I believed Olivia was rescuing me. The last person, the only one who still saw me for who I really was. It turns out Adam was right to distrust my claims: I was medicated. And as Olivia sat with me on those long, empty nights, giving me strength to carry on, she was stealing it all straight back with God knows what chemicals. No one else had been here to see, I guess she'd seen to that.

'I'm just topping up your clonazepam to keep you nice and relaxed as the paralysis wears off, which it will, soon. You shouldn't feel much — I'm not completely heartless — that's the point of doing it in the bath, isn't it?'

A question I couldn't answer. A picture, though, starting to form in my mind. I have no idea what clonazepam is.

'I'm sorry for all the extra drugs, but I needed you fully unconscious for a bit to set this all up, obviously. You weigh nothing by the way. You've always been so petite. I admit I was a bit jealous.'

Nothing about anything she was saying was obvious to me. I've been so blind; I had no idea. The drugs must be wearing off, as I feel my eyelids flutter I start to open them once again, and as I do I feel a familiar sting. Tears for myself, tears for my marriage, tears because this might be the end and I'm just not ready for that. Tears, absurdly, for Olivia.

'Don't cry, it'll all be over soon, and you know that we'll be happy. You always said you wanted me to be happy. You wanted him to be happy. Didn't you?'

I try to speak and this time it works.

'I'm sorry, please don't, please stop, we can work this…'

But then I tail off as I see what she has done. There is a cloudy red path forming from my wrists floating in the shallow water, journeying to the bottom of the bath, expanding. My brain tells my arms to move, my back to straighten, I must get out, I must stop this, but I can't. My body is still a dead weight, as I watch my own life leave it.

I don't know if it's the drugs or something within me that no longer wants to fight, but my mind starts to fog over again. Pictures form and dissipate, I can't hold onto them. There's no order, no sense.

The first time I saw Adam — he's so handsome. I adored that cheeky smile. The first time we had sex; his touch was like electricity. We fell in love so quickly. I love him still. I can't believe Olivia's testimony, her lies about him, and me.

Nights with Bea at our messy university house flash in my mind, drinking cider, smoking cigarettes, plotting our glamorous future lives.

My childhood horse, Solomon, and falling off him as I tried an ambitious jump, and my father, kissing my cut knees better. I've missed him so much.

My darling mother laughing with a gin and tonic when they visited our first home, her happiness for us shining through her eyes, before the spark died, and all that remained was a lookalike in an institution.

Olivia and I, years of memories flashing by. What was she really thinking all that time?

And now Olivia, sat by the bath, saying goodbye, forever.

Adam

Adam held Olivia's hand as they left the church. Megan's funeral. He could not believe it. His mother held his other hand.

'I'm so sorry Adam,' she'd said earlier, 'I never meant for you to leave her alone when she was recovering. I didn't mean it, I am so sorry.'

Adam's mother had convinced herself she must have phoned the secretary, and she must have given the impression of urgency. She promised to see a doctor, sure she must be losing her mind. Adam told her it wasn't her fault, but he couldn't muster the strength to fully reassure her. When he'd relayed his secretary's message to Megan, she hadn't questioned his urgent need to drive to his old home. They both assumed things had changed since Megan had taken the brief phone call earlier that week. There was no malice here, just misunderstanding and misfortune. Megan had been ill. No one was to blame for her death.

Olivia had cried and cried. She blamed herself, she said. She should have been there to stop her. She should have seen it coming. If only she hadn't cancelled Saturday morning's get-together, she repeatedly told him. No one blamed themselves as much as Adam did. The husband who tried to cure serious mental illness with seven days in Corfu. He retched for the hundredth time at least that day, and coughed into his hanky, trying to keep nothing much down but bile.

He'd barely eaten since he'd found her.

The nightmare plagued him night and day. The post mortem had been quick to conclude suicide yet the police were conducting an inquest after the funeral. Adam didn't know what they hoped to discover. A large quantity of alprazolam had been discovered in her system, along with a far stronger member of the benzodiazepine family, clonazepam — a bloody tranquiliser — which would have prevented her from fighting any primal urges she had to live after slitting her own wrists with the small kitchen knife. Small, yet lethally sharp, the Robert Welch knife was part of a set they'd been given as an anniversary gift. Eleven years for steel. Adam wondered why he remembered that now, when before he'd made great efforts to demonstrate his disdain for silly old traditions.

Drugs, and a knife to her veins, but in the end, it was the bathwater that had killed her. She didn't stand a chance. The report called it a 'determined and successful' suicide mission. Adam hated them for that. She wasn't being appraised at work. There was no promotion to come. There was nothing at all to come. Megan had drowned, most likely having fallen unconscious through a combination of the drug overdose and the loss of blood from her wounds. How ridiculous, Adam had thought, that a Saturday afternoon bath had killed his wife despite her efforts at more traditional, more certain, methods. She'd lied to him about her medication, not that it mattered any more.

The wake was to be held at home, though it didn't much feel like home any more. Bea, Elizabeth and Antonia had prepared a spread. He almost hadn't called them. He was wretched with anger and guilt and pain. Where had they been as Megan fell apart? In the end, he called Antonia, the first name to come up as he scrolled through his contacts hoping at least one of her friends would have found their way into his contacts list. Her anguish was palpable, even over the phone. She insisted on driving over. She hugged him tight.

'Oh Adam, I didn't know she was so ill, I'm sorry. We didn't want to stay away, but we understood. And of course, it's been difficult with—' she stopped. Her mouth was poised in position. Adam knew she had been about to say 'Olivia'.

'It doesn't matter,' she quickly said, 'I thought we just needed time. That we'd figure it out. We've rowed before and we've always sorted it out. I didn't know how bad it was.' With that, Antonia started to cry. He held her, without affection. 'I'm sorry, look at me. Look, we'll organise everything for you here, Adam. Just tell me the date and numbers. It's the least—' Before she could finish her sentence, she'd started to weep again. He'd given her a cup of tea and ushered her out of the house.

Adam had not wanted company, but today, he had no choice. There was a large turnout at church, and it appeared most of the congregation wished to come back to the house for a buffet meal and to reminisce. Adam didn't understand. This wasn't a celebration of life. Megan's life wasn't complete. This was a mourning of everything lost, and everything that they would never lose; everything that had been stolen. By who? Adam debated: by Megan herself or by the illness. The anger at himself fought his anger with Megan. His guilt fought his heartbreak. There was no room for small talk.

They'd gone, just close family and friends, to the cemetery, before making their way home to Megan's wake.

To the rest of his life without her. People shook his hand and patted his back. He wished they'd all fuck off. There was dirt underneath his fingernails from where he'd grabbed the earth and thrown it onto her coffin. He did not really believe she was inside it. That didn't make sense. He noticed he had a drink in his hand, whisky if his nose was correct. He sipped it and it burned his throat. A relief to feel something else, less unpleasant, other than the incessant wrenching of loss.

Peter was sat alone on Adam's favourite armchair by the fire, which someone, Adam didn't know who and he didn't care, had managed to make. It was a rather good fire, Adam thought, as he watched the flames dance high above the expertly built pile of logs and kindling beneath. Earlier he and Peter had tried to shake hands and pat backs but had fallen into each other into a heap of sobs. Now, they both felt the same urge: to be alone. Fuck off, fuck off, fuck off. He didn't know where Olivia was, though he thought he remembered her drifting towards the garden. He'd go to her, later. Bea, Antonia and Elizabeth were bustling, keeping busy, they claimed.

A hand on his arm startled him, and he realised he was stood awkwardly, in the way, eyes glazed. He turned to see the owner of the hand. As he did, his temper rose through his belly, but he forced it back down. He kept his voice low, but he could not keep the bitterness from it.

'Dr Lewis, I'm surprised to see you here.'

'Mr Sykes, my deepest condolences. Mrs Sykes was a wonderful woman, I'm so sorry for your loss. I'm so sorry there wasn't more I could do.'

'Yeah, me too,' Adam muttered under his breath, staring at the ground, considering shuffling away without another word, social etiquette be damned.

'I was concerned to have not seen Megan in recent weeks, I did write to try to make an appointment.'

Adam had seen no such letter, and Megan hadn't mentioned it, though if she was lying about her recovery, her medication, she could easily choose not to mention a letter.

'So you haven't seen Megan recently? You didn't give her all those drugs?'

Dr Lewis looked uncomfortable.

'I had challenged Megan about her intake of medication, but she was adamant she only took as I prescribed. Addicts do lie, Mr Sykes, please don't blame her.'

'I'm not blaming *her*, how dare you? What are you doing here?'

Actually, Adam had given serious consideration to blaming Megan's doctor. He'd toyed with the idea of suing Dr Lewis for negligence as he tossed and turned alone in bed at night. As Adam saw it, Megan's psychiatrist had provided the tools to allow a sick woman to kill herself. He was supposed to know better — he should have seen what Adam could not. He, like Megan, was an innocent, let down by the system.

'I simply wanted to pay my respects, Mr Sykes, I felt I got to know your wife. I'd hoped to see her make a full recovery. She was a good person. It's devastating to not be able to save a patient.'

Adam was unmoved by Dr Lewis' words. He didn't know the meaning of devastated.

'So where did she get all these drugs if not from you, tell me that?' Adam demanded, irate now, knowing this wasn't the time or place, affronted by the doctor's presence, and yet unable to prevent himself from driving forward the awkward confrontation. He was desperate to understand.

'I don't know. Perhaps the inquest will turn up something. I do hope so for your peace of mind,' Dr Lewis went on. 'I'd prescribed benzodiazepines, but only Xanax, and sleeping medication.'

'Only Xanax!?' Adam seethed, almost shouting the whisper, outraged by the use of the word 'only' in its dismissal of the seriousness of prescribing a previously healthy woman Xanax, and in the suggestion that he hadn't prescribed the other toxic substances that led to her life bleeding out of her, all over their freestanding bath. Of course, he knew deep down that the inquest would tell him the same. The list of meds the report detailed did not match up with even the broadest, most cavalier Google diagnosis of his wife's symptoms. Adam had clung onto the hope of pinning the blame on someone accountable nonetheless. Dr Lewis quickly moved to speak, to redeem himself over his last careless words.

'But I suspected your wife may have been getting extra prescriptions, from less reputable doctors, even online. I read in the post mortem she'd taken Clonazepam shortly before… before.' He paused, clearing his throat, and taking his quiet voice to almost imperceptible levels, natural shame controlling his vocal cords without instruction. 'I didn't prescribe that Mr Sykes. It wouldn't have been safe. It's highly addictive, you see. I was keeping Mrs Syke's prescriptions to less potent therapies, at the lowest dose I could, without abandoning her medical needs entirely. Her anxiety and suffering were too great to ignore or leave to talking therapies. I was working based on my notion that she was drinking too much and potentially taking additional doses of the drugs I prescribed, before she'd stopped her sessions.'

Adam stared blankly ahead, mouth partly open. He couldn't process the words and their meaning fast enough. Dr Lewis was charging ahead, no thought for the destruction in the wake of his words. By now he was almost as confused as Adam, tying himself in knots.

'Mr Sykes, I'd asked her about self-medication on a number of occasions. From her response, and her continued relatively high functioning lifestyle, despite her symptoms, it was my professional opinion that the situation was under control, that with a little more time, I could gain her trust, and—'

'There is no time though, is there Doctor Lewis?' Adam interrupted, his voice rising. 'You let her down. Why didn't you do something? Why didn't you reach out to me? And don't give me your patient confidentiality bullshit. She was clearly a danger to herself. Isn't there some kind of exception to your damned ethical chains?' Without realising, Adam had grabbed onto Dr Lewis' jacket sleeve. He was pleading. 'Even if you didn't know about the other drugs, even if you simply suspected she was taking more than recommended of the ones you did prescribe, surely, surely, you could have done more? How could you just abandon her? Why didn't you come here? You should have come to me. I called you! I gave you an opening! You should be fucking ashamed, Dr Lewis. Don't pretend you give a damn when you're just trying to alleviate your guilt for doing the bare fucking minimum.'

Adam knew he was being unreasonable but he didn't

care. It had only been a couple of weeks since Greece, since Megan had stopped going to see Dr Lewis. She'd been a couple of weeks before they went, Olivia had told him so over dinner. The doctor claimed to have written, and was waiting for their response. None came and now none would. Suddenly Peter was next to him, guiding him away. Peter turned to the doctor.

'Perhaps, Doctor, you should leave.' It wasn't a question.

Later, Adam lay in bed alone. His mind whirred away, but made no progress. Where the hell had Megan found a potent drug like clonazepam? Why had she sought it out? It was bad enough she'd relied on any prescription drugs, but for them not to be enough, for her to look for harder drugs? That wasn't the woman he knew. The woman who had never even smoked a joint when they were younger.

He drifted in and out of sleep, dreams of Megan first granting him brief respite, before whipping it from under him with cruel nightmarish visions.

She was smiling in a floaty dress she'd worn on that last, precious holiday, collarbone protruding and hair flowing, fragile but no less beautiful. But then suddenly she'd be in a grey corridor talking to hooded shapes, frightened and alone, and Adam could see her but not reach her, and as she backed herself into a corner, he'd see she was taking a knife from the shapes, and slicing into her own tiny middle, the sheer top layer of the patterned dress turning a dark red as she slumped like a sack of bones.

His eyes sprung open, he sat up sweating. He no longer could find rest in sleep. He found Olivia in the kitchen when he went downstairs to make a cup of tea in the middle of the night after the funeral.

'I thought you'd be back at the flat,' he said.

Adam had not noticed who was left still clearing up when he'd went to bed, not bothering to thank anyone or say goodnight. He sat with her, and together they let their tea go cold in companionable silence. The kitchen was big, empty and soulless without Megan. Eventually, Olivia tired of his endless silence. She kissed him goodnight, and told him in the morning that he would start to feel better. It was almost as if she was giving him permission to get over it, to move on. She meant well. It angered him nonetheless.

'Today just needs to end, the whole horrible chapter finely at a close,' she said, as she wrapped her arms around him.

His body was limp to her embrace, arms dangled by his side. He knew he was wrong to deprive her of comfort, but he had nothing to give. He'd silently nodded and kissed her hands, though he disagreed. This would not be over that quickly, perhaps never. Adam wouldn't throw her words back at her. She was trying to help, although she couldn't know she didn't stand a chance of saving him, not now. He'd been blind to think that she ever could.

Olivia

I've saved him. From himself, and from her. Finally, we're both free from her tyranny, her plotting, her manipulation, her naturally controlling nature. It took me so long to see it, no wonder he doesn't realise it yet. He's in shock, but he will. It's a good job I've been in such a good mood, otherwise I might start to feel a tad irritated with the persistent lack of effort on Adam's part to cheer the hell up, given how much work I've put into rescuing him. A little gratitude wouldn't be too much to ask. Sometimes though, you've just got to be the bigger person. I understand that now.

Yesterday I heard him wittering on to some aged relative on the telephone about how she'd used their anniversary knife, as if the knife held special memories. He made such a fuss I wish I'd chosen something of less symbolic importance, but how was I supposed to know? Anyway, I bought a new one and left it in its proper place, so he can stop banging on about it being 'conspicuous in its absence.' What total tosh.

It's been a week since the funeral. I'd at least have expected grief to move to anger by now. Anger at Megan for leaving him, and anger at himself for misjudging her so badly. At least anger would give us something to talk about. The silence is beyond irritating. He mopes so extravagantly, he's permanently in the way in whatever room he occupies. It's almost like he's doing it on purpose. It wasn't so long ago he'd moved out, ready to start a new life, with me. Now she's cleared the way, he needs reminding of the long-term plan. We mustn't forget that he only came back to stop her from going mad and dying. That failed. Now, he can focus on us, guilt free. No one could say he hadn't tried.

He finally went back to work today, perhaps getting back to the routine will do him good. I am alone in Megan's kitchen. I'm wearing her apron, and I'm using her recipe book. I'd deliberated carefully between cooking steaks (every man's favourite, I'd heard him say once), or roast chicken (the taste and smell of a happy home, as she used to tell us). He used to love Megan's roast chicken on a Sunday. It's Monday, close enough. I decided on homely chicken. He said the smell of a roast in the oven was pure heaven. His expectations of heaven are pretty low, but whatever.

I've taken charge of the house this week. He told me it wasn't necessary, that I didn't have to stay with him. It is entirely necessary. Someone has to get him back on track. Obviously New York is cancelled, and this time Adam didn't argue. Peter offered to come and stay, but I insisted he'd be in the way.

'Charming, as always,' he'd rudely quipped in response to my quite honest and well-meaning statement. Then, for probably the first time ever in his arrogant life, he apologised, remembering that he and Adam weren't the only mourners in this charade.

But life is for the living, they say. Grab it by the horns, they also say. A million and one dreadful inspirational quotes for awful people to hang on their walls and post on their Instagram pages. Not something that had appealed to me before, but then again, I hadn't had to save someone from the depths of deep depression before. So I googled them. Who writes this shit? *Don't let yesterday take up too much of today.* He needs to work on that one. *It's not whether you get knocked down, it's whether you get up.* Ditto. Luckily he has me to drag him up off the floor of self-pity. *Things work out for the best for those who make the best of how things work out.* Quite. *The best time for new beginnings is now. Live each day as if your life has just begun.* And so on, and so on.

I heard the key in the door. The smells emerging from the cooker were not everything that I'd hoped to greet him with. The chicken is dry but at least it won't kill us. I cheated on the roast potatoes by getting the frozen ones. Same with the carrots. The gravy is instant; can't go wrong with that. I doubted he'd notice anyway at the moment. Whilst I enjoyed Megan's dinners, it was obvious she valued the self-satisfaction of cooking from scratch more than the end result.

'What's going on?' I'd surprised him.

'I made a roast. On a week night.' Pride swelled.

'You shouldn't have.' Perhaps not, if this is all the enthusiasm he can muster. He carved the chicken, I served up the rest. We ate in silence at first. It wasn't bad, though rather more reminiscent of school dinners than I'd imagined it would be. Nothing really wrong with that though. I'm not a cook; no one's perfect. Then he spoke, ruining the peaceful atmosphere.

'I'm not going to just accept her death. Someone is to blame. The inquest will show that, I just know it.'

I didn't know there was going to be an inquest. Nobody ever tells me anything.

'No one is to blame, she killed herself. Pass the salt.' I didn't love this turn in the conversation. Sullen silence was preferable.

'They were too quick to label her death suicide,' he persisted. 'I want to know where she got all those drugs from. I want the inquest to overturn the post mortem's assumptions. What is wrong with a system that just chalks it up to suicide without a thought for how the suicide was made possible? Whoever gave her those drugs needs to answer for that. It should at least be misadventure! She wasn't in her right mind.'

He was raising his voice. He rarely raises his voice, but I know how to turn down the volume, transform his anger into regret and sympathy. Positivity is the key to life, after all, said someone really stupid. My lip quivered, and I blinked a tear to life. I was fuming internally. Until she died, he was happy to think that their romantic jaunt to sunny pebble beaches had corrected her malfunctioning mind. Always thinking the best of her. She's perfectly fine one minute, but the second people are using a dirty word like suicide, she's no longer mentally capable. She is no longer required to take responsibility. People like Megan rarely do. They do good things, but bad things simply happen to them. Convenient.

'I'm sorry, Liv, I really am. I don't mean to upset you. And you've gone to so much effort tonight. I do appreciate it. I'm just so angry. I don't mean to take it out on you, I know you're devastated. You're right, we need to look after each other, don't we?'

He stood up and circled the table, and by now his arms were around me, where they ought to be. I sniffed.

'I thought the doctor gave her the drugs. No one gave her the knife though, did they?' I ventured.

His eyes darkened. I wanted to retreat, take a new

256

position. I was not blaming Megan, heaven forbid.

'I'm not blaming her, I loved her so much.' I couldn't think of a quick way out. The tears and snot came hard and fast and his grip tightened. I felt his love, but his anger was sure to leave finger marks on my upper arms, where his embrace finished each side.

'Dr Lewis thinks she may have been taking additional drugs for weeks, ones he did not prescribe. She wasn't herself when she took that knife upstairs.'

He was adamant that there must be someone to blame, but not him, of course. In a way he's right. Dr Lewis ought to be struck off for being bloody oblivious.

'Why are you so convinced she didn't just store them from months of prescriptions? People do that. I read about it. I've been looking for answers as well.' I looked down at my plate. Obviously, I am no longer looking for answers, but it's insulting to almost Peter's levels to assume he's the only one to show an interest in science. 'She drank too much, I realise that now. It might have increased the effects, mightn't it?' I added. I could hear the approval-seeking tone start to appear in my voice. I pinched my arm to remind myself of my new role and persona: the totally together woman who makes roast chicken on a Monday night. She, the new me, is not the type to need approval. Megan never did.

'I just know there's more to it. It's so out of character. I just can't get the picture out of my head of her desperately buying or begging some quack for these dangerous drugs.' He stopped and looked at me, as if suddenly realising I was there, that he wasn't talking to himself. 'I'm sorry, I shouldn't be saying these things to you. You don't need to know all of this.' Quiet and considered.

257

The chicken was getting cold, but I was losing my appetite. Adam had lost interest in the meal. I started to clear away, harnessing every bit of my restraint not to throw the damn plates on the floor, food and all.

'I'll do that.' He got in my way; he was starting to make a habit of it. 'Honestly, Olivia, you've done enough. Just forget this conversation, okay? You need to get some rest yourself. Leave me to it. Go! Relax! Catch up on your own stuff.'

I was incensed with rage. He's ordering me to go. Pushing me away. What the hell is wrong with him? Can he not see I'm all he has left now? Does he not realise that everything around him is disintegrating? Her friends were long gone at the first sign of trouble, and I'm pretty sure that holier-than-though Perfect-Peter who was definitely a bit in love with Megan, thinks less of Adam for his casual desertion in her, *our,* hour of need.

'No wonder she gave up on herself, if even solid old Adam had given up on her.' I imagined them whispering in the spacious aisles in Waitrose. 'We all doubted Olivia's intentions, but in the end, she was the only one who stayed loyal throughout.' I hope they feel guilty. I hope they can't sleep.

'I'm only trying to help.' My rage was folded neatly in the pit of my stomach. Now was not the time for rage.

'Oh God, I know!' he replied.

It was heartfelt, and I unclenched my fists, which I hadn't realised had become tiny white balls, giving me away.

'I am so self-absorbed,' he continued, 'I just don't want you to burden you with all of this. It's not fair. It's appalling of me. It's horribly inappropriate of me to allow you to care for me like this, after everything you've been through, everything we've been through together. You just need some time to yourself.'

If he thought that was what I craved — time to myself — then yes, he was correct: he *was* self-absorbed. That was the last thing I have ever wanted. I immediately forgave him, all the same, because unlike Adam, and unlike Megan, and all the rest of the hateful crowd, I am not self-absorbed. I pay attention, and I can tell when he needs me. I was once told I lacked empathy. I guess they were wrong about me. It wouldn't be the first time.

'It's okay. I'll just finish up, and then I'll go get some rest, and leave you to get some too. Work tomorrow?' I said with great, undeserved kindness.

He simply nodded. I busied myself with scraping, he loaded the dishwasher. I didn't try to help and instead wiped crumbs from the table top. It had always been a running joke in this house: Adam's anal obsession with the order that plates must be stacked in the dishwasher meant no one else bothered to try to meet his military standards whenever he was around. I wondered if they had dishwashers in the military or had to clean all the plates by hand. Probably the latter. If I didn't know Adam so well, it would have surprised me that despite the state he was in, he took just as much care as always, the origami master of cleaning crockery.

We worked in steady silence, which was a relief. The tension in the room was starting to evaporate. I decided I'd tried hard enough for one night. He'd feel bad later for failing to see how much I was doing for him, and perhaps he'd even start, as he rested and dreamed, to see the future for the beautiful bright thing it was. He just needs time. I kissed him on the cheek as I bade him goodnight. He stroked my hair. My fingers tingled with joy, and real tears pricked my eyes, as we stood as one for moments that I wished could have lasted forever. He was thawing. He was coming back to me. I know he'll find his way, and I'll be here every step of the way to guide him.

'Goodnight, Olivia.' He pulled away and looked me in the eye. 'I promise I'll be better. I just keep thinking if I knew how this all happened…' He tailed off. 'I'm just looking for *closure* —' he made bunny ears with his hands '— as they say in those dreadful sitcoms you and she used to love to hate so much.' He smiled at me, genuine for the first time since everything happened. 'I don't know what I hope to find though, and whatever I find, what does it matter, really? I'm just trying to figure out who she was, at the end. I can't imagine her doing anything illegal, never mind anything so dangerous.'

I smiled back, ready to help him put this to bed. 'You're right. It makes no difference now, all it will do is upset you and muddy the wonderful memories,' I gently told him. 'Besides, Klonopin isn't heroin, you know? It's not illegal. She could get that from any doctor.'

Adam

Tap, tap, tap, went the knife against the marble table top, as Adam passed it between his shaking hands. The blade was sharp, brand new. The design sleeker than the one the police had taken and never returned but it was the same brand, the same style, the same coloured handle. But it wasn't there yesterday morning, he was sure of it. This bothered Adam. And Olivia was bothering Adam. Of course he hadn't expected a normal reaction from Olivia, whatever normal meant anyway. Olivia wasn't normal, and previously that had been part of her charm, despite what other people thought. He thought they were small-minded, and intolerant. He, and Megan, had seen something special in her, and adored sharing the quirky lens through which she saw and interpreted the world. He was prepared for a different perspective but he wasn't prepared for this.

One minute she was devastated, in competition with him for most wretched, but the next she was crudely trying to fill her shoes, acting as if Megan had never existed, as if it were possible to continue on as before, with her death and all the guilt and pain that went with it hanging between them. For him whatever had been possible before, whatever future they had imagined, was no longer conceivable. Olivia had cruelly reminded him in one of her outbursts that not so long ago he had left Megan, and had been ready to live without her. Could she not see that living without Megan and living in a world in which Megan had killed herself, in which he had failed her, were two very different things?

He clearly didn't know Megan, and now perhaps he would have to admit he didn't know Olivia either. The charade of the roast dinner was weird enough. Had she no sense of social norms at all? She couldn't pretend to play the role of his dead wife. It had been a horrifying and bizarre evening, but in his fugue, he'd allowed it to continue without question. But this was becoming significantly troubling. Why did she buy the knife? How did she know about the knife? He might be able to rationalise that, he'd talked about the knife. But he hadn't talked about the drugs, so how did she know which brand of potentially black-market prescription drugs Megan had used to dull her senses before she slit her wrists? Even he didn't know the name of the specific brand. They'd found no packaging amongst her things, adding to the suspicion that they were procured in a less than legal manner.

Megan had been fiercely secretive of her anxiety meds, even when she was on the regular stuff an actual doctor had prescribed legitimately. He couldn't fathom a reality in which Megan had confided in Olivia not only in her increasing reliance on her prescribed benzodiazepines, but on her escalation to darker, more potent members of the drug's family. As far as he knew, only he, Dr Lewis, and the authors of the post mortem report knew what Megan had taken. He'd not told a soul. The words wouldn't have come out even if he'd wanted them to. They cut like razor blades in his throat. Then again, what did Adam know about reality these days? He needed to ask Olivia. If Megan had confided in her, perhaps she knew who was guilty of allowing her addiction to bloom. Maybe, her refusal to enter into any conversation about opening up an investigation into how Megan got hold of the drugs was part of a misplaced sense of loyalty. Was Olivia keeping Megan's last secret?

Olivia had told him she'd see him around nine, which was over three hours away. He could hardly contain himself. Anxious, apprehensive, jittery. He knew if he asked her outright, she couldn't lie to him. She'd see how important it was to reveal what she knew. Together, they could get justice for Megan. Olivia must need answers too, she had said so herself. He would make her see that she was no longer protecting Megan's secret but someone else's: the person responsible for Megan's death.

Adam made tea and sat in the kitchen, then in the living room. He switched on the television and then switched it off again. Tinned laughter echoed in his ears. Then, as his jumbled thoughts messed up his blank mind without forming any real meaning, suddenly an idea struck him: Bea. If Megan had told Olivia, of all people, what was really going on, without a doubt she would have told Bea.

Megan adored Olivia, but she always said she wasn't the best listener, her world experiences too narrow to comprehend those of others. Olivia may have overheard snippets of confessionals, but perhaps wouldn't really know or understand the full story, which might explain her hesitation to discuss it at all — troubled by her own lack of insight, misplaced guilt for not asking more, just like him. Adam scrolled through his contacts in his phone. No Bea. He shrugged, he'd rarely had any reason to call Megan's friends directly. Social arrangements were organised by his wife.

He marched into the hallway, positive that the old address and phone book they'd had since they were given it as a house-warming gift by one of Megan's elderly aunts would be still sat there, rarely opened. Piles of recycling were mounting up on the lower shelf of the table as well as on the very top. A couple had fallen off the back and were wedged between the table edge and the wall. He needed to sort this out, he thought, practicalities never completely leaving him, even in crisis. He pulled the table out to release them and bent to retrieve them. As he did a batch of partially torn, crumpled, thin-lined pages, full from top to bottom of blue-inked words, fluttered to the floor.

Adam automatically gathered them and the words jumped from the page straight into his horrified eyes as Olivia's unmistakable handwriting told its despicable lies. He read them once, and then again. An excerpt from a diary, crudely torn and stashed. He was on every page, countless times. The words put him in places he'd been to, and attributed words he'd said to him, but everything else was different. He and Megan were monsters in this story. Olivia, a victim, over many years. What were these pages doing here, stashed, seemingly torn roughly, hurriedly, without thought or care? Not the beginning nor the end, but right in the centre of the most squalid reincarnation of hell imaginable. Olivia was sick, far sicker than he could have ever imagined.

He must have asked himself a hundred futile questions in whatever time it took for the world to stop spinning. Seconds, minutes, hours? And then he knew. Megan had found the diaries. Had she confronted Olivia? Had Olivia convinced her that he had done these things? Megan was also painted as a demon, so surely she hadn't believed a word. But Megan was ill. Her mind wasn't functioning. Had she only seen the Devil in her husband? Had she killed herself because of these lies?

Because of Olivia's cruel words? Was it a betrayal she couldn't stand in her fragile state? A state he'd forgotten she remained in, when he drove to his perfectly healthy mother. No wonder Olivia wanted nothing more to be discussed about her death, when her part in it was obvious to her, and now to him. His palm squeezed the sheets, causing them to crumple even more, and he staggered into the living room, collapsing onto the sofa in a heap.

His head was in his hands. On the deep windowsill, the clock ticked dutifully, each minute lasting hours. Thoughts swam in circles. He watched the hands of the clock near nine. His gaze drifted left, an ornament of a ballet dancer, missing a finger. He heard Olivia let herself in through the front door rather than retreating to her flat first — a habit she'd taken to increasingly since Megan's death. The heavy thump of a bag being dropped in the hallway followed. She carried her diaries and her sketches wherever she went. The rest of the story was in reach. But how could she ever explain her warped mind, a mind that could think, let alone record, such horrifying lies. She walked in with trepidation, or perhaps he imagined it. He put on his best smile, causing Olivia to pause. It didn't fit here, not now.

'How are you?' she asked.

'Could kill for a cup of tea,' Adam lied. Delighted to be useful, Olivia headed straight to the kitchen to put the kettle on. Adam silently went to the hallway, not daring to breathe. He opened the large bag, recalling that his wife had a similar one, before she died. He looked inside, and there they were. The leather-bound sketch book, and the moleskin books, three of them.

He took everything back into the living room, burying the books of lies behind the cushion, before leaning back on it.

Olivia handed Adam the cup, and he placed it on the coffee table in front of him. Palpitations of his broken heart reverberated through his ribcage. At first no words would come. He didn't know where to begin. He was afraid of how Olivia would react, and what she might be capable of. The diaries were lines of sick fantasy, creating monsters and victims where there were none, romance where there shouldn't be any. Drugs, abuse, control. If this was art, he was happy he didn't understand it. He feared it was something else.

'Have you lost some pages of your work?' he asked, his voice shook.

'I only realised the pages were torn out today. I take it you have them.' Olivia's voice was calm, and Adam wondered if she had recognised the look in his eyes, he'd greeted her with; the one Megan would have first shown her having read the pages. Her eyes pierced his own. She offered no apology. 'Please don't over-react. It's an experiment about truth and perspective, that's all.'

Controlling his voice, Adam asked, 'Did she read the pages? Is that why they were torn? What did you say to her to make her do it?' He inhaled back his sob.

A strange sound escaped from Olivia's mouth. A shocked snort tinged with the beginnings of laughter. With a reserve of energy Adam didn't realise he had left, he propelled his body upwards to standing and grabbed Olivia by the shoulders, shaking her, screaming at her, words tumbling forth, demanding an explanation for her lies and for the unnerving hatred that burned through her pen, all the way from her rotten soul. She didn't answer, or cry. Her silence was enduring, and in the end it outlasted Adam's rage. He fell back to his seat, the diaries were now visible.

'I see you have the full set,' she said, a quiet observation, rather than an accusation.

'More of the same?' he asked.

'Yes.' They stared at each other for a while.

Finally, Olivia spoke. 'Megan's gone, we only have each other now.'

No longer attempting to hold back his sobs, Adam sniffed and spluttered as he choked out his questions. 'What did we do to you to deserve this? What happened that day? Were you here? How did you know what drugs she used? What happened, Olivia?'

'I can't tell you. I don't trust you right now. You won't understand,' she said, deadpan.

Adam sat up straight and composed himself, rearranging his face to the calm, competent one that he knew she found reassuring and safe.

'Yes, yes you can. I just need to know what happened that day. All I want is to understand. I promise this isn't about blaming you.' He was earnest.

Olivia's face softened. 'I promise never to share my story unless I have to.'

'What does that mean?' Emotions were blurred: pain, anger, shock, fear.

She didn't answer.

Adam tried to find the pieces of the puzzle in the corners of his mind. The torn pages, a defiant Olivia, Megan dead and full of drugs he couldn't imagine her sourcing herself, a suicide just at the moment she was in recovery. The smiles she'd rediscovered in the last weeks of her shortened life had not been faked. His wife had not been suicidal. Even the discovery of Olivia's diaries could not have changed that so suddenly. She would have talked to him about it, he knew that. He suddenly knew that Olivia had got to her first.

'It wasn't suicide, was it?' he almost whispered.

'I'd say that anyone reading the diaries would believe she had every reason to kill herself, wouldn't you? I have another copy.'

A threat, Adam recognised.

'I only wanted what was rightfully mine but she wanted to take everything from me. Including you. I just wanted to be accepted, loved. I just wanted to belong.'

Adam's eyes looked past Olivia as he blinked back tears and found the clock, next to the broken ballerina on the windowsill. Without him meaning to, his eyes moved to the mantelpiece above the fire, to a photograph in a silver frame of Megan and Olivia. In it Megan was laughing, her hair blowing into her eyes from the wind. Olivia looked serious, she always had. She was shielded from the wind by Megan's protective arm. He had taken the photograph, many years ago.

'You killed her. She loved you. I loved you. And you killed her.' Adam's voice was getting louder. 'And your threats, what are they, to keep me quiet? To protect you?' Olivia shook her head, then nodded, then shook it again. Adam gagged, so deeply disturbed, his head was spinning. This would kill him, he was sure of it. 'You're insane.'

'I just wanted you to love me like you loved her!'

Rising to his feet once more, Adam roared, 'I loved you

268

like a daughter!'

Olivia reeled back and knocked into the mantelpiece. The silver frame fell onto the fireplace, the glass smashed. She collapsed to the floor. Adam towered over her. She was heaving now, her chest rising and falling too quickly, sobbing, tears and snot running down her face. Still, just a girl, really, he thought looking at the young woman before him, but not the girl he had thought she was. He needed a minute. He needed her gone.

'Go and wash your face, calm down. We need to finish this tonight.' He meant it.

'Will you tell them I did it?' she asked, meekly.

Adam looked at her, and surprised himself by offering her the promises she craved, 'I promise I'll never tell a soul. But go and clean yourself up, so that we can talk.'

A tear escaped. She saw it, a flash of relief crossed her treacherous eyes. She also looked taken aback. She'd never seen him cry before, but what was she expecting? Olivia obeyed silently. Adam crouched down by the fireplace and, holding the frame, brushed the shattered glass from the photograph, before picking up the box of matches that lay in the basket of kindling and returning to the sofa, where he placed the diaries on his knee.

He didn't have long but he allowed himself a moment. He still loved her, no matter what she had done, and he hated himself for it. He could never throw her to the wolves, and he could never allow these vile accusations to leave this room again. Moreover, he would not allow Megan's memory tainted, nor would he watch Olivia rot in jail. He had no choice.

Adam lit the match, and watched the pages curl. He

didn't move for a while, inhaling the smoke, hypnotised by the flames, staring at the photograph in the broken silver frame. His beautiful wife, Megan, holding Olivia, then aged three.

Their cherished daughter, Olivia.

Part Three

2019
The present day

Olivia

I'm surprised at Lucy's staying power. I underestimated her. She just seemed so flaky. She doesn't love him, my father. She just likes the idea of him: the wealthy, suave banker with the expensive apartment he doesn't have to share with a load of self-righteous vegan twenty-somethings who think eating avocados will change the world. Does she believe in miracles, I wonder? That it would be possible to find a man like him, in his forties, no wife, no children, no baggage? She might not be as flaky as I thought, but she's just as stupid.

He's a liar. He's allowed her to believe in miracles. Would she be so keen on him if she knew our history? Of course not. His love for me, back then, even she could not have competed with. His jealous, crazy wife, determined to oust her own daughter for fear of losing her greatest prize, and me, his whole world. Creator and destroyer of. My note to Lucy was fair warning. I might loathe the lithe little idiot, but surely she deserves some insight into the man she's swooning over like some halfwit. But he promised he'd never tell, and he's kept his word. So don't try and tell me he doesn't still love me.

I told her women in Adam's life tend to get hurt. That's no lie. Poor Megan, my darling mother, who ripped me from her womb and would have ripped me from my home, my world, if I hadn't been clever enough to see her betrayal coming a mile off. The world is a dangerous place, and loving Adam is a dangerous vocation. Oblivious, he plays us off one another, vying for his attention. He hurt me; he broke my heart. I thought he'd understand and even if he didn't, at least at first, I never thought he'd destroy us. And for what? A dead wife? What use is a dead wife, when you could have a living, breathing daughter whose only real crime is to love you too much? He will forgive me because that's what parents do. My mother forgave me, I saw it in her eyes. She loved me until her last breath.

I followed Lucy to the apartment and waited outside while she confronted him about the note. I didn't expect it to take so long. I sat and waited, and time seemed to stop. I imagined he'd have no choice but to tell her the truth, and I had no doubt that she would immediately run from it. She wouldn't have the stomach for our world. He'd get over it, and he'd forgive me, and I him. There could be a future for us, even after everything. We just needed time, of which we've had plenty, and space, which is currently overcrowded with unhelpful additions, like Lucy. I couldn't imagine Peter being much help either. He never liked me.

But she didn't emerge. She stayed there all night. I did too, alone, out in the cold. From my mother's point of view, if she still had one, you might call it poetic justice, or irony, as in my quest to stay safe in my home with my father, I ended up on a dark street, sat on a wall, alone, as he gave his love to someone else. I'd tried to force him to think about me, and where I was now instead of where I should be. My actions were designed to make him remember me, feel guilt over his treatment of me, but so far it seems my efforts have not yet come to fruition.

He believes in his own lies, no doubt, as Lucy had when

I guess he spun her a tale and took her to bed. Adam, the innocent party, robbed of his perfect life by cruel, indiscriminate insanity and unstable females. Poor, poor, widowed Adam. Not, as I see it, nor as my diaries recalled it until they were almost entirely turned to ash by a stricken and desperate man. My father, the villain, who as well as reducing my truth to dust, went on to discard me, the last person alive to love him truly, in my moment of need. He erased me from his life as if I was never there.

He's tried to wipe every trace of me away. He deserves for me to forget *him*, avenge myself, reveal his dark past to the world, but fool that I am, I still love him, and I will make him see that. I know, as well, it's his visceral pain that's causing him to block out the past. It isn't who he really is: a cold man, an unloving man, who would leave his own daughter out in the cold, to fend for herself, not caring one jot what happens to her. He does care, but he's suffering. He blames me for Megan's death, but he'll see one day, if he'd just listen, how she invited war, and then lost. We could have all been happy together, and now, because of her, that's not possible. At least we can make up for that by the two of us reconciling and finally being a family again. A family of two.

The yoga-slut finally surfaced in first light, wearing yesterday's clothes, her hair unwashed, and make-up smudged. It was still early, and I figured she was going home to shower and change for work. A single light glowed from his bedroom window. He was probably snoozing still, warm beneath his duvet. Lucky for some. I thought about waiting a little longer to see him. I desperately wanted to confront him, have him see me again. I haven't changed. I'm still the girl he adored until that terrible night.

Lucy fished her phone from her bag and she dialled. Without planning to, I fell into step behind her, ready to listen to her analysis of the note and find out how he had managed to persuade her to stay the night after all of his lies. She perched on a wall near the bus stop. I crossed the road, to watch her from a distance.

'Hey Tom, it's me.' The flatmate with the fixie bike and stupid, overly groomed beard. It made him look like he had a jutting Disney chin, which no doubt he thought attractive. I saw only a cartoon of a man.

'Did you feed William last night?' The beloved cat. She smiled. I guess he fed the cat. Good old Tom.

Silence for a few moments, the smile faltered and then disappeared altogether. A frown manifested on her forehead. She took a breath, about to speak, but Tom clearly wasn't finished. She swallowed it.

'He doesn't understand it either. His wife died, and he says there's been no one else. He wonders if it is just a stupid prank. He said he'd assume it was the tosspots he's just started working with, except how would they know who I was or where I lived?'

A sharp intake of breath as she was cut off. I couldn't hear but I imagined Tom's voice increase in volume.

She was firmer now, clearly talking over him. The kind of loud that is still contained in a whisper, like a mother threatening a badly behaved child in the supermarket. Like my mother's voice when she'd take me to one side and implore me to stop being so defensive, stop pushing buttons, to just be normal for once.

'Look, Tom, I do appreciate that you're worried about me, but it's just a stupid childish note, probably written by a stupid child! Maybe some silly girl in our building has a crush. In the end, it all seemed so ridiculous, we even laughed about it. It's classroom behaviour, it's so obvious now. Ridiculous really!' She laughed.

I'm going to fucking kill her.

'I know, I know, but he explained that too. He took the day off to sort out some paperwork about his old house, you know, it burned down, but it's on the market?' The last two points intoned upwards, like a question. A trait belonging only to Americans and imbeciles. 'Of course I'm being careful. You met him. You know he's a decent guy. I've blown everything out of proportion.'

Wow, he's good, I'll give him that. Threatening note, lies about whereabouts, mysterious previous life never mentioned, and somehow lovely Lucy has worked out that somehow this is all her fault. I'm impressed. Despite my irritation at the ongoing situation, which frankly, I thought would be easier to rectify, it is moments like these when it's clear to see why we belong together. He's brilliant; we both are. Together, we could rule the world. We really could. And that isn't some childish notion, that's called ambition.

I've always had ambition, but never managed to fully realise it. When I went to start art school in New York (on my parents' dime, as they both joked in silly Bronx accents, unkindly evoking guilt and probably trying to ensure I didn't scarper home too quickly), I struggled to fit in. I thought that artists were encouraged to be experimental out there, but obviously not. My flatmate didn't appreciate the blood on the walls, although she also claimed to be an artist. It was disappointing. The department were up in arms about my so-called plagiarism, and before that about my actual work.

277

They called me a pretender, and then they called me a cab. I came home, the only place I ever fitted, and found that I no longer did. They'd banked on being empty-nesters. It was a very upsetting time.

I wait for a little longer before watching Lucy jump on the number 277 bus and disappear out of view. I know where she lives. She may think my methods are childish, I'd say that was just a lack of imagination, but either way it's not like I have much choice. I can't confront her, or him, not yet. It's too complicated. And as for Dad, he knows the truth. He knows I'm far more capable than any stupid child. At least his lies and his lack of fair warning about his crazy life shows that he doesn't actually give a damn about her, or maybe he really does believe in his ability to ensure that I was gone for good, just like he wanted.

Lucy may live to regret underestimating the girl who writes notes.

Adam

Adam was lonely, even now, wedged in between two large men vying for the barman's attention. He'd been lonely for months, really, despite starting to believe in his own marvellous propaganda that a corner had been turned. Great job, sexy girlfriend, tragedy in the past, time to look to a future. When Megan died, he was devastated, but not lonely. He'd thought he was lonely, lying awake in their king-size bed, alone, perhaps forever it seemed then. Now he felt silly. Back then he hadn't known what loneliness was, didn't know the meaning of the word. With his wife gone, he thought life had hit him with all it had, but it was holding its punches.

His daughter's betrayal, then needing to wrench her from his life, that was the source of the purest loneliness imaginable, caused not only by the absence of those he loved most, but by the weight of the secret he carried, with not one person to confide in. Adam had previously thought of loneliness as a passive state. Wrong again. It was a violent emotion, gnawing at his internal organs, hitting his brain with an invisible hammer. The headache had been constant and sharp for months, and Adam had spent most of this year in a stupor, exhausted. His only respite those cherished moments with Lucy, or even with a spreadsheet. Moments in which he could hide from the pain and the lies and all that went before. Even evenings with Peter drained him. The sympathy he couldn't bear, the truth clambering to crawl out of his mouth, washed down with too much wine, worsening his headache, and causing evenings to end earlier than they had used to. A rueful Peter, head shaking, a wobbly Adam, head nodding.

For months, he'd spent most of his days alone, occasionally meeting Peter, licking his open wounds, which never ceased to sting, avoiding his guilt-ridden mother, his confused brother. They thought he was isolating himself due to grief. In some ways they were right. He was overflowing with grief. He knew they could deal with that though. His mother would mop his tears as if he were a child again. The problem was the contents of the grief, and what she might find when she looked closer. They mourned him like he was dead. Perhaps he was dead, he'd thought in those early dark days. Perhaps better off dead, at least.

Adam hated his new self-pitying state of mind. So did his work colleagues. James, the contemptible Head of Equities had even bored of baiting him. Adam kept his head down, concentrated hard. His strategy wasn't failing but it wasn't flying either. Just yesterday, a reflection in the floor to ceiling glass walls in his open-plan office had tricked him, illuminating Olivia's accusing face with dappled sunlight skewed by clouds.

'Olivia, I—' he had started, automatically.

'Fuck you Adam, I'm Leanne. Or do all skirts look the fucking same to you?' She stalked off, tutting.

He'd meant to find her to apologise, but it had slipped his mind. He thought he might go along to the drinks later that week, on Friday night, and try to act like less of a freak. It was as if the last few weeks had been a dream, and now he'd awoken to find he still resided in the same sordid nightmare. He had dared to think he deserved a second chance. A third chance perhaps, as he had let down both Megan and Olivia, without meaning to. He recalled his newly energised legs almost skipping down the street just weeks ago. He grimaced with shame as he imagined his stupid grin as he acknowledged strangers in the street and bored checkout girls with pathetic dad jokes.

Just when he thought he couldn't have any reserves of foolishness left, he scolded himself, sipping his water, accidentally swallowing a pip from the turgid piece of lime casually thrown in from a dirty saucer by the till. He coughed violently, and then again. A pat on the back startled him.

'Don't you go dying on me, mate!' Peter laughed, and then rearranged his face, ashen, as he saw Adam's eyes widen. No one joked about death around Adam anymore. It was rather a shock.

'I'm so sorry,' Peter began to stumble over his words.

'Stop.' Adam held up his hands, a visual gesture to negate the need to keep tiptoeing around him. 'You just took me by surprise. As you can see, I was busy choking.'

They both broke into wide, familiar smiles. The gap between them had erupted after Megan's death, tectonic plates leaving a grand canyon between them. Adam's apparent recovery and return to work had begun the shift that could bring them closer together albeit with a few hiccups along the way. It wasn't like before, but it seemed they may be close enough to build a bridge that wouldn't crumble under the weight of pain between them. Today, that bridge felt secure, and they automatically hugged and grappled and shook hands in such a fashion that a casual observer might think them masonic.

'What are you drinking there? Gin and tonic? What's got

281

into you?' Peter asked, one eye on the stern-looking barman, waving his suit-clad arms.

Adam was drinking sparkling water tonight, determined to keep a straight head. He didn't want to imagine where Olivia was, or see her where she wasn't. He certainly didn't want to entertain the notion that Olivia was writing notes to his girlfriend. A small corner of his mind was still quietly trying to find the fight within that would convince him that he had not completely lost his tenuous grip on that briefest period of happiness, but if he had, at the very least he was determined to keep it together. He would keep his pain private, his secrets hidden, and he would live at least what would appear from the outside to be a normal life.

The bar was sticky and smelt of stale beer. The music was too loud; generic old school heavy metal. Overweight men with greasy hair jostled for space at the bar. This was not Peter's usual style, and Adam was faintly irritated. Bad week, in fact, bad few weeks, and now perfectly polished off with an evening being jostled by poorly groomed, ageing rockers.

'Meeting on Wardour Street, some start-up I might invest in. There's some old pub, The Ship Inn, apparently it's no longer a grotty rock pub, but an actual Soho icon these days,' Peter had tried to convince him when he called to arrange.

Adam was not convinced. The barman sauntered over to Peter, eyeing his suit suspiciously. He flicked his long fringe out of his eyes and raised an eyebrow.

'I'm fine with water mate,' Adam said.

'Two pints of lager please,' instructed Peter, resolutely ignoring his old friend, as it began to dawn on him too that they really didn't fit in here.

'Go sit down in that corner — look, they're leaving.'

Peter elbowed Adam who shuffled off through the crowded bar to the corner by the toilet as Peter continued to brazen out his presence at the bar, surrounded by people who, to him, looked ridiculous, but in a strange twist of reality, clearly thought that it was he, in his new season Pal Zileri suit — which had set him back almost two thousand pounds — who looked odd.

Adam took his seat in the corner. The wooden chair was lopsided and the seat too small for any reasonably sized grown man. He could smell disinfectant each time the toilet door swung open, and if he breathed too deeply, something unpleasant tried to break through and find his nose. He yawned, quickly covering his mouth in case some invisible fume should slip inside. He hadn't slept well since Lucy's note. He was hugely relieved that she'd accepted his explanation, for what other explanation could he give?

He convinced himself it was nothing, he believed the note was a prank, a one-off, because she just couldn't be here — he had done everything he could to make sure of that. Yet, there was no denying that Olivia was back, even if only in his increasingly muddled mind, breaking through the pieces of his poorly stitched together broken heart. In his fitful dreams she spoke to him, promising she'd love him forever, and never leave.

Those words had once been woven of innocence and adoration, now they were sinister. Her reflection appeared next to his when he looked into a shop window with the glare of the sun glinting across it. She crept into his consciousness, popping up when a deadline loomed, distracting him, making him look incompetent. He chastised himself silently. His thoughts, his imagination making him *look* incompetent?

Surely that just means he is, in fact, currently incompetent, and would be until he got this under control.

He'd been avoiding Peter lately, along with most other people, other than Lucy, who he was beginning to think he should avoid because much more of his last minute cancellations, glazed eyes over dinner or sub-par bedroom performances and she'd soon start to tire of him. Sometimes, in his lower moments, he wondered if he really cared that much now. Perhaps the nasty little note was right. Maybe he'd be better off keeping his head down, plodding on alone. He'd be stoic, get into something solitary, such as stamp-collecting, or birdwatching.

His thoughts produced an involuntary snort: as if he'd have the attention span for something so uninteresting. In his youth he had thrived during the chase. Beguiling girls fascinated him. Megan had captured his youthful heart, and Olivia had stolen it, as she'd transformed slowly from a dead weight lump of a dribbling baby he couldn't understand, to a precious girl he adored. His job was hard, he'd liked that. He liked to win so solitary pursuits had never given him much satisfaction. He wished now he'd adopted a different temperament a long time ago.

Finally, Peter appeared at the table and sat down, rather clumsily, overestimating the sturdiness of the stool and the stability of the table. The drinks sloshed over the rims and they quickly grabbed already sodden, frayed cardboard beer mats to soak the spilled liquid from the scratched, sticky table between them.

'So,' Peter said, gravely, with a serious look in his friendly eyes. 'What's going on?' As Adam opened his mouth to speak, Peter raised his hand; a traffic warden of pointless excuses. 'Don't answer that. It's obvious. You're missing work, you never seem to leave your flat. Are you even still seeing that gorgeous young thing Louise?'

'Lucy,' Adam correctly, quietly.

'Well, I haven't even been honoured with an introduction yet!' Peter protested. 'What's happened this last month? Just as you took the job, met me for dinner all pleased with yourself. Frankly, you looked rather smug, if I'm brutally honest.'

'Please don't hold back.' Adam was forlorn, but a sulk had started to appear through his features.

Peter sipped his pint slowly, and replaced it on the torn beer mat, with precision, right in the centre, staring down intently. He inhaled, ready now, to say what needed to be said.

'You don't seem well, Adam. Perhaps it was too soon. You should take a break, better that than lose the job, altogether.'

At that Adam looked up. He thought he'd hidden his despair, and his confusion, better than that.

'You're pale, you've lost weight. Even your shirt is crumpled. You look old.'

'Fucking hell, Peter—'

Here came the stop sign hand, this time from Sergeant Peter, 'No Adam, mate, you know I love you. I loved Megan. What happened, to Megan, with Olivia...' Peter didn't know how to continue. He'd never been very good at hiding his feelings about Olivia, but now wasn't the time. That time might never come.

If only he knew how much he understood, thought Adam, reading his mind, but he couldn't find the words to share the sickening truth. He couldn't destroy the history they'd created. Better he was seen as a lost widower than the father of a monster, the man more guilty than anyone. So it continued to eat away at him: his decision to allow his wife to be branded weak, and his daughter lost to her own grief. A family torn apart. Everything was his fault, they'd think if they knew the truth. Or would they just think him pathetic? After all, what could they have expected of a man like Adam? A simple bloke, easily manipulated, average in every sense. Predictable. He'd thought he had it all, but he'd been the puppet on strings.

As Olivia had said the last time he'd talked to her, the death of Megan — wife, mother — should have brought them together, the last of the family, closely guarding one another to keep further tragedy at bay. But he didn't have it in him to forgive her, he hadn't even been able to look at her. Adam had spent days afterwards vomiting. During the following days, he thought about ending it all, but Megan's voice in his head had told him that now it was down to him to be the strong one. He'd listened to her, ironically, for the first time properly in a long time. If only he'd listened sooner, instead of believing her capable of such deception. As usual, she'd been right all along. He wished Megan had listened to him when he wanted to take their empty-nester status by the horns and start afresh, instead of allowing Olivia to be so dependent and clingy when it was her time to fly, and when their marriage depended on hard work and time alone.

'I'm still seeing Lucy, Peter, and I've been putting the hours in. There's not been a lot of time. I swear, all this,' he gestured to himself, 'all this is working too hard, not needing a bloody therapist.'

'Bollocks.'

Peter wasn't smiling anymore. His patience was thinning. Adam couldn't blame him. Through Peter's eyes, he could see he had clearly lost whatever slippery grip on himself he'd previously successfully pretended to have.

Since the showdown with Lucy, he'd felt dreadful. Olivia had infiltrated the dark nights, telling him it was his fault, he'd driven her to despair with his controlling behaviour, his false promises. She was a victim of vile emotional abuse on the part of both her parents. Didn't her diaries prove that? He was in denial. If they were childish fantasy, why destroy them? What was he afraid of? Confronting the truth, seeing what he'd done?

He'd toss and turn, sweat turning the sheets to yellow by morning, when she'd whisper to him that she forgave him anyway, as one day she hoped he'd forgive her. He'd wake with a start to an empty room, sunlight slithering through the cracks in the blind, and try to forget. He'd arrange dates with Lucy, then after a sleepless night and falling behind on work he'd cancel. She was becoming a little frosty, but true to the ridiculous note, her distance from him had brought with it an absence of any more threats.

'I'll book an appointment with a quack, okay? But you know I don't hold much faith in them these days?' Adam managed an upbeat smile, but his eyes gave him away.

Peter, however, was resolute, his voice deep and firm, 'Take voluntary time off, as of tomorrow, on medical grounds. That way they can't sack you. Well, not strictly true, they can do what they like, but HR will hold the vultures off for a few weeks, and if you go back and smash it, you may just get another chance. James is gunning for you. I stopped by last week for drinks. Jean Paul was doing a zombie impression of you. Wasn't very funny, to be honest, but we were quite well-oiled, and anyway, well, you get the picture. They're all working all the hours, making money, and you're coming in and then going home hardly noticed. So don't tell me you're putting the hours in, mate. There are guys half your age, expecting half the salary, champing on the bit for your job. You've got to earn it, and if you can't, you bloody well need to get out of the way so they can't build up any more of a case against you.'

It was relentless, Adam thought, this conveyor belt of chances that he was determined to fuck up.

Olivia

It came naturally to me to be invisible. I'm quiet, my features are plain. I took nothing of any great value from my parents' gene pool. I used to think I dressed in a striking manner, but the so-called friendly taunts, the theme tune of my life, come back to haunt me now. I'd never really grown out of being just another teenage loser, too ashamed of my body to clad it in my mother's couture style, opting for artist bohemian instead. Might as well have worn a sack. But he used to like my style, I hope he still does, because I'm past experimenting with new looks now.

Since my mother died and my father rejected me, time has at once stood still for me, while everything around me changes too quickly. I'm not used to the city, or the way that there seems to be no discernible difference between night and day. I used to like my routine. It's not such a full schedule these days. Waiting, watching. It's no life really, but it won't be forever.

Lucy hasn't been around much lately, which is at least one positive to report. Easily bored no doubt, and proving me right: I always knew she lacked dedication. Whatever else she offers up to him, I have the edge when it comes to commitment, and to loyalty. I imagine he's pushed her away, and she hasn't resisted much. Bit of a running theme with him really. First leaving Megan, then spurning me, and now Lucy. At least her lack of fight comes as no surprise. At times like these, some semblance of predictability can be hugely reassuring.

It's natural for me to be silent too, unheard, unseen, like all good little children. Perhaps that's why I took to art. The paper heard me, the paints saw me. I used to feel such fierce jealousy of Megan and how the spotlight followed her so faithfully. She was never unnoticed, unheard, or invisible. But then I learned something. If you're not talking, you're listening. If you're not seen, they talk more freely. In the end, they knew nothing about each other or about me. I knew it all. Still do. Invisible, silent, but very much present.

I'm getting closer to reconciliation every day, I can feel it, he can feel me. My father still loves me, I can tell by his haunted expression. He thinks of nothing else, no one else. Just like it used to be. He told Peter he blames himself, which I guess means he doesn't blame me anymore. Or not as much. I just knew he'd come around and realise that he and I did this together, for love. I spend a lot more time in his apartment now, looking at his things, leaving no trace. It will never be my home, but it's the closest thing I have to one since mine was hollowed out by flames, blackened by smoke.

He's there and that's what gives me a faint reminder of what it was like to have a home. Familiar clothes fill the wardrobes, and are draped over his bedroom chair. His brand of strawberry jam is sticky, and his cornflake box on the kitchen island is not properly sealed, which used to drive Megan mad. These small reminders of a life I loved give me something like, but not quite, happiness. But it isn't where we belong. When we are together again, we'll go somewhere else.

Earlier tonight, I was in my usual hiding place in his

large bedroom, the door to the spare wardrobe the only thing separating us. I expected him to fall into a restless sleep as soon as he'd eaten his dinner of toast, or omelette, or his most depressing new habit, a microwave meal for one, when he shocked me by striding with purpose towards my little den, in which I was imperceptible, and opening the wardrobe next to it. I was completely out of sight, I didn't breathe. He didn't see me. But I saw him. He looked smaller close up, but he was still big enough to reassure me that he was the one who would eventually remember that his job was to protect me. He quickly changed, and sprayed some aftershave on his wrists, ruffled his rapidly greying hair, and grabbed his keys and phone. I waited until the door shut behind him and I could hear the lift arrive to take him down to street level before I let myself out and followed him.

I've started to feel like his guardian angel. I patiently follow him, keeping him focussed on his future, warning off distractions. I feel powerful, but in a magnanimous way. A fairy godmother, or goddaughter. He heads to a part of town I'd never been to before and fittingly aligned with my positive outlook today, I persevere with the awful underground tunnels, the jostling people, the putrid smells, only allowing my anger to bubble up into my consciousness once or twice in the whole thirty-five minutes it takes to get to daylight once more. Not for long, because the sun is setting, and soon I find myself in a pub last decorated before I was born, hiding in a corner, watching him, waiting once again. I wish so badly he was waiting for me.

When Peter arrives my heart sinks. Still has his talons in, still pulling his strings, turning him against me. Is it any wonder I had to take drastic action to keep Adam? When everywhere I turned, people who should have been there to protect me tried to poison him against me, leaving me to fester alone. I only catch brief snippets, but Peter definitely tries to stick the knife in. I heard my name, and that can never be a good sound coming from Peter's lips. I'm happy when Adam looks angry, and combatant. He is defending me, I presume. He's angry about how things turned out, but he's still my dad. He won't take that shit from that ageing, portly buffoon with the skinny-fitting trousers. Peter suggested boarding school once. Thought I needed socialising, like a fucking puppy.

After what seems like a lifetime, I follow him as he leaves the grubby-looking pub, which I now understand from fragments of drunken conversations and kooky signs above windows, is in Soho. It's late, and the streets are crowded with people drinking and laughing. Some bars sell more than alcohol to relax the local men in suits and entertain gangs of lads on stags. It disgusts me, as I pick my way through the debris thrown carelessly to the floor, forgotten already, like most of their sordid night time experiences will be by morning.

Peter hails a black cab immediately, but Adam walks on. He lives miles from here, but he's walking away from the tube that deposited him into this small corner of hell and his arms are dormant by his side, not protruding at the road. Until he waves Peter off, and with him out of sight reaches for his phone.

It's too noisy, I can't hear him but I already know that something Peter has said has prompted him to find his Lucy, and try even harder to forget me. I've always hated Peter. He leads me all the way down, down, into a square, and then beyond, a cocktail bar called Mabel's. Strikes me as a pretty stupid name for a bar. And there she was, all legs and hair, though no hair on her legs. That was all just flowing over her bony, brown shoulders. She looked like she belonged on the top shelf of some dated newsagents in Yorkshire. Adam didn't agree. He held her and I wanted to cry; I miss those arms.

I didn't go in, and they didn't stay for long. I can't bear to think about the way he was touching her as they left. Has she no pride? He pretty much ditched her for days and now he's allowed free reign. I believe in taking control. When Adam and I reconcile, he will forgive me, and I him, and our future will be on my terms, just as our past was, when life was good, before I'd been forced to follow him to London instead of being taken to our capital by him, as a treat. Before I'd met any posh, bike-riding eco-warriors. Long before my own father abandoned me, selfishly looking for redemption that doesn't belong to him.

The streets were dark and quiet, so I heard him demand his fare to Canary Wharf, as she stepped into the back of the cab, he not far behind her. Perhaps in a different life I could muster some happiness for them, after all they both regularly display a level of fickleness I haven't seen in many other people. Perfect match in another world, maybe. He leaves Megan, then me, and Lucy forgets all about poor William the cat whenever he clicks his fingers. The wretched feline and I have something in common too then. Perhaps while Daddy-Dearest and his sequinned whore enjoy their evening, Wills and I should get more acquainted.

Adam

It was six p.m. on a grey, drizzly afternoon, and Adam was in his pyjamas bursting tiny balloons on his phone gaining unfeasibly large numbers of points as he scaled up through the levels like King Kong on the Empire State. It was a mindless game and he was very good at it. He'd been on leave for four days now, and thanks to those speedy little mopeds carrying delivery drivers and their spoils, he'd only had to leave his apartment twice since he and Lucy had arrived back after their short but entirely successful date last Thursday night.

He didn't know if somehow Peter's brutal pep talk had, against the odds, made him feel better, or if it was eight pints of lager they'd shared, but the broken coil of that fleeting spring in his step seemed to have hope of repair that evening, as he strolled towards his forgiving girlfriend at far too late an hour to earn him any real brownie points. Lucy had accepted his apology for his distance, his grumpiness, and his lack of explanation. Adam was grateful, and in awe of her ability to live so firmly in the present moment, refusing to let the past of even a week or two ago interfere with her positive mindset.

'Happiness is a choice, old man,' she'd jokingly told him, perhaps with the slightest hint of an edge, a suggestion to tear a leaf from her neat little book of life.

He'd kissed her in the late-night bar, and felt surges of

horniness he hadn't managed to summon since the nightmares and the note had started to haunt him. He'd allowed his hands to wander, and it was only when he noticed the look the barman was giving him that he'd seen himself once again from the outside in: a middle-aged man groping a beautiful girl in a club. Where was his wife, his family, they were probably all thinking? Before melancholy, self-awareness and self-loathing could worm their way back to the forefront of his mind, he'd growled into her ear that he needed to take her home, and Adam had been surprised to find that she was happy to be taken. He hadn't stopped kissing her the whole way home, even as she texted someone asking them to feed her cat. Tangled within his sheets, worries temporarily forgotten, it suddenly hadn't felt so impossible to live in the moment.

When she left him the following morning, he promised to call later that week. She waved goodbye as if she didn't care. Perhaps she didn't, Adam had thought, which was for the best really. Or she could be playing the 'I don't care game' to make him want her more. He hoped not. Currently he wasn't capable of mustering any more enthusiasm or desire than that which she had already borne witness to. If she was hoping for more, it was premature, yet, even now in the midst of his constant mood-swings, confusion and turmoil, he wanted to believe the day would come when he might have more to give.

He'd waited until Lucy had shut the door behind her to call his GP. Miraculously he'd got through straight away and managed to get a same day appointment, one reserved for emergencies. He'd felt a little bad, but it was this act of taking control that could save his job. His GP had been fairly unsympathetic to Adam's toned-down account of the symptoms that required a sick note, but efficient nonetheless. Dead wife, grieving process, nightmares, insomnia, guilt over failing his daughter; he may as well have said 'blah blah blah'. The sick note was printed and signed within his maximum of seven minutes' clinic time, and was agreed with HR by ten thirty. By noon, Adam had tidied up loose ends, and was walking out of the office door.

Peter was pleased he'd listened, and texted him Friday afternoon to tell him he was proud of his brave decision. Lucy was content that he still wanted her, and that they still had something worth pursuing, and seemed a little excited by what she viewed as his complexity. As she said, her previous boyfriends didn't come with much baggage. He was a challenge, and Lucy loved a challenge. The GP had ticked off another task in human form and was one step closer to his monthly target. Adam was in the system and should be invited to meet a psychotherapist in the near future. He'd promised Peter he would, and he would indeed, so long as he could work a few things out for himself by then.

He wouldn't allow himself to be dragged into some confessional in his exhausted and emotional state of mind, which was desperate to confide. A stranger bound by confidentiality might be too hard to resist. Adam didn't dare google it, but he suspected his whole story may be exempt for any good doctor's ethical handbook and the truth would be out, and they'd know what he'd done, what he'd created, and forever the small mercy of Megan's memory, and of a tragic but not monstrous family, would be replaced by sensationalist scandal. The dirty, nasty truth of failure, deceit and warped, sick minds. They all looked so normal, people would say, but you never know what goes on behind closed doors.

He'd promised he would never reveal the truth, and he wouldn't. It no longer mattered who had run Megan's last bath as in the end he was guiltier than anyone. He wouldn't give up his daughter's name, and for that reason, he couldn't correct Megan's damaged one. Adam believed she would have understood, and that she would have done the same. They'd both loved Olivia too much to condemn her to a life in prison. She'd never have survived it; it would have been torture for her.

Now, almost a working week into his leave, he still hadn't called Lucy. He made a mental note every morning to and then put it off. What would he tell her? More lies? He had, however, flushed antidepressants down the toilet, and resolved to put off any psychiatry appointments offered via his GP's obligatory referral letter until he was well enough to handle himself properly within them and that required being able to forgive himself, and forget Olivia. He knew he must also try to forget Megan, for memories of her were now forever tied to the secret he needed to erase from his mind. Despite Peter remaining ill-informed, his familiar perception and gut instinct had reminded Adam of that long-lost feeling of being, if only a little, understood by another human being. He'd craved more of that and sought it in Lucy. Temporary ecstasy, ephemeral relief.

And so, at six p.m. on that quiet, damp afternoon, Adam was working hard on thinking about nothing, in the hope of training his mind to fog over without ceasing to function altogether. He was simultaneously winning at the balloon bursting game and considering which takeaway to order in later. Multitasking and proud of it. Soon, he promised himself, he'd feel confident enough to spend another evening with Lucy, reasonably sure that he wouldn't drift off into his own world, see his daughter's illusion in the shadows, or forget how to connect, both mentally or physically. Lucy had been patient so far, but she had her limitations. It was one thing being party to someone else's tragedy; the brooding banker with issues in some lights could look almost appealing. It was quite another to feel undesirable in bed, as he rolled off back onto his back, apologising and weakly admitting to having a lot on his mind. So he focussed on not having anything on his mind, not even what clothes to wear, as pyjamas were sufficient for his current daily schedule.

The intercom loudly interrupted the silence. Adam jumped slightly. Peering through the screen next to his door was Leanne, who out of the context of their shared office, or mid-cackle in the bar across from it, looked younger than he'd previously noticed. Or perhaps he was just getting old. He pressed the green button, and said hello, except for it came out as a hoarse, unintelligible grunt. Adam realised he hadn't used his voice in a couple of days, and now he came to think of it hadn't drank much water either. His throat was suddenly so dry it hurt. He cleared it anyway.

'Leanne, hi, what are you doing here?' He imagined her having come to taunt him, steal his job, or perhaps as a messenger carrying his P45. All far-fetched, but his mind had had plenty of rest and his imagination was on top form.

'Let me in, dickhead, I've come straight from work and I haven't got all day.' She no longer looked or sounded young. That hard-edge veneer, her armour, would see her fight her way to the top, Adam had no doubt.

He pressed enter and the door buzzed and she disappeared from his screen. He stayed by the door, eagerly listening for the tell-tale sound of the lift doors opening, and as they did, he swung the door open to greet his colleague.

'Fucking hell, so they weren't exaggerating then? You really have gone off the fucking rails.' Leanne was appraising him, not bothering to disguise her disgust.

Adam looked down to try and see himself through her eyes. He'd forgotten about his pyjamas in his shock at seeing her on his doorstep. Leanne brushed past him and found her own way into the open-plan living area. She passed him an envelope. Maybe his premonition wasn't as far-fetched as he'd thought.

'What's this?' he asked, feigning nonchalance. She looked at him as if he was stupid.

'A card, saying *Get Well Soon Pussy*,' she cackled. He actually quite liked her cackle. 'I don't know why I bothered really, seeing as you can't even be bothered to remember my name, and you're a mental fuck, but hey, guess I was in the mood to do a good deed.'

Adam took the card gingerly, realising that it should come as no surprise to him that in this moment he felt wrong-footed, baffled, and confused. That was the status quo for him nowadays, yet, he couldn't quite shake the emotion threatening to reveal his weakened state away. He willed himself not to cry.

'Thank you,' he managed, quietly, and as he opened it he saw indeed it did say *Get Well Soon Pussy*, with pussy written crudely by hand in black marker pen on the otherwise rather traditional floral design. An involuntary laugh escaped him, and he started to cry.

'Jesus, I'm sorry,' he uttered, inadvertently wiping snot onto his dressing gown sleeve. As he rolled it up to hide the smear, he noticed an egg stain on the underside. Leanne, the renowned ice queen, embraced him tenderly, quelling her urge to make a snide comment about the egg, which she had noticed.

'You're alright Adam, but you seem to be a mess. Do you want to talk about it?' It was disconcerting, and not only for Adam.

'Most definitely not.' Adam straightened himself. 'You probably heard some of it, but I had a family tragedy last year, and I probably didn't deal with it properly. I'm taking a couple of weeks to sort my head out, and then I'm moving forward. No more dwelling in the past. This isn't who I am.'

Leanne smiled at him, 'I know.' She paused, about to say something, then started to turn back towards the door. 'Got to run, Ads. See you in a couple of weeks. Let's see if you can handle your drink better next time too, eh?' She left without saying goodbye but called over her shoulder as the door started to slowly close behind her: 'And get dressed, for fuck's sake.'

She'd only been gone ten minutes when he texted her thanking her for popping by. A beep responded within seconds:

Let's have a drink soon, and I'll fill you in on all the office drama. Dave still hasn't managed to shag anyone, by the way.

The following day, Adam woke up smiling, and luxuriated in the fragments left over from his pleasant dream.

Lucy and he had been lying in bed. She was laughing at nothing in particular, before she gently morphed into Leanne. The dream was uneventful, with the faces of the two women who had occupied his clinical space for one with him merging, smiling, and captivating him. He woke up smiling and clinging on to the rapidly fading memory not ready to open his eyes and accept reality.

Slowly, he lifted his lids and allowed the room to sharpen into focus. The sharp edges of the room looked blunted, smoothed, and it seemed the knots in his stomach had loosened. He opened the blinds to see blue skies and sunshine, a welcome change from yesterday. Adam hadn't really expected his fairly unimaginative and certainly unscientific approach to curing himself to work yet, somehow, could it be that the old-fashioned much-mocked mind over matter method had worked? Perhaps he didn't need to talk about it, and digest mind-numbing medications. He simply needed to take some time and focus entirely on nothing.

In the months following Megan's death and Olivia's devastating confession, his silence on the matter externally had beat continuously in his head. Yet, he reminded himself, over time he had begun to learn to mute the internal accusing voices. He'd started to say hello to shop assistants, he'd stopped refusing Peter's invitations, and he'd found a flat. His selective memory loss had been so effective he'd even joined a dating app, met lovely Lucy, and somehow managed to convince both Peter and his new boss that he was fit for work.

Now, he realised, he'd become complacent. He was functioning so well because he was working on pretending to feel normal every single day. He pretended so hard and achieved such remarkable results he'd fooled himself along with everyone else. He'd lost focus and started to live as if he was a person with a normal life. That was his biggest mistake: he lost sight of the fact that he had to actively forget every second of every day. When he forgot to forget, she came back, haunting his sleepless nights, taunting him for daring to think he could never be happy without her. Happy might be too far a stretch, but he could, with a bit of effort, achieve some level of fine. These past few days proved that; not once had she entered his dreams. With renewed focus he had reconquered his demons, and this time he intended to keep them at bay for good.

Adam got dressed and called Lucy. She was distracted, but not unhappy to hear from him. He invited her over after work but she insisted she had to go straight home. She explained her cat still hadn't been home since the last time she'd stayed over with him, and she was worried sick. She and her flatmates were trying to keep the flat occupied at all times, in the hope that he would come back and if he was injured or scared that someone would be there for him. Later, Adam reluctantly left his flat and headed to Lucy's, at once mildly irritated at the excessive reaction to a missing cat — after all cats are independent — yet at the same time, realising the opportunity was there for him to make an effort, get out of his flat, and potentially redeem himself in the eyes of the judgemental flatmates.

Lucy collapsed into his arms when he arrived and, taken aback, he realised he couldn't recall the last time he had been required to comfort someone else. She was truly distraught about the missing cat, and while Adam couldn't understand such heightened emotion over a pet, he was content to offer a shoulder to cry on. They ordered a pizza, and he made countless cups of tea as they speculated over the whereabouts of the elusive feline.

'Probably some old lady buys a better brand of cat food than you, he'll be back for cuddles soon though. I know I would be.' He raised a smile from her, and as he stroked her hair on the sofa, he'd bent his head over hers and kissed her open mouth. She hesitated a moment before kissing him back. Adam pulled away, he didn't want to give the impression he only ever called her for one reason. 'You should get some sleep and I should leave you to it.'

'Thanks for coming over and hanging out,' she said.

He knew he was right to leave, and show her that this wasn't just about the sex, but that he could be a good friend to someone too. It mattered to him as well. He understood, with sadness, that since that fateful night he'd either been fixated on his loss, or concentrating on his need to forget his loss. Either way, it had all been about him. Even his relationship with Lucy had been ticking off a necessary task to enable Adam to prove to himself that he was moving on.

He'd left Lucy's place late enough in the evening to risk taking the bus home. There was something charming about viewing London's twinkling bustle from the top deck, long after the stench of disenchanted commuters had dissipated. Lucy's flatmate, Tom, had cheerily waved him off from the hallway. Adam couldn't be certain that Tom's intentions towards Lucy, and his corresponding protective nature, were entirely pure, but at least tonight he'd not given the jumped-up twerp any reason to bad-mouth him to her.

It was dark when he arrived back in Canary Wharf, past

eleven, but the muggy evening combined with the Friday feeling of abandonment in the banking world had kept beer gardens full to the brim. Large half-empty glasses of wine were being sloshed and spilled as young women with slightly smeared make-up talked too loudly to men with crumpled shirts hanging out who responded oafishly. Adam smiled to himself. Those days might be gone for him, but it was good to feel a jab of nostalgia for a simple time, when hitting a target and then getting purposefully pissed were his main goals on a Friday night too. He walked past another bar, standing room only for the smokers, and idly gazed at the crowds. All happy, all drunk.

'Oi! Watch it!' A stern, slightly slurred female voice berated him as he turned to see who he'd walked into, failing to pay attention on the pavement ahead.

'Oh, I'm sorry,' he started to say, and then paused. 'Leanne!'

She focused her eyes on him and took a moment to adjust. Her pupils were dilated and she seemed unsteady on her feet.

'Well, well, Adam's out and about. Care in the community, is it? Coming for a drink?'

'On my way home, actually, and I'm avoiding booze. Where are you headed?'

Leanne pulled a comical face, sticking out her bottom lip and pretending to wipe away tears, 'Boo hoo you're sooooooooo boooooooooooring!' She sang it over and over, 'Boring, boring, boring!' while she did a strange little drunken jog around him, prodding him, annoyingly, again and again.

'Shall I get you to the taxi rank?' Adam interrupted.

'Boring, boring, boring!' She repeated, and then she fell over.

'Oh Leanne! Shit! Are you ok?' Adam pulled her up but she was still very unsteady, and so he kept hold of her arms, keeping eye contact, trying to help her refocus and rebalance.

Her balance did not return and it took Adam a moment to realise that she was now standing on one tiptoe, her other leg coyly kicked out as she lunged forward, unable to master the move she intended, and yet somehow her lips found their target and she kissed him forcefully, catching him off guard, and for just a moment it felt so good, that he opened his mouth and found her small wet tongue.

Olivia

William and I weren't really surprised to see him kiss a drunk girl on his way back from Lucy's. It has already transpired that loyalty isn't his strongest attribute. I guess I got mine from my mother. I'm fiercely loyal: to him, and now to William, my new cat. Having been alone for so long, ignored, the invisible girl, it was an emotional moment when I called to William and he looked straight at me. He's never left my side. Fickle little thing. Let's hope it's as easy to take my father back from Lucy's clutches as it was her daft old kitty.

I've missed being close to him. The cat can't be trusted yet, so I've had to stay with him pretty much full time, which means I've been on the outside of his walls all week, instead of in my usual hideout, not that I could sneak in when he never leaves. It's dreadful timing as because he's hardly left the apartment block at all, I've been pretty bored. In fact, I'm starting to get bored of my new pet. I guess I only have enough loyalty in me for my old dad after all.

William has a tag with a mobile number on it. Lucy's, of course. I find her on WhatsApp: last online ten minutes ago. I ping her the compromising video from a phone I stole from a drunk banker. From this angle the whole thing looked pretty steamy. I cropped the end where he pulled away, crestfallen. He never ceases to be amazed at how easy he finds it to make mistakes around women. You'd think he'd learn. At the very least he might learn not to be surprised. The video prepares and sends and seconds later, it is received. Two ticks. I quickly send a follow up.

I told you that you'd get hurt.

William and I walk back at the same slow pace as my father, across the road from him. He doesn't spot the missing cat, he probably wouldn't recognise it if he did. Paying attention, it transpires, is not a particular strength either, though that can be an advantage, for me at least. My feelings are torn about this latest development. Drunk girl saves me a job: Lucy will wash her hands of him, and I won't need to kill her stupid cat to show her that I'm serious about people getting hurt. But, if Lucy ditches him, he might hook up with drunk girl.

My window of opportunity seems small. I need him, alone, focussed on me, in order to win him back. He's getting too good at pretending I never existed. Peter mentions my name in their chats more than he does, and then he just quickly dismisses me and changes the subject. Girlfriends, jobs… these things help him forget me, allow him to ignore me. It seems as soon as I extract him from one distraction, he finds another. I'm afraid of my next step, but I can't leave it much longer. I must face him, and he must face me before I'm no longer even a distant memory.

William is trotting along happily next to me. Cats are known for being sneaky. It's possible he could make it into the apartment unseen, as I do, but I daren't risk it. As I cross the busy carriageway towards the river, nearing my father's apartment, a few footsteps behind him, I scare off William. He tries to follow again, making it to the centre island of the road. Standing there alone, he looks so small, I almost feel sorry for him. Cars and trucks whizz by and he cowers. I consider calling him to me again but change my mind. He should have stayed with Lucy, he should have been loyal. He might be miserable now, but at least he's alive. I don't turn back as I cross the second road, and follow my father into his home.

Dad doesn't turn the light on at first, heading straight to the toilet. I find my place in the corner of the room, knowing he'll sit in his usual place, where his line of sight will not cross me. When he returns to the main living room, the sounds of the flush rolls through the open bathroom door. He puts on a lamp and pours a brandy but doesn't look at me. As I suspected, his eyes bore straight out to the view beyond the large windows. So much for his vow not to drink. He looks sad. I watch in silence. The glare of streetlights and light pollution creates slithers of light dancing with shadows as he moves across the room and places the bottle on the coffee table, before sitting and sipping from his glass.

He doesn't notice me so I bide my time. I can't speak. Not yet. The stakes are too high. Besides, I'm used to waiting, and I can't rush this. He has to be ready to take me back and to forgive. When he realises how quickly he is forgotten by the other people in his life. Written off as a nut job by Peter, dumped by Lucy over a misunderstanding, estranged from everyone else he can't face. Soon, surely, he must see that it's just the two of us. It always was. His phone flashes and vibrates, illuminating the side of his face. He'd missed a bit of stubble in his rush to pretend to be a normal functioning man earlier tonight. He seems to read the screen for the longest time.

'Shit, what the–' he mutters, he stands, and he sits down again. I expect that was Lucy. He clumsily fingers his screen for ages. He's too poorly illuminated for me to see but I sense he's shaking.

That moment when you're caught makes your stomach flip, doesn't it? All we can hope for is for someone to understand why we did what we did, and that we didn't mean to hurt them. I'd say I hope she's more forgiving to him than he was to me, but I'd be lying. It's time he saw everyone else for what they are, as I always have. They're not like us and they don't feel as deeply as me. They offer nothing, not one of them. Mother and her hateful clique, Bea, Antonia and Elizabeth, the ever-present Peter who clung onto our family because he couldn't be bothered to make one of his own. *Luce*, and the drunken workmates he thinks offer him a new start. Vacuous and superficial, instagramming their smoking cocktails and yoga mats, and talking around in circles about their unremarkable lives.

My father isn't special to them, he's just a piece of periphery jigsaw to help complete the picture they think their lives should be. The handsome boyfriend who can pay for dinner, and maybe a mini-break down the line. The oldest friend to keep you company whilst you drink your expensive wine so that you look distinguished not desperate. The colleague you can tease or flirt with. Banter, as they say. It's all so meaningless. To me, he is everything. He promised me he'd never leave me, but he did. I promised I'd always love him, and I will.

My mother once said that sometimes people don't know what is good for them. I think the patronising cow was actually talking about me, as if I wouldn't notice. I suppose she was right in theory, though. My father has been left alone to his own rubbish choices for too long, and look at him now. About to get sacked, about to get dumped, living alone in a soulless shell, as miserable as I've ever seen him. We used to laugh so hard it hurt. I miss him, even though he's sat not twenty feet away.

He finally stops fiddling with his phone, the screen is still bright, creating strange contortions of his face, so that he doesn't look like my father any more. He's reading the screen again, and then he's tapping away again. Finally, he stands and puts the phone to his ear. But I guess she doesn't answer as he doesn't speak. He looks at it again, presses again, and the phone is back to his ear. Again, he doesn't speak but a long sigh escapes him. I want to roll my eyes dramatically at him, like I used to, as he repeats the futile exercise for a third time. This time, however, he does speak.

'Lucy, please call me back, or at least pick up next time. I know it's late, but I promise you I can explain. I don't know who sent that to you or why, but it's not what it looks like. Jesus, I sound like a fucking cliché. I... I'm sorry. She took me by surprise. She was drunk, I was trying to help her. I pushed her away, I put her in a taxi. I promise. Please, can we just talk?'

He sinks back into his chair and knocks back the brandy in his glass in one gulp before immediately refilling it almost to the top. He glances at his phone. It's no longer illuminated though he holds it and stares at it obsessively, giving the impression he plans to watch it all night until a flash and a vibration offer him atonement. A watched phone never beeps though. Social cues aren't my forte, but even I know this is the end for the happy couple's new romance. My father is full

310

of drunken hope, oblivious to the repercussions he will inevitably face. Luckily, he'll still have me.

I don't move, I don't make a sound, even in the emptiest of silences, like this one here tonight, he can't even hear my breath escape my body. I hear his though, it's slow and heavy, punctuated with a gulp every few seconds, a small thud as the glass hits the table, the tinkle of the next pour, a final thud to end the routine as the bottle is replaced, and the cork pushed in. I feel bold, to sit so close before he falls asleep, but I have nothing to fear, he is blind to me. That used to make me feel sad but tonight I feel in control, and optimistic.

We sit in silence for hours. For him it seems comfortable. I thought he might at least sense my presence, a bit like when you feel someone looking at you. A sixth sense burns our skin and tells us to turn around and catch the stare before its owner has a chance to whip it away and hide it beneath feigned interest in something else. I imagine him walking towards me, seeing me, opening his arms, yet he doesn't move, except to bring the glass back to his lips again, and again.

I don't drink, never have. Well, you see what it does to people. I don't care about the physical impact on the human body but instead the way it reduces people to their most dreadful selves and the way that a person can be completely condemned because they drink is an intolerable idea to me. My mother's doctor assumed so much because she liked a few glasses of wine. Your testimony is worth less after half a bottle of plonk. What's it worth after a bottle of brandy? I wouldn't know, but as he stands, I can see tonight isn't the night for a sensible conversation. He wobbles, spills the dregs of his glass onto the floor, but doesn't notice. That will be sticky by the morning.

'Ah! Fuck!' His voice was tinged with pain and he was reeling back from the kitchen island, as if it had purposefully attacked him. That corner looks sharp, I imagine it will bruise his hip. He should have turned the lights on instead of sitting in the semi-dark, being all melodramatic. The early morning light had started to creep down from the sky, but the flat was still cloaked in shadow, and regardless, his vision didn't appear to improve. I hear him bumping into walls, accidentally slamming doors, and knocking God knows what off their surface homes, before I finally hear nothing. I wait a while longer to hear something, anything, until I don't and I'm certain he's asleep, and then I wait some more. I can't confront him tonight, not in this state, but I can leave him a message.

I used to write notes for him. I'd hide them in his suit jacket. But he doesn't wear a suit jacket these days, and frankly I want him to find this note before he leaves his flat tomorrow. I don't want him to leave at all really. I always liked it when we could stay home, just us. Out there, in the world, I used to always feel so self-conscious, so conspicuous. I never fitted anywhere expect for in his arms, or in their kitchen. Now, I no longer feel self-conscious out there, or conspicuous.

Everyone in this city is a stranger, to me and to one another. It's not weird to be the odd one that no one notices in London. Everyone is equally anonymous, and equally unimportant. It's a sad, lonely city for anyone but tourists, and I don't know why he came here. He was never one of the invisible people. Perhaps he wished he had been now. It's all very well being observed when your captive audience is clapping. It's less fun when they start to boo. At that point, you'd wish the curtains would close around you and they'd all get bored and turn away forgetting you were ever there.

He tosses and turns, and talks in his sleep, the deepest, alcohol-induced coma passing. Then he'll dream, but in his dreams, unlike a happy puppy chasing squirrels, he is the prey, and I'm getting closer. He mutters something over and over, and with rage I realise he's calling her name. Guiltily dreaming of Lucy. Not of me, and not of his poor dead wife, the one he must realise could have lived if he'd done his job properly.

His job was to love us both, and to protect me from her jealousy, stop her from casting me out. But he didn't, he let her toss me aside, he allowed her and her friends to bully me, and then he left us both all too easily, only to come back and make his final choice: her, not me. He refused to see her for what she was, and he left me with no choice, and frankly I get angrier as he dreams of Lucy and forgets that he has far more important regrets to feel guilty about. It's unbelievable really, how easy it is for him to concentrate his energy, even in his subconscious, on some minor dating misfortune instead of the real tragedy of his life.

I write the note on the full-length mirror. I use Lucy's lipstick; she'd left it one time and I'd taken it. I don't wear lipstick, so old-fashioned. I really thought Lucy would have known that. She was probably trying to look more like the sort of woman she imagined her older lover should be with. How could she not realise that he was looking for someone far less daunting, and that her attraction lay precisely in her lack of sophistication? Not that it matters now, because predictably, Lucy thinks that a kiss is everything. Fairy-tale perspectives, typical of people like her.

I write the note, and my words are few, and not as kind as I'd originally intended. Maybe, I think, in the morning he'll remember what really matters. And although I forgive him, if he's going to feel guilty about something, it should be about what he made me do to Mum, and what he did to me. Just before I leave his room, I can't help myself. I'm already feeling bad about the note, and I don't want him to be too upset, so I crouch down, and I whisper in his ear, my face just inches from his own.

'Daddy, I forgive you, I love you, don't be sad.'

His eyes open with a start and he stares straight at me. Before he can gather his senses, I get the hell out of there. I wander the streets for a while. William didn't make it across the road, but he has made a mess of it. Someone has moved him to the pavement. They most likely got his blood on their hands. Fortunately, I didn't.

Adam

Adam's eyes were crusty with sleep and his head was banging. He didn't open them. He longed to sleep again. He turned onto his side and his stomach lurched, his heart was racing. Bile tickled his throat and he coughed a deep gagging, grisly bark. Swallowing the phlegmy mucus, he lay perfectly still and tried to slow the beating palpitations thumping through his chest. Only a few seconds passed before his body came alive and propelled him upwards, his feet landing on the floor with a crash.

He ran to the en suite and vomited a burning liquid that tasted like brandy. Groaning, he wretched again and again, knelt on the floor, clutching the splattered bowl with white, shaking hands. He pushed himself up, a staggered to the sink, where he splashed cold water on his face and stared at his reflection. As he came into focus, he saw his bloodshot eyes, encased by pale, puffy skin dappled with yellow dry flakes. The taste of brandy was still on his tongue and memories of last night started to surface, drawing horror onto his face.

Olivia. It was as if she'd been here. He'd had nightmares like this before, but she'd never seemed so real. He shouldn't have drunk all that brandy. He couldn't handle it right now, the stress was too much. Adam felt an urgent need to speak to Lucy. He wondered if she'd heard his message, if she'd replied, or tried to ring. He had no idea what time it was, although the sun was pretty high. The bedroom blinds were still open, forgotten about in his drunken stupor.

His jeans were crumpled in a heap next to the washing basket on the bathroom floor, he was still wearing his shirt and boxers. The phone was on the floor, half concealed by the jeans from which it fell. Picking it up, Adam gasped, as a shard of glass cut his finger. The screen was smashed, and the blood trickled gently, but continuously. Adam tore of some toilet paper and haphazardly tried to stem the flow from his index finger. The cut was deeper than he'd first thought, and the blood soaked through the paper in seconds. He grabbed more paper, throwing the disintegrating red piece to the toilet and missing. He bent to retrieve it and his blood dripped onto the floor. It stained last night's creased, slept-in shirt as he attempted a more successful bandage. Adam didn't own a first aid kit. He needed to go to the pharmacy.

He carefully unlocked his phone to check for messages. The screen was badly fractured, and every swipe dislodged another fine piece of the glass puzzle. Still, he could see there were no messages, no missed calls. He'd get dressed, go to the pharmacy, eat something, drink some coffee, and then with a clear head, he'd call Lucy. He re-entered his bedroom, and walked towards the wardrobe. Out of the corner of his eye, the mirror winked at him. Something was wrong. He turned to face it. Smeared in a deep blood red were nine angry words over three lines, each line messier and larger, and harder to decipher than the next.

You killed her.
You killed her.
You killed her.

What had he done? The room spun and the light pierced his eyes turning everything a bright and painful white. He fell back onto the bed, then in a panic sat up again and looked again. The damning hateful words still there, accusing him. His own words? He remembered little of last night. Is this what it had come to? He looked away, disgusted with himself. What kind of behaviour was this? Writing self-loathing messages on his mirror in lipstick. Who's lipstick anyway? This wasn't the behaviour of a middle-aged man. This was the behaviour of an immature girl.

Olivia.

Was it so impossible that she had come back, found him, and let herself in? He saw her, didn't he? Just a dream, he's assumed. Adam had been sure that he'd made certain she couldn't follow him here. He thought it was over and that she had gone for good, but it wasn't over and she wasn't gone for good. It suddenly became clear that his nightmare hadn't ended; it was only just beginning. The words she'd whispered in his dream came back to him. She forgave him. She was back, she was here, and she forgave him.

Was she still here, Adam wondered, his breath quickening, panic rising up through his stomach, his chest, swirling around in his head, making it impossible to find a single thought that made any sense at all. What did she want? She forgives me, he thought. But he couldn't see her in his mind. Those once innocent brown eyes, her unkempt hair, her beaming smile when he gave her his full attention. All he could see now was Megan, in a bath full of blood, her blue skin stretched over her skeleton. Adam ran back into the bathroom and pulled on his jeans, he needed to breathe fresh air.

He stumbled out of his flat, not registering the ride down in the lift, and found himself on the pavement, sun shining straight above. He checked his watch, finally: eleven forty-five. He never slept this late. Mind you he had no idea what time he'd finally stumbled into bed. Adam didn't know where he was going but placing one foot in front of the other was soothing. There were people on the streets. Normal people. Some shopping, carrying paper bags with tissue paper poking out of the top, some carrying gym bags, wearing stylish leggings and expensive trainers. Normal people living normal lives, not walking the streets afraid to be in their own home, in fear of the return of their psychopathic offspring.

As Adam walked with no firm idea of where he was heading, ideas tumbling across his mind, bumping into each other. He bumped into an old woman, who stepped back, eyes wide at his appearance. He'd forgotten to take the stained shirt off, he dared a quick smell. Brandy, body odour. He needed to get off the streets before someone he knew saw him. He walked until he found himself at the wrong end of Westferry Road, down near some old boozers in which he doubted his appearance would seem so out of place. Sat on an old ripped bar stool, Adam sipped his coke, and carefully took his phone from his pocket. The barman, shuffled over with a slight limp, and collected the empty tumbler.

'Another brandy?' he asked, casually.

'Er, no. Yes, actually, yes. Please.' Adam didn't want another brandy, but he thought he needed one.

'Bad day?' The barman asked.

Adam noticed he had a neck tattoo, but his kind eyes seemed genuine. Still, probably not quite ready to hear his sorry tale, Adam thought, whatever else he must have born witness too in this place over the years.

'Yeah, just personal stuff.' Before he could elaborate his phone lit up. In his haste to open the message, he cut his thumb. 'Damn it!' he cursed, wiping the shallow cut on his jeans. This time, the blood didn't flow though it left its mark on the expensive denim, and across the tip of his thumb, finding its way to the palm of his hand before giving up. It was a text from Lucy.

> *Stop calling me. Don't contact me again. This has all got too weird. In case you care, someone found William last night. He's dead. And your friend texted me again telling me she took William. So that note, the threats, they were all real, and you knew but you let her target me anyway. Well, the psycho bitch is welcome to you. I hope you're very happy together. Now fuck off and die.*

Adam froze. Olivia. How could she? If the writing wasn't quite literally on the wall, would he think Leanne had set him up? That she was the psycho prankster? She couldn't have known he'd be there. She had been drunk. Until today any explanation would have seemed more feasible than Olivia being back. Yet again, he thought, he'd underestimated her. He smiled as the next wave of dizziness passed and he allowed himself the luxury of just accepting the crazy situation. Olivia had come back, she had found him, and she had killed his girlfriend's cat, broken into his home, and fuck knows what she was planning next.

319

He needed to speak to Lucy. He needed to make sure she was okay. Maybe he also needed to make sure she didn't go to the police. He'd kept them out of this mess for so long, getting them involved now wouldn't solve anything. It would only destroy whatever remained. Adam no longer knew if any of it was worth saving but he instinctively wanted to preserve something of what he had fought for, lied for, suffered for. She didn't answer. The brandy had appeared on the table without him realising it had been delivered. He drank some and dialled again. No answer. Adam knew it was time to stop, but he couldn't. He dialled again, and the call was accepted.

'Lucy, I—' Adam began, but he was immediately interrupted by a male voice.

'Adam, this is Tom, Lucy's flatmate?' His questioning intonation irked Adam, even in the middle of crisis.

'Tom, can I speak to Lucy? I just need to—'

Tom didn't allow Adam to finish his sentence, 'No Adam, you can't. You need to get out of her life. You're clearly involved with some very shady people, very shady indeed. I've had my suspicions all along. You've never been up front about who you are or what happened in your past, and it seems you're still up to your neck in shit, and now poor Luce is as well. The cat was found dead around the corner from your house. We've called the police and given them the number of the threatening texts.'

Shit, Adam thought, 'Tom, mate, it's not like that I swear. I'm not involved with anyone. I have no idea who sent those messages. I told Lucy, that girl in the clip, she's from work, she was drunk. It was a misunderstanding. The cat—'

'William,' Tom solemnly interrupted.

'Yes, William, I'm sorry. William's death is awful, but I promise I don't know who sent those messages or what he was doing here. Did the police find out who it was? Then you'll know it was nothing to do with me. Perhaps someone you guys knew? I know you had a fairly fluid living arrangement there, people coming and going, drugs sometimes...'

Tom's voice became clipped and sharp. His usual drawl clearly affected; a disguise to hide those years of private education, make him more approachable in Pilates. 'Adam, don't bother trying to pin this on us. Millennial life might be alien to you but I can assure you we aren't animal murderers. Most of us don't even eat animals. We don't know who the number belonged to. The phone was reported stolen. So have a word with your girlfriend mate, tell her she's won, and never call or message this number again, or we'll report you. Got it?'

Tom didn't wait for an answer. Adam heard the phone go dead and drained the last of his brandy. He dropped a twenty on the bar and left the pub. He wasn't really ready to go home, but right now, he didn't know where else he could go looking and smelling like this.

He pushed open his door and walked into his spacious flat. He didn't have a lot of clutter so at first the mess took him by surprise. He hadn't realised he'd left the place in such a state last night. He hadn't noticed in his haste when he left earlier, and he hadn't known so few belongings could create such mayhem. He took it in, scanning the room three hundred and sixty degrees. The glass he'd used last night had rolled onto the hard floor and was smashed. The cushions were on the floor, and the windows were covered in the same writing as his mirrors. He steadied himself against the back of the sofa and took a cautious step forward to read the messages. As he did, a voice cut through the quiet.

'Hello Daddy, I've missed you. I'm sorry about the mess, it was an accident.'

He turned around, and there she was. Olivia was back. The shock, the brandy, the lack of sleep, the sheer horror all hit him at once, causing him to take a sharp intake of breath, choking on it. Olivia slowly stood, and started to step towards him. Adam stepped back tripping over an upturned bar stool, and as his head crashed against the kitchen counter, his body heavily slumped to the floor, and everything went black.

Olivia

I really didn't mean to make a mess, or for the notes to look so violently painted. It's been hard for me after so long of being alone, my hands don't always seem to do what my mind tells them these days. My emotions overtake me. I intended for it to be my best artwork yet. All my love shown in words and lipstick strokes, poetry illuminated on the windows by the summer sunlight. He used to love my art. He used to love my notes. He used to love me. I studied his form on the floor by my feet. Blood circled his head, but otherwise he looked peaceful. I asked him if he still loved me and if he could forgive me now. He didn't answer, so as usual I waited. I thought maybe this was the end, but it wasn't. He stirred, he was clearly confused.

'Olivia. Help me,' he said.

I asked my question again, but he only repeated his demand. I waited for the answer I deserved. It didn't come. Eventually, he managed to sit up against the wall and dial a number, before slipping back down to the floor. I decided it was time to leave. For now.

Adam

'Adam? Adam?' A familiar voice.

His eyes opened even more slowly than the last time they dared, earlier today. Peter's face came into view. Adam opened his mouth to speak, but words did not come.

'Don't try to speak old friend, don't move, the ambulance is on its way.'

He whispered something, a croak.

'Shhh, mate, don't worry.'

'Olivia...' Adam mustered.

'She's not here Adam, it's just you and me.' The voice was soothing, and everything started to go dark again. Peaceful relief.

When Adam woke up again, he could no longer feel the cool, hard floor. His head hurt, but the throb this time was different. He was woozy, but not from brandy, at least he didn't think so. He wanted to know where he was, but his eyelids wouldn't obey his brain's command to open them. He heard voices.

'He's physically stable. A nasty wound to the head, and high blood-alcohol levels, but he's sedated. We'll need to run some tests.'

'He called me, but he didn't speak, I got there as soon as I could. The concierge let me in, thank God, took some persuading.'

'You did great. Thank you. He's been trying to talk about

his wife and daughter, saying things that clearly don't make sense. He'd been drinking, and we have put stitches in the cut to his head, but we are probably most concerned for his mental well-being at this time, given his family history.'

'You think he's had some kind of breakdown?'

'Possibly, but we'll know more when we can properly examine him. We'll need to talk to him, but maybe not tonight. Let's just allow him to rest.'

Who were these people? Adam thought, confused, and afraid. He clutched at something, sheets perhaps.

'Oliva is…' he began.

'He's waking up again. Stand back please sir.' The woman's voice was stern, but not unkind.

'Oh God, I should have known. I did know, I didn't do enough…' The man's voice was quiet, and choked. Adam recognised that voice, remembered the face he'd seen last. Peter. Peter had come to his rescue.

'Mr Sykes, I'm Dr Pearson. Can you open your eyes?' He could it seemed, one obeyed, then the next. A bright light blinded him but now they were prised open.

'Do you know where you are Mr Sykes? You're in The Royal Hospital. Your friend, Peter, called an ambulance to your home earlier. It seems you had a fall.'

Adam tried to speak again. It was too late to protect her. Where was she now? He found his voice.

'Where's Olivia?'

'Don't worry about that now. Your mother is on her way, she'll be here soon.'

Adam's limbs were heavy and his mouth was dry. He drifted in and out of sleep, not dreaming, not fully waking. Sometimes a small piece of plastic would penetrate his cracked lips and water would tickle his tongue. A warm sponge on his forehead dripped small droplets of water onto his face. The voices came and went, and then a door would click shut and silence would fill whatever room he was in. He couldn't sit up yet. He tried once or twice, when the voices came back.

'You'll be strong enough to sit up later Adam, just rest now.' They'd say, as a foreign hand gently melted him back into the bed.

Hours passed, and Adam started to feel something awaken in his mind. His thoughts reappeared at the same time as the throbbing pain taking a sharp turn for the worse in his head. He must have cried out, because suddenly a door swung open and hit the wall behind it. A cool liquid swam up his arm, and the pain subsided.

'There, there, it's just a little something for the pain,' an unfamiliar voice said. 'Ah Doctor, he's coming around. I've administered pain relief, and topped up his sedatives.'

As the voice addressed the new person in the room it went from kindly matron to stern professional. Rubber shoes squeaked loudly then faded to nothing and the door thudded once more.

Adam rested a while, his mind on standby. When he slowly and dreamily opened his eyes, he wasn't surprised to see Olivia, sat on the chair next to his bed. Her fingers traced the scar on his arm.

'Do you forgive me?' she asked again. 'Do you still love me?'

Adam was weak, too tired to fight. 'I'm sorry,' he said.

'Do you forgive me?' she repeated. 'Do you still love me?'

His scar started to tingle, painfully, as it had used to when it was fresh, after the fire. Was she pinching him, he wondered. He looked, but she was still just lightly running her fingers over it.

'Does this scar remind you of me every day? I forgive you.'

The scar did remind him of her every day no matter how hard he tried to forget her. He started to speak, but felt extreme drowsiness overwhelm his thoughts, and when he awoke, somewhere between five minutes and five hours later, she was gone.

'My Sykes, it's me again. Dr Pearson.' This time Adam opened his eyes quickly. 'Are you ready to sit up?' He nodded assent and the woman supported him and reorganised some pillows behind him as he awkwardly shuffled to seating. He was in a small room. A computer screen beeped, its tubes connecting him to it.

'Adam, can you tell us what happened this afternoon? You were found unconscious, with bloodied clothes. Your head injury has required stitches, but no permanent damage done. We are more concerned about your mental state. You had been drinking heavily. Your flat was turned upside down, and there were disturbing messages written on the wall. Did you write those messages?' Dr Pearson asked.

'It was Olivia. She's back. I fell, I was shocked, I didn't expect, I can't explain, there's so much I can't explain.' Adam didn't know where to start. He was getting agitated. He could see the look in the doctor's eyes. She didn't believe him.

'Your friend Peter found you alone. Do you remember what happened exactly?'

Adam started to hyperventilate. 'It was Olivia. She wants to hurt me, because of what I did. But then she said she forgave me, so I don't know what she wants.'

The doctor whipped an oxygen mask from nowhere, and put it on. He did not resist. She put her hand on his.

'Don't strain yourself, Mr Sykes. Don't try to explain just now. We have been very worried about you, but we can help you get well. We'll just take this slowly. Your mother has come to visit. I'm going to bring her in now. Okay?'

Adam hadn't seen his mother for months. Too afraid to look her in the eyes and somehow manage to keep the truth concealed. It would all come out now, though, he supposed. Olivia had seen to that.

'Darling, darling!' His mother ran to his bed side. 'Oh, look at you, you poor boy. I'm so sorry, I'm so sorry.'

She was weeping, and, as usual, Adam could do nothing. He looked at her pleadingly. The doctor took her gently by the arm, and walked to the door with her, almost out of earshot. He caught some words, half-sentences.

'He's in shock.' Dr Pearson's voice was calm. 'Serious episode... could have been building for some time... Was prescribed anxiety medication and it's all gone... blood-alcohol levels... dangerous combination... head injury looks worse than it is... he should be up and about in a few days... keep him in... refer to psych unit...'

'He did everything he could. He has the scars to prove it. He's never forgiven himself,' his mother's voice said in hushed tones.

After what seemed like an age, Adam's mother was back by his side. The oxygen mask was removed. He was feeling calmer and his mind had reorganised itself, the sedation

328

making way for clarity. Adam was finally ready to tell the truth, no matter how difficult it would be to hear, or for his mother to accept.

'Mum. Listen.' He said his words with a purpose that surprised him. 'Olivia came to my flat. She wrote notes on the wall.'

His mother put her familiar fingers on his dry lips and wept a silent tear.

He paused.

She took a moment, and a breath before she said, 'Adam, Olivia died in the fire.'

'She's still here, Mum.' Adam started to sob, his scar started to come alive with pain.

'She was very unwell, she couldn't cope with her mother's suicide. She was so fragile, you couldn't have done anything. You couldn't have stopped her. She only wanted to burn her artwork, her diaries, darling, to cope with the pain — she didn't mean it, and I know you can't accept it, but you must, my love, you must, because you're making yourself ill, and we can't bear to lose you too. Olivia died in the fire, Adam, she can't come back, my darling, she just can't. You tried to save her, but you couldn't, no one could have.'

Olivia

She's right, I did.

I tried to escape the burning building but he pushed me back in, so determined that I should die for what I did that he didn't notice the flames licking at his shirt sleeves. But what does the truth matter anyway? Who decides what the truth is? Did Megan kill herself? Did I? In the end, we're two peas in a pod, my father and I.

Adam

They were keeping him sedated to limit his hysteria. Nobody would listen to his claims. He knew he sounded crazy, he didn't blame them. His mother, Peter, and now even his brother, were taking turns to hold his hand, tell him mundane facts about the weather, and shut down any attempts to talk about Olivia, or even Megan. In the end he stopped trying to speak. He ate the grapes, he lied about feeling better, understanding where he was. He told them that he knew that his wife and his daughter were dead. He did, but he also knew Olivia had come back. Reassured, they'd leave him occasionally. He lay in his small, hard, hospital bed, and, he waited for Olivia. She always came.

'We'll always be bound by our story, Daddy, don't fight it. They'll never believe us, and they'll never understand us or why we had to do what we did. That's how I can forgive you, and you can forgive me. We're all we have now. They didn't even see me when I was alive. Only you saw me, really, only you see me now. Not so much has changed, in the end. I'll stay here with you, Daddy, you'll never be alone again.'

Adam knew very little, he thought, but he knew with certainty that Olivia was right: she would never leave him alone and she would never allow him to forget her. He also knew the only way to make her wrong, to make her disappear. All he wanted now, all he could hope for, was to escape this agonising fate.

He was allowed one final decision, no matter how poor all the ones that went before had been. His hospital door was shut, its handle prominent, and the bed sheet strong; hospital issue. He carefully knotted the noose.

Olivia

I knew he'd never leave me, and I never stopped believing that he'd find his way back to me. In the end he chose me and my world, and finally we are together again.

This time, forever.

The End.

Acknowledgements

Thank you to my parents, Susan and Roger Jeary, who along with my mother-in-law, Valerie Nicholas, patiently read early drafts of *Don't Forget Me* and provided invaluable feedback. Thank you to Claire Fuller for being a wonderful writing tutor and mentor — your encouragement and feedback helped me more than you know. Thank you to Dr Tapas Mukherjee for the medical insight and for helping me get away with murder. Thank you to my dearest friends and family: my sister, Natasha Jeary, for always being there, my best friend Lauren McAughtry for always believing in me, my stepchildren Cade and Ellie Nicholas for being the loveliest stepchildren I could hope for, and special thanks to Cade for the cover design. And most of all, thank you to my husband, Steve Nicholas, for making life such a wonderful thing to live.

Printed in Great Britain
by Amazon

66115698R00199